EVER THIS NIGHT

EVER THIS NIGHT

A NOVEL

M.J. SIONS

Brandylane
Publishers, Inc.
Publishing books since 1985

ISBN (Paperback): 978-1-966369-06-6
Library of Congress Control Number: 2025905402

Designed by Sami Langston
Project managed by Haley Simpkiss

Published by
Brandylane Publishers, Inc.
5 S. 1st Street
Richmond, Virginia 23219

Brandylane
Publishers, Inc.
Publishing books since 1985

brandylanepublishers.com

For Katie

1

Sylvia's hands were steadier than she'd expected. During the previous eight months, when she was taking cold showers and ingesting maca root, watching her zinc levels and seeking out red foods, she'd been so frightened by the possibility of going off hormones that she'd assumed she would shake if—when—this moment came. She thought she'd be shaking so bad that Danielle—who had accompanied all of Sylvia's homeopathic dead ends with dead ends of her own, namely Yellow Stork tea, fertility yoga, and lunar calendars—would have to be the one loading the pill cutter.

Sylvia wouldn't have been surprised if she had to leave the room while Danielle slid the little oval under the blade. She could've been out there in the hall, contemplating the fruitless optimism with which they had tried wheelbarrow, legs-on-shoulders, reverse cowgirl, and side-by-side scissors, each time hoping that a change in position would beget a change in the result. But each month the result had been the same.

They still weren't pregnant, and it was time to move on to the obvious solution. It didn't matter that Sylvia was afraid of the obvious solution. It didn't matter that the contours of the obvious solution doused her in primal fright. What mattered was that a day ago she had walked out of a bitingly cold shower and lied to Danielle that she was no longer afraid of the obvious solution, and Danielle had hugged her so warmly that she forgot it was January.

An hour later, Sylvia had confessed she was lying, but their trajectory had already become immutable. It was like telling a rocket she had lied about fearing the moon.

Now she was in the bedroom with Danielle, looking down at her hands. Danielle's hands were on hers, enveloping them from the outside. Maybe that was why they weren't shaking.

"It's only going to be a little while," Danielle said. She rubbed Sylvia's knuckles with her thumb.

Sylvia nodded, looking down at the materials on the dresser, transfixed. She'd said all those Hail Marys, all those Our Fathers, all those St. Michaels, and all those Glory Bes, all to avoid this.

"Temporary," she said. The winter air had dried out her throat.

"Mmhmm," Danielle said, looking at the same objects on the same dresser.

The pill cutter's exterior was translucent blue, and on the inside it was pink. The pill itself was green and ovular and the pill cutter was a rectangle. Sylvia's veins were long blue tubes, and her blood cells were tiny red disks.

Danielle rubbed her thumb across Sylvia's knuckles again, firmer this time. "Do you want me to cut it?"

Yes.

"No," Sylvia said. "I should do it."

She pushed down gently, but the ovular pill continued to hold itself together. That shouldn't have surprised Sylvia, given that it had been holding her together too. It was estradiol, but to Sylvia it might as well have been holy water. Together with spironolactone to lower testosterone, it washed away all of her foggy-headed conundrums, untangled all her spiky misconceptions. But with the wave went her sperm count, and she needed that back.

She pushed harder, and finally the pill snapped. Its two halves rattled as they hit the plastic walls. Newly divided, the pill seemed more material than it ever had, more chemical than abstract, more fixed quantity than infinite flow.

On their church-themed calendar, Sylvia and Danielle mapped out a schedule of reductions. On today's date, Sylvia wrote, "-½ Est." On the date two weeks out, she wrote, "-½ Est; Spi." and so on. The reductions would be routine and gradual. They would only go as far as required.

On the same church-themed calendar, Danielle wrote out speculative ranges of ovulation dates. When they had finished, they looked at their handiwork together for a moment. A baroque painting of the Holy Family loomed above their plans, partially obscured by a glare from the kitchen light.

Sylvia noticed an unfinished champagne bottle from New Year's Eve sitting on the counter by the calendar. She took it to the sink and poured it out, surprised it still had so much fizz.

"Think of it like you're pregnant," Danielle told her the next morning. "You'll remember this as a rite of passage."

"I like that," Sylvia said. She smiled. "I like that a lot, actually."

Danielle was on the bed, sitting cross-legged in a pool of morning light, her hair blown dry for the workday.

"You know, that's perfect," Sylvia said, her smile bigger now. She climbed onto the bed on her hands and knees. Danielle extended her hands, taking her in. They could never resist each other in the mornings, while Sylvia was still in a towel.

Did Sylvia want a baby as badly as Danielle did? She pondered the question later that day on her drive home from work. She thought the answer was yes. When she had first transitioned, images of babies and their parents tore at her. They summoned a sense of loss, a sense that the path she had chosen was not a better one but merely adjacent to the one she'd left, every step laced with the same isolation that had pervaded her life to that point.

So the answer was yes. She wanted a baby as badly as Danielle did, so she could put her fixations on those bright images out of her history, and with them, the fear that her hard-won peace was temporary. Sylvia remembered the rush of excitement with which her transition had begun, the reckless novelty of everything. Then slowly, the novelty had given way to peace; but every peace had its little cracks, its lurking troubles. If Sylvia wanted to remain well, then she had to stay ahead of those troubles. Family meant purpose, stability, direction, a place in the world that had existed as long as life itself. She knew that every day they went without a baby would bother her just a little more, until soon enough it would be all she thought about. Sylvia knew exactly how that worked. And besides, did she want Danielle to carry a stranger's baby?

The music playing on the radio stopped, then three jagged pulses seized control of her speakers, making her whole face scrunch up. A crackly male voice informed her that a winter storm warning was now in effect for her area. Three more awful pulses sounded, and the crackly male voice repeated its message.

A trail of silence drifted by, then the radio resumed, Sylvia's thoughts resuming with it. Of course she didn't want to subject Danielle to surrogacy. Of course she wanted the baby to be hers. Her conclusions were sound. She knew that. But she was scared. She was really, really scared.

"It's like grocery shopping in purgatory," Danielle said, inspecting a can of black beans that went out of its way to announce, "No salt added." With the shelves picked over and getting emptier by the minute, their cart had quickly become a collection of unfamiliar packaging. They had margarine instead of their usual butter, a gallon of whole milk instead of two-percent, brown eggs instead of white, and several bread products of unusual grains.

"Virginians panic over snow," Sylvia said.

Danielle dropped the black beans into their cart. "I'm used to that, but these mad store rushes always leave me wondering why they make products with such insignificant variations." She walked ahead of the cart, charting a path through the crowd.

"People like things to be customized," Sylvia suggested.

Danielle bent down. For a moment she turned her head away from the shelf, burying it in her open black coat. When it emerged, she returned to scanning the shelf. "I mean look at this." She held up a can of crushed tomatoes. It said, "With Basil" in scripty green letters across the label. "Fresh basil is the best basil, but you can't get it year-round. So they make dried basil to keep in the kitchen, and you put the dried basil in the crushed tomatoes when you make spaghetti sauce. So then why do they also make canned crushed tomatoes where the basil has been stewing in there for months?"

"People are lazy," Sylvia said.

Danielle added the Crushed Tomatoes With Basil to their cart. "Lazy people buy sauce that comes in a jar. Who are these people that are industrious enough to make spaghetti sauce on their own, but consider dumping in the basil a bridge too far?"

"Maybe they're neurotic," Sylvia suggested.

Danielle stopped walking, confusing an old couple who had plotted their path around her. "I'm considering how horrifying that is," she said.

"Some people like having everything the same," Sylvia said. "The amount of basil in the can is always consistent. It comforts them."

"Stop it," Danielle told her. "You're going to make me question my faith." She opened her coat again and buried her head in it, then emerged and continued walking, Sylvia pushing the cart behind her.

"Potatoes!" Danielle said. She accelerated her steps, losing Sylvia in the process.

The cart made Sylvia feel unwieldy as she attempted to catch up. Every turn presented an obstacle, with overfilled carts weaving slowly between empty display stands that stood at odd intervals, as though the staff had hoped to create a roadblock to slow the horde of shoppers down.

Danielle was holding two mesh sacks of potatoes when Sylvia reached her. "What do you think? Little sack, or big sack?"

"Make it the big one. I'm eating for two."

Danielle looked again at the potatoes, then at the price listed on the shelf. "These are the expensive organic potatoes."

"Small sack, then," Sylvia said.

Danielle put the bigger mesh sack back on the shelf. She opened her coat again and buried her head in it.

Sylvia said, "Why do you keep doing that?"

Danielle's head popped out hastily. "The inside of my coat smells funny."

"Everything smells funny. The whole parking lot smells like snow," Sylvia said. But before they left the house, she had seen Danielle filling up a flask—had watched her twist the cap back on and tuck it into the inside pocket of her coat.

Danielle began leading the cart again. "The thing I like about potatoes right now is that there aren't any minute variants. Potatoes are potatoes; our friend, potatoes."

"What about sweet potatoes?" Sylvia said.

Danielle stopped walking, blocking the path of a muscular man whose cart contained eight bottles of barbecue sauce. "I'm considering how horrifying that is," she said.

"We need to get out of here," Sylvia told her.

"After the wine." Danielle tugged on the cart. "The thing about wine is that wine is all about the minute differences. The blizzard is wine's natural habitat."

Sylvia nodded. "I think you've been inhaling too many coat fumes."

They turned down the wine aisle. Danielle spread her arms wide, slowly so as not to hit anyone. "French, Italian, Californian, Argentinian, Oregonian, or Spanish tonight, my love?"

"Whatever smells the least like your coat and costs less than twelve dollars," Sylvia said.

"Oregonian it is, then! My coat is very East Coast. It's an East Coat. An Eat Coat. Don't eat my coat."

"I will not eat your coat."

Danielle inspected a bottle. She held it up to the light and rotated the label. "Not eating each other's coats is essential in marriage. That's free advice."

Sylvia was beginning to feel watched. "Let's go check out."

Danielle kept the wine in her hand. She held it by the neck, swinging it as they walked.

Sylvia watched her. It was possible that, of the two of them, Dan-

ielle was the one being watched right now, with her tipsy proclamations and ballet footsteps. She was oddly graceful for a drunk. It *was*
possible, Sylvia thought, but she had trouble believing herself.

To Sylvia's relief, there was one checkout line open, and they made
it through without much forced lingering. Out in the parking lot, the
snow had begun to stick to the pavement, dissolving the regular white
lines of the spaces into a nongeometric pattern. Cars were pulling in
and out with noticeable urgency, their wheels skidding as they turned.
Danielle took a sip from her flask and then caught a snowflake on her
tongue like a chaser.

Sylvia drove slowly on the way home, pacing the car through the
crowded streets with the same steady attention she had given the cart.
After they reached the house, she told Danielle to relax while she unpacked and made dinner, but Danielle followed her into the kitchen
anyway. Sylvia put the perishables in the refrigerator and then selected
an onion while Danielle opened the wine.

Sylvia liked to chop onions in a deliberate sequence: horizontally
first, and if the onion was big, store half in a plastic bag. She would
then take the other half and place the flat side down, using her left
thumb and index finger to hold it together while her right hand made
a series of incisions.

With the pinstripe incisions made, she rotated the onion, maintaining pressure with her left thumb and index finger.

"It's not actually faster that way," Danielle said, swirling her wine.
"Especially not when you move like you're playing Jenga."

Sylvia was busy crossing the pinstripes with perpendicular slices.

"I like this wine," Danielle said. "We should visit Oregon."

"Ow." Sylvia had nicked her left index finger.

"I told you," Danielle said. She put down her glass and reached for
the knife, then nudged Sylvia away from the cutting board with her hip.

Sylvia tore a paper towel off the roll and held it tightly against the
wound. The blood spread outward through the quilted surface. "We
forgot to get Band-Aids."

Danielle cut with a rocking motion, one hand on the handle of the
knife and one hand on its spine. She paused, reached above her, and
pulled down a copper pot that had been a wedding gift.

The paper towel continued to soak up blood as Sylvia wrapped it
around her finger tight enough to stay. She reached for the olive oil
with her good hand and poured it into the copper pot.

Danielle smiled. "Don't get blood in the pot."

Sylvia turned on the burner and went back to holding the paper towel with both of her hands while Danielle poured the onion shards into the olive oil. They sizzled, filling the kitchen with their scent, warm and full-bodied with a touch of sweetness on the finish.

The clink of the mail slot and a subsequent thud in the front hall announced the arrival of something heavy. Probably a catalog, but maybe the issue of *R-Home Magazine* they had been waiting for.

Danielle pulled out a can of crushed tomatoes and slid it down the counter to Sylvia's waiting hand. "Nearly got the wine glass," Sylvia said, retracing its path with her wrapped finger to show how narrowly the can had missed.

"Didn't, though," Danielle said, pulling the pot off the burner to jostle the onions. "I should be a bartender. I can slide stuff without hitting other stuff."

"While drunk," Sylvia added. The can opener was tougher to turn with her index finger held away from the handle.

"Not drunk," Danielle said, setting the copper pot down and reaching for her wine. "Professionally jovial."

"There," Sylvia said, passing her the opened can. "Get me the tomato paste."

"I'm glad we stocked up some before the bizarro grocery trip. Our tomato paste doesn't have any basil, oregano, fennel, or eggplant in it."

Sylvia opened the tomato paste and put the can opener down. "I'm going to check the mail," she said. She wanted to know if the magazine had arrived. They had been told the article about Danielle would be in the January issue, but they hadn't been told what day it would come out.

"Don't bloody up the bills," Danielle called after her.

A catalog lay on the hardwood with an outdoorsy couple looking up from the cover. They wore identical hiking boots, though Sylvia knew if she opened the catalog she would find women's boots and men's boots sold separately. And she knew the man on the cover would be embarrassed if one day he pulled off his boots and found he'd been wearing the women's ones all along, even if he'd never noticed before. Beneath the catalog lay an insurance ad addressed to the house's previous owner, and beneath that was a late Christmas card from Preston Ellridge IV, who had been in love with Danielle for eight years.

Sylvia picked up the Christmas card and carried it to the kitchen. "Your mistress would like to wish us yet another merry Christmas," she said, holding it out in front of her.

Danielle added salt to a pot of water and covered it, then took the envelope. "He addresses them to both of us now, you know. He really does feel bad about the way he used to talk to you when you and I were dating."

"*About* me, you mean," Sylvia said.

Danielle shrugged. She opened the card and glanced at it, then put it aside. "I'll read it later. His cursive is too dense for me in my state."

Sylvia poured a glass of wine for herself. "I don't mean to make too much of it. But I'll be less on edge about him when he stops sending cards."

Danielle waved her hand, shooing the sentiment away. "He's harmless. And even if he wasn't, he's in Tuscany, or Argentina, or Rioja. The closest he's been to us in the last year and a half is the West Coast."

Sylvia gathered plates and napkins and silverware and set the table. They ate mostly in silence. Danielle polished off her wine and moved on to gin. She had developed an affinity for straight liquor in recent months. Sylvia had put herself in charge of hydration.

"Put it on ice," she suggested.

Danielle looked at the cabinet, wrinkling her forehead. "We're going to be nearly dry after tonight."

"The hardship will do us good," Sylvia said. She looked at her wine and considered pouring some of it out. Alcohol was bad for sperm production. Some nutritionists called it "liquid estrogen."

"Don't go and get that open wound infected," Danielle said, stacking Sylvia's empty plate atop her own. "If you get gangrene, we won't have any hard alcohol to sterilize." She walked over to the sink and began washing the dishes.

"I think you need to slow down anyway," Sylvia said.

Danielle continued scrubbing the copper pot. "We'll have to call in the finest apothecary from two farms over, and he'll say, 'I'm afraid we have to amputate.' But I'll have to tell him, 'I'd love to have you amputate my spouse, but we don't have any alcohol to sterilize.'"

"Stop," Sylvia said.

Danielle turned the water off.

"I mean it," Sylvia snapped.

Danielle looked at her, surprised. "I'm sorry. I was just having fun."

Sylvia bit her lip. "I didn't mean to do that."

"You're not stressing about the snow, are you?" Danielle sipped her gin. "Or is it the Christmas card? Here. I'll take care of that."

Danielle yanked the gin bottle out of the cabinet, removed the cap, plucked the card off the top of the refrigerator, then poured a shot's worth of eighty-six-proof gin over Preston's dense cursive. Then she pulled a lighter from the junk drawer and said, "This will take care of it."

Sylvia got there first. She wrenched the Christmas card away and secured it in her shallow pocket.

Danielle said, "Oh, you're not having any fun," cackling as she held the gas down on the lighter to keep its flame burning. "We won't be able to have fun like this when we're parents."

"Let's go in the living room," Sylvia said.

Danielle said, "It would have been okay. The snow would have put the fire out."

Later that evening, while Danielle and Sylvia were upstairs sleeping, enough snow fell to put out an entire neighborhood's worth of fires—much more snow than the two to three inches that had been predicted. In fact, nearly seven inches of snow fell and was still falling when Sylvia woke the next morning, slowly burying Richmond as the sun struggled upward.

* * *

On the first day of the snow, Sylvia waited. The reduced hormone dosage did not shock her system, but the knowledge of it discolored her thoughts. She tried not to think at all. The power had flickered overnight, and all their clocks were wrong. She made tea with Danielle and the two of them watched the swirling snowflakes until Danielle fell asleep, her laptop neglected on the floor beside the couch.

Sylvia made more tea and watched her breathe. The mail didn't come.

They went to bed at nine.

On the second afternoon, the snow stopped. Sixteen inches waited outside their door. Sylvia watched for the plow. She needed distraction. She was struck by how hard it was to be distracted at home.

Sylvia soon came to feel like a caged animal. Hypothetically, work could occupy her thoughts, but most of her meetings had been canceled. Many of her coworkers were still waiting for their power to come back. The predicament was ironic, given her job title. She was a risk manager who worked with other risk managers, yet none of them had managed the risk of a snowstorm disconnecting the team. Big miss on that one.

She and Danielle tried making their own bread, but the bread did not rise. Sylvia found this hilarious. She couldn't stop laughing at the flat brown lump on their oven rack. Danielle agreed that it was funny.

"I'm stressed," Sylvia said on the third day.

Danielle was sitting cross-legged on the couch. "Remember what we talked about."

Sylvia said, "First I have to admit that change is okay."

Danielle lifted one foot from her lap. "We could have sex."

The possibility made its way from Sylvia's ears down to her abdomen, where it dissolved in a pool of anxiety.

On the fourth day, Sylvia took a hot shower, relieved the work week had ended. Idleness was natural on the weekend. Everything was steady.

She washed and conditioned her hair and moisturized her face. She rubbed coconut cream on her hands and put on gloves, a scarf, a coat, snow boots, a T-shirt, a sweater, wool socks, a cami, jeans, and a bracelet, then went downstairs and announced, "I'm going to the liquor store."

Danielle was sitting cross-legged on the armchair. "Check if it's open first."

"I'm in the mood for a surprise," Sylvia said.

The snow on the roads, still unplowed, had been packed down and frozen to a glassy sheen. Sylvia had to look down as she walked to avoid the blinding glare. The snow suppressed every sound and deadened every echo. Sylvia walked, grateful to be in public again. Snowmen of varying size and artistic merit marked which houses had children in them.

The sidewalk widened and narrowed in accordance with how much effort each homeowner had put into shoveling. Sylvia resolved to shovel her and Danielle's section when she returned home.

The liquor store was in Carytown, on the other side of the highway. Sylvia walked over the highway bridge and along the path that passed in front of Ellwood Thompson's, the big organic grocery store situated at the far end of Carytown. The adjacent liquor store sat around the back of the building, like a secret cellar. Glancing down Cary Street as she passed, Sylvia was surprised at how busy it was. The Christmas decorations were still up, and residents were strolling up and down the sidewalks, looking in the windows of snow-closed stores while parents pulled little kids in sleds down the center of the icy, carless street. Sylvia smiled. It was rare to see this neighborhood so relaxed. Normally it was clogged with shoppers from surrounding counties, who had heard Carytown described with words like "quaint" and "vibrant" and "safe." Everything responded to them, from the flower stand outside Charleston 1925 to the homeless man who taught bewildered drivers how to parallel park, buskers and colorful shops filling every space not taken up by pedestrians. Equally absent from the icy sidewalks was the adversarial parade of punks and hipsters, walking in clusters of cigarette smoke as if to drive away the suburbanites. Years ago, distracted by a window display, Sylvia had bumped into one of them, and in response he had called her a prettyboy. Danielle hadn't understood why it bothered her so much, at least not in that era, before everything.

The liquor store was indeed open, and packed. Stir-crazy adults perused the aisles, whose shelves were as picked over as the tomatoes in the grocery store had been. Sylvia looked at the liqueurs, the rums, the gins, the vodkas, the bourbons, the scotches, the cordials, the bitterses, and the schnappses. She knew what she wanted, and part of what she wanted was to be out in public for as long as it took her to want to go home.

After she had looped the store enough times to feel suspicious eyes on her, she went to check out. The cashier did a triple take with her ID, then asked, "How old is this picture?"

"I was sixteen," Sylvia said.

She always felt a tinge of malicious enjoyment when she got carded. She had discovered early on that she could either be embarrassed by what her ID revealed, or smug about the unsure reactions of the people she handed it to. It was either her problem or their problem, she figured, and she didn't really want another problem.

"Thirty-three eighty-four," the cashier said.

Sylvia felt the cashier's eyes tumble down her back as she left, carrying a bottle of scotch in a black plastic bag. Holding the bottle by the neck so the label remained hidden while the cork protruded, she tore the plastic off, popped the cork, looked down, and said, "Hail Mary, full of grace, the Lord is with thee. . . ."

As she passed over the highway bridge and reentered her neighborhood, Sylvia was struck by a sense of sudden, aimless gratitude. It was a wonderful neighborhood in a wonderful city, budding with collective energy. People who lived in Richmond loved Richmond. The city had undergone a renaissance in the last decade, and everyone here considered themselves a contributing factor. They disagreed over what to do next, but those disagreements made things lively. She was glad her child would grow up here—if she had one. So what if this place held a few unpleasant memories from before her transition? It didn't matter that someone had called her a prettyboy. She and Danielle were a beautiful couple. What they were doing was correct.

And the neighborhood they had chosen was correct, too. They had settled on the Near West End because it was inside the city limits but had front yards and kids and dead-end streets that nobody could speed through. It was a sleepy neighborhood, dreaming softly in the shade of ancient oak and beech trees. They'd been giddy for months after they moved in, awash in the optimism of a new start.

Then they started trying to conceive.

Danielle opened the door for her before Sylvia got to the stoop. Sylvia paused in their walkway and whisked the plastic bag away from the bottle like the conclusion of a magic trick. The wind blew just then, and she let the plastic bag fly from her hand and down the street, twisting above the snow.

"I love you," Danielle said.

Sylvia's smile broadened. "Now say it to me instead of the bottle."

It was miraculous, given how she had used alcohol in the past, that Sylvia could drink at all. Whenever she reflected on the era that preceded her relationship with Danielle, it was with a sense of grim admiration at how many spiritual thoughts she could produce without landing on a single productive one, even by accident. Like most of her generation, she had grown up fairly agnostic. Her parents, both ancestral Catholics, had dutifully enrolled Sylvia and her two older brothers in First Communion and Confirmation but otherwise considered Mass attendance to be extra credit. The family had said grace only when they remembered to, and never at restaurants. Every once in a while, Sylvia's mother would attribute an occurrence to "God."

Over time, Sylvia had developed a free-verse approach to spiritual engagement, her prayers a mix of mild confessions and petitions. They often took the form of something nebulous about being a bad person or a problem child, followed by a plea for an equally nebulous notion of guidance. When she'd first met Danielle, the Our Father was the only prayer she could recite from memory.

It was fine. Sylvia had never found herself trending toward atheism. But she was wary of death regardless of what awaited after. She had feared eternal thoughtlessness with as much intensity as she feared eternal thinking. As a child, religion, God, and the like had vaguely comforted her, but not nearly enough.

By the time she started drinking in her late teens, Sylvia had become so uncomfortable with thoughts of death and spirituality that she drank almost exclusively to forget the subject until she sobered up. She was no fun at all at parties. Danielle had changed that. Most of the way through college and feeling sure she had met every type of person one could meet, Sylvia had been stunned by how singular Danielle was. Creative and curious and astoundingly devoted to her religion, Danielle brought Sylvia into a period of spiritual convalescence, the extent of which only became clear years later.

That afternoon, Danielle poured herself a generous portion of scotch while Sylvia recited a Hail Holy Queen under her breath. After she had finished praying, Sylvia poured a drink of her own. Together they chopped ingredients for a hearty soup as the sun went down, diffusing into luminescence as it struck the icy roads.

Sylvia liked to look out onto the dimming street while they cooked. They had been in this house for a year now, long enough for her to observe her street in every season. That she could do so while making dinner was one good aspect of their house's unusual layout, with the kitchen in the front rather than the back. Another good aspect had been the price; apparently no one wanted to buy a house with rooms in strange places, which had dropped the house into the very top of their affordable range. They had handed over their savings before the chance could pass them by. Then Danielle had set about making the odd layout livable. She told Sylvia it was a personal challenge, an opportunity to use the talents she usually sold to her clients on a home of her own.

The flow of money into their hands had improved some since their purchase, but not enough to rebuild their savings. They had built up enough to pay for insured prenatal care and delivery, and that would nearly run them dry. That the Catholic Church did not permit IVF treatments aligned oddly well with their current finances. They couldn't afford it anyway.

Danielle and Sylvia chopped on identical cutting boards—accidentally redundant wedding gifts they'd received three years before. Each of them moved to slide their pile of ingredients into the pot at the same time, bumping the boards.

"Mine first," Danielle said.

Sylvia downed a burning sip of liquor. She wondered if the changes in her hormones would soon bring back the existential cacophony that had made her drink so ferociously in a previous era. She was not sure, exactly, when she realized her relationship with alcohol was different from the other faux-adults around her in college. After all, they'd all said things like, "It's not alcoholism until after you graduate," and regularly drank past the point of throwing up. It was possible she had only realized it in hindsight, after the true problem presented itself.

After they had dumped the vegetables into the pot to simmer, Sylvia and Danielle went out on the porch with their bottle of scotch. Danielle liked to drink cold liquor, so she had put their glasses outside in a bed of snow to chill. The neighborhood was lively in the sunset. Other people's children were out in their small front yards, throwing snow at each other and digging tunnels that crossed property lines. "I like that mom with the little blond boys," Danielle said. "I'm targeting her to be my mommy mentor."

Sylvia laughed. "I'm glad you added the word 'mentor' to the end of that."

"Hush," Danielle said.

Sylvia took a sip of her cold scotch, holding it by the heels of her hands to keep her fingers from freezing. "'Hush' is a good parent word."

"Hush," Danielle said again.

Sylvia wanted to be more fully on this porch, in this moment, with her attention on Danielle, but her mind kept drifting. Another thing she wondered about was whether or not her changing hormones would cause the world to once again lose structure. Before she fixed her hormones, she'd had trouble convincing herself objects were 3-D and stationed inside of real space. She remembered worrying that she could watch a tree branch fall and leave a hole in the space behind it, as though torn from a painting.

Sylvia spoke aloud, hoping to bring herself back to the present. "We should get a fire pit out here."

Danielle threw back the rest of her scotch and tossed the glass into a snowbank. "It would work better in the back. Otherwise we'd need enough fire for everyone on the block."

Sylvia walked into the yard. "Not for relaxation. For shoveling."

A low-flying plane scooted overhead. All the kids stopped running, throwing, and shouting to look up at it. The sound touched the ground in a muffled tone, wrestled downward by the spongy earth and crumpled snow.

Sylvia stopped just short of the sidewalk. She was projecting now, though not quite shouting. "Two pits, equidistant from one another, and we get them burning right as the snow starts. Nothing sticks in their radius, and we end up with the clearest sidewalk in the neighborhood."

The mother of the two blond boys was watching her.

"Come back over here," Danielle said. Her glass was full again.

Sylvia was present now, aware of the neighbors, feeling the cold. "Just consider it," she projected.

She walked around to the backyard to get the snow shovel. Stepping over the gate, she heard a woman call out, "She's very innovative!" Hopefully it was the mother of the blond boys.

There was one other thing Sylvia was wondering about, and she tried not to wonder about it as she used her hands to dig the shovel out of the mound it was buried in. She was wondering, despite her efforts, if any of this would work.

"We've been meaning to get our upstairs floors redone," Danielle was telling someone when Sylvia stepped back over the gate. "They creak more than we would like. It's very loud at night."

Sylvia held the snow shovel against her shoulder like a soldier's rifle as she came back around the side of the house. Spotting her, Danielle held out a hand in Sylvia's direction.

"This is my Sylvia," she said, addressing an unfamiliar woman in their snowy walkway.

"Nice to meet you," said the neighbor woman. Sylvia recognized the voice; she was the one who had called her innovative a moment ago. The mother of the blond boys had gone inside.

The neighbor woman said, "I'm Harriet. My husband and I just moved into four-five-oh-six over there."

Sylvia's eyes followed her gesture to a big brick house with a snowy crepe myrtle in the yard. "Welcome to the neighborhood," Sylvia said.

Danielle put her glass back down in the snow. "Harriet and her husband grow their own jalapeños."

Sylvia turned the shovel perpendicular and hung her arms from the shaft. "We've tried vegetables a couple times, but the squirrels get to them. Maybe you guys can give us tips."

"Hopefully the things we learned down in Charleston will carry over to our yard here. My husband is excited about how much more gardening space we have now; he absolutely loves hot peppers."

"Sylvia's the same way," Danielle said.

Sylvia nodded. "I should probably shovel before we run out of daylight." She walked away.

The very bottom layer of snow had frozen, and Sylvia had to bash the corner of the shovel against it in powerful bursts to reach the sidewalk. The work was hard, and the repeated impact made her elbows ache. Between stints of breaking ice, she watched Danielle and Harriet on the porch. Danielle was swirling her drink while she listened, laughing with her head tilted back. The sunset brought out the red tones in her dark hair. She was speaking to Harriet with that intense focus of hers; she had a gift for making people feel as though she had never cared about anything quite so much as she cared about what they had to say. Sylvia remembered her mother fawning over Danielle after they met, how on occasion she called her "my daughter" instead of "my daughter-in-law." Sylvia continued chipping at the ice. She could see why Preston Ellridge was in love with Danielle. She would not begrudge Harriet for falling in love on the porch right now. It seemed impossible not to.

"We're going inside," Danielle called as she opened the front door, flicking the porch light on as she and Harriet exited the snowy twilight. Sylvia continued to work as, one by one, the children went inside. Sadness came over her on the cadence of dusk.

Harriet's husband, Tyler, joined them later that night for soup. He brought with him a surplus baguette, purchased during the pre-snow grocery dash and promptly forgotten in the pantry.

"We had to stock up on all the strange versions of things," Danielle said. She slung a sideways glance at Sylvia. "We had a lot of fun at the store."

"Count yourself lucky," Tyler said, waiting for a spoonful of broth-soaked carrots to stop steaming. He was a big man with enormous hands that made the spoon look small. "By the time we got there, it was like society had collapsed."

"Tyler and I differ in our feelings on crowds," Harriet said. She put her fingers on Tyler's knuckles.

Danielle said, "Sylvia and me, too. I like the bustle, but she thinks it's constricting."

Tyler turned to Sylvia. "Imagine being my size."

Sylvia couldn't think of a worse thing to have to imagine.

"People get out of the way of angry-looking men," Harriet said. "We women don't have such a luxury."

Sylvia sat up straighter. "It's true."

Tyler leaned back in his chair, holding his hands up. "Help! I'm outnumbered."

Danielle put her finger up. "I haven't voted yet."

"Isn't that just like a man to ignore a woman's vote?" Harriet said, turning to Danielle. "I'll tell you, men are quite hard to love."

Danielle looked down into her soup.

Sylvia put her hand on Danielle's back. "We should try to get the fireplace going tonight."

"Is it gas?" Tyler asked. "Electric?"

"Wood," Sylvia said.

"Kitchy," Harriet said. "Very quaint."

"We'll need to start with little sticks," Danielle said. "The firewood's big, and everything is wet."

"I can help gather sticks," Tyler said.

They all went outside to gather sticks. The streetlights had come on and the snow reflected their light, along with the light from the moon, dousing the street in inverted twilight, like the surface of another planet. They fanned out over the front yard and onto the sidewalks, sweeping the ground with the flashlights on their phones as they gathered small twigs in fistfuls and piled bigger branches by the porch. Back inside, Danielle arranged a bouquet of newspaper and twigs in the fireplace, then reached in with the lighter. While the fire took hold, Sylvia went into the kitchen and reached on top of the fridge for the scotch. Her wrist brushed Preston Ellridge's Christmas card, still on top of the fridge where Sylvia had placed it after saving it from the lighter. She had only intended to put it out of sight for the evening. Once they had the fire going steady, she would put the lighter away and put the card somewhere it wouldn't be forgotten again. That way she wouldn't feel petty for having hid it.

Turning, she found that Harriet had followed her into the kitchen. "We're so glad your wife invited us tonight."

Sylvia poured a finger of scotch into a mug she had used for tea earlier that day. She pointed the neck of the bottle at Harriet and raised her eyebrows.

"Too smoky for me," Harriet said. "I assume Tyler would love some, though."

Sylvia nodded and poured a glass from the dwindling bottle. In the living room, Danielle and Tyler were collaborating uneasily on the fire.

"We need more newspaper to get the twigs to catch," Tyler said.

Danielle said, "The embers are glowing."

"We brought drinks," Sylvia said as she entered.

Danielle knelt by the fireplace and lowered herself onto her hands.

She arched her back, extended her neck, and blew. The embers flared, and when they faded again, a twig had caught on fire.

"You could be an Eagle Scout," Tyler said.

Danielle returned to her feet, grinning. She reached out for the glass of scotch in Sylvia's hand. "Thank you."

Sylvia looked at the burning twig and began to form a thought about the difference between fire and snow. "Let me get you a glass too," she said to Tyler.

As she turned around to go back into the kitchen, Harriet leaned in toward her ear. "You handled that well."

Sylvia nodded. She fetched another glass and poured another finger of scotch for Tyler. No one was looking in her direction as she approached the living room again, and she lingered in the doorway, taking a long look at Harriet. Odd, she decided; just an odd woman. When she stepped back into the living room, Danielle asked, "Was that the last of it?"

"Surprisingly no. There's still a respectable amount left," Sylvia said, taking her seat next to Danielle on the couch.

"Good," Danielle said, swirling her drink. "I've paced myself well enough, I think. I don't think I'll be nursing a headache all through church if we go at eleven."

Harriet was reaching for the glass of scotch in Tyler's hand, and Sylvia thought she saw her back stiffen at the word "church."

"Unitarian?" Harriet asked. "Episcopalian?"

Danielle and Sylvia looked at each other. Sylvia felt a twitch of the same malice she had felt handing over her ID at the liquor store. She turned her gaze back to Harriet, smiled, and said, "Catholic."

Scotch came out of Harriet's nose. "Still?"

"I'm afraid so," Danielle said, swirling her drink harder.

"We really didn't mean to be," Sylvia added.

"You have to believe us," Danielle said.

Tyler put his hand on his chin. "Come to think of it, I did notice the crucifix in the kitchen."

Danielle slapped Sylvia's wrist. "I thought I told you to hide that before company came over."

Sylvia dropped her jaw. "You told me you were on crucifix duty!"

"You two are so interesting," Harriet told them. "We love interesting people."

Sylvia glanced sideways at Danielle, suppressing a smirk.

The majority of the twigs had now cast their votes to continue the fire, and Sylvia deposited one of the thicker pieces of kindling on top of them. She wished she had held on to that thought about the difference between fire and snow. It had felt like a good one. "We get a little defensive about it sometimes," she said. "Catholics tend to be misunderstood."

Harriet lifted her hand. "No no, no need to be defensive. Tyler's family is very spiritual."

"We have advent candles," Tyler said.

"You guys are so interesting," Harriet said again.

A mouse scurried out from under the radiator. "Get out of here," Danielle told it.

The mouse did not seem to comprehend. It stood there by the radiator, looking at Danielle politely, ears perked up so far that they appeared too big for its head, as though it really would like to understand.

"You two should get a cat," Tyler said. "We had terrible mouse problems in our apartment until we got Winston."

Sylvia's hand tightened around her glass.

"Winston is our saving grace," Harriet said.

Sylvia tried to steal a glance at Danielle's face, but she couldn't look without making it obvious. Instead, she put her hand on Danielle's knee in a controlled motion. Her knee felt cold and stiff, but knees were usually cold and stiff. What could she touch instead that would tell her more than a knee?

Danielle loved the name Winston. She wanted to name the baby Winston.

"We'll have to introduce you to Winston one day," Tyler said. "He's been a bit skittish about the new house."

Harriet nodded. "Winston's a shy cat. He'll probably hide behind me the first time you meet him, but he'll warm up."

A few drops of scotch landed on Sylvia's hand. Without moving her head, she shifted her eyes to see how hard Danielle was swirling her glass now.

Tyler reached for Harriet's hand. "Winston always warms up to people once he decides he knows them. Once he decides you're one of his friends, he'll follow you around."

"We're letting him acclimate to the house right now," Harriet said, "but we'll let him out soon. If you see a slinky orange cat around our yard, just say, 'Good morning, Winston!'"

More drops of scotch landed on Sylvia's hand. She kneaded Danielle's knee harder.

"I think it's ready for the logs," Danielle said, speaking to the fire.

"Seems a bit small for that still," Tyler said.

Danielle stood. "No, it's ready. I'll get them. They're in the backyard."

Sylvia felt proud of her. She put another thick stick on the fire, hoping it would catch before Danielle got back with the first log. "What do you guys do?" Sylvia asked.

"I'm a data scientist," Tyler said. "Working on machine learning models."

"I'm an artist," Harriet said.

The back door hinge signaled Danielle's return. She appeared in the entry to the living room, cradling a snowy log in her arms. "They were buried out there."

Harriet plucked Tyler's glass from his hands and swilled a small amount. "I hope it's not too wet to burn."

Danielle put the log down next to the fireplace. She put her hands on her hips. "I guess I could hit them with a hair dryer."

"Sounds clever," Tyler said, taking his drink back.

"Does it?" Danielle asked. "Does it sound like a good idea?"

Sylvia's pride dampened. Danielle was overdoing it.

"I think it sounds like it would work," Tyler said.

"I should get the hair dryer, then?" Danielle said. "It's right upstairs, but the cord isn't very long."

"There's an outlet right here," Harriet said. She was holding out her hand near the outlet.

Danielle said, "So that's our plan, then. I'll go get the hair dryer and I'll plug it in right there in that outlet."

They could've laughed together later on—took turns imitating the way Harriet said "interesting." Instead, Danielle was doing this, the same thing she did every time she'd been drinking and someone pushed her—only, the pushes it took to set her off had been getting smaller and smaller lately.

Sylvia said, "I think we should just throw it on and see if it catches."

The mouse emerged from beneath the radiator again. Its disproportionate ears made it look lost and dumbstruck.

"What kind of art do you make?" Sylvia asked Harriet.

"I freelance professionally," Harriet said, drawing out the word professionally. "It varies from client to client."

"She did the illustrations for an archaeological journal recently," Tyler said.

"I learned much more about early human sea vessels than I wanted to know," Harriet said.

Danielle put the wet log on top of the struggling fire, extinguishing it. She turned around. "Could you draw me on an early human sea vessel?"

Harriet laughed mechanically. "I'm not sure about that."

Danielle continued to push. "I can model for you." She craned her neck and put her hand horizontally above her eyes. "See? I'm looking out for early human sea marauders."

Harriet looked over to Sylvia. Sylvia shrugged.

"I suppose I could," Harriet said.

Danielle said, "Don't draw the sea marauders in the background. I'm looking for them out of caution."

There was a pen and a legal pad on top of the bookshelf. Danielle went to go get them.

Sylvia couldn't wait for the trudge to church tomorrow, followed by the melting of the snow in the afternoon. "I think Harriet's commission is out of our price range," she said.

Visibly relieved, Harriet sunk down into the couch.

Later, when Tyler and Harriet had gone, Danielle sat on the couch, her shoulders back and her knees together. "I'm sorry," she said.

"I don't think they noticed," Sylvia said. She could still hear Harriet's voice moving away from the house.

"It wasn't the cat name. It was that comment about loving men," Danielle said.

Sylvia nodded and looked away. "I'll cut half a pill out of the spironolactone dose tomorrow."

She went upstairs without waiting for a reply.

Sylvia woke in darkness, and all she could think about was math. She had been doing the math as she fell asleep, and while she slept, a part of her brain must have remained awake, doing the math still. Danielle was snoring a little beside her, and the digital clock on their long wooden dresser said it was just past 1:00 a.m.

Sylvia sat up. She was aware that she was still trying to do math, but in her half-awake state the numbers ran in endless loops. Her feet touched the carpet lightly so as not to wake Danielle, and her sweater found her shoulders. She left the room with her jeans and her socks slung over her elbow and went down the stairs to find her snow boots. Taking her phone with her on her way out, she closed the front door carefully behind her.

She walked in the same direction she had walked earlier that day when she went to the liquor store. There were probably a couple bars still open if she went all the way to Carytown, but she hadn't brought her wallet. That was okay. The idea of people struck her as odd just then.

The moon was bright and the sky was pale purple, palest where it fell below the roofs of the houses and met the snowy ground. She walked along, more awake now, wondering if her surroundings resembled an Alaskan winter, dark in the middle of the day. Pacing herself carefully on the ice, she tried to do the math again.

Sylvia's prescribed hormone dose consisted of two estradiol pills and one spironolactone in the morning, plus one of each at night. She had subtracted half of one of the estradiols already, and tomorrow she would subtract half of one of the spironolactones. If she subtracted half of each medication every two weeks, how many until she would be down to zero hormones a day? Right now, she was taking one and a half spironolactones, so three halves of a spironolactone, minus one half every two weeks, that made it six weeks until zero. Right now, she was taking two and a half estradiols, so five halves of an estradiol, that made it ten weeks until zero. Six weeks would be one and a half months, so just before the end of February she would be down to no spironolactone and one remaining estradiol.

She looked into the pale purple sky and thought, *Is this what it feels like to be an astronomer?* Somewhere out there, an astronomer was surely walking along the way she was, dividing and multiplying, charting and deducing, under the same bright moon.

After she got to zero-dosage, it would take sixty more days for her sperm to be fully healthy again. And that was if she assumed that reaching zero spironolactone—the word "zeronolactone" occurred to her and she laughed at it, creating a puff of steam in the air—if she assumed that reaching zeronolactone would be enough, and that her body wouldn't need additional time to undo any atrophy in her fertility. She laughed again at zeronolactone. Things were funnier to her when she was alone. Sixty days from the day of zeronolactone would be sometime in April. If Danielle cycled in early April, then they would need to wait an additional month to try again.

Sylvia nearly tripped over a tree root that had broken through the sidewalk, jarring her from her thoughts. Gathering herself, she looked around for landmarks. She could see the enormous silhouette of an inflatable Santa outside the house across the street. So she had gone four blocks so far. She resumed walking, the darkened Santa watching her from afar.

So the earliest they could get pregnant would be May, assuming it worked on the first try. Assuming two tries—and zeronolactone working immediately, and an early cycle for Danielle—it would be June. Assuming it would have to be zeronolactone, plus an additional four weeks of tapering down estradiol, plus an early cycle, plus two tries, it would be . . . she didn't know.

Sylvia shook her head. She knew she needed to taper down faster, but she was scared. Her thoughts drifted back to when she first went on hormones; back to how it had felt to be in her head. She could remember how quickly they took hold, almost from the very first dose—the sudden feelings of openness, possibility, freedom.

But she couldn't remember what she had felt like just before then. She had tried many times over the last half year as she built her courage to taper off, but she'd eventually accepted those memories were beyond her reach. It was one thing to take medicine for palpitations in the heart or pain in the arm. She could use her brain and her memory to feel the difference in her body, to understand what the medicine was changing. But with hormones, she had realized immediately that the effects would be different. Changing her hormones changed more than her physical being—it changed the way her brain assessed the present, and it also changed the way her brain assessed the past. Minute to minute, hour to hour, week to week, month to month, year to year, Sylvia couldn't track changes to how she thought. It was like an astronomer trying to assess the speed of a comet from the surface of a different comet, one whose speed was unknown and changing in real time.

She knew it had been bad, and she remembered the words she had used to describe how she felt then: Like bumper cars. Like someone else was having thoughts for her. But the words didn't make the feeling real for her now, the same way those phrases had never made it real for anyone around her. It was all abstract and distant.

By now, Sylvia had nearly reached the bridge to Carytown, but between her and the lighted bridge stood a tunnel of tree-shadowed darkness, like a void in the pale sky—one that she could fall into. She turned around.

She remembered it had been bad, but still, it hadn't been all bad. Her past self had achieved the most magnificent accomplishment of her life: that person had fallen in love with Danielle. There was one particular night that stood out in her memory, another winter night, but different in every way: warm for the season, the ground all dry.

It was back in Charlottesville, toward the end of fall semester. She and Danielle were taking a walk after dinner, and they turned down one of the paths between the pavilion gardens, between the serpentine brick walls. The sky was open, the stars were close, the weather was mild, and Sylvia didn't yet know she was trans.

The rabbit started it. They came across it on the garden path. It hopped away from them and landed in a puddle of bluish light from the LED bulbs overhead. As they approached, it hopped down the path again and stopped to stare at them. Danielle had bent down and asked, "Are you confused?"

Sylvia put her hand down on her shoulder. "Seems more like he wants to lead us somewhere."

"They're crepuscular," Danielle said, looking upward. "They're supposed to go back into their holes after sundown, but they can get confused in well-lit areas and on clear nights."

"I didn't know you were such a scholar on rabbits," Sylvia had said.

Danielle tried to approach the rabbit non-threateningly. It hopped farther down the path before stopping again. She stood straight up. "I want to take it home."

Sylvia was standing a few feet behind her now, hands in her pockets. "I'm not sure how much luck we'll have running it down."

She had wanted to appear so pragmatic back then. So austere and controlled, unmoved and even-tempered. A fact-oriented realist with the demeanor of a judge. Cool under pressure and always under pressure. She looked at the rabbit, thinking that she could run it down right now, just burst forward and be free for a second, dive for it and come up with her heart pumping. But it wasn't right. It wasn't the right image to cultivate. She didn't want to blow this. Not with the lady in front of her.

Danielle was far from a guarantee then, maybe not even a fifty-fifty proposition. She was headed to a wedding the next day with a friend, a grad student she knew from her major who had asked her along, ostensibly as a platonic outing.

Danielle flung herself forward, the soles of her flats scraping the path as she lunged, body almost horizontal to the ground. But the rabbit darted easily out of her reach, then vanished. Sylvia had laughed. "The goddess of the hunt comes up empty."

Danielle reached up to the bough of an evergreen that protruded from behind the serpentine wall. She snapped the end off and lodged it behind her ear. "I answer only to the title of Hunt Goddess now."

"How blasphemous a thing to hear from such a Serious Catholic," Sylvia said, taking her by her waist.

"Blasphemous is talking to the Hunt Goddess that way."

Sylvia laughed and reached for the evergreen. Danielle swatted her away.

They had walked along together under the open sky. Sylvia suggested paths that didn't pass directly under lights to avoid making the evergreen too visible. She had devoted so much attention to avoiding attention back then, never asking herself why it mattered so much to be discrete, never interrogating her hatred of being looked at. Did it make more sense to her at the time? It must have. There must have been some reason she had concocted for avoiding everyone's eyes all the time, even when Danielle's were the only ones that mattered. They continued on toward Danielle's apartment until they came to an old university building that was under renovation. An enormous scaffolding had been erected by one side, with stairs leading up to the roof. They stopped without a word, exchanged a look instead. If either of them had said no, the other would have followed where they led. But neither did, so together they went—up the stairs of the scaffolding and onto the roof. They sat on the perch together, Danielle still wearing the evergreen but no longer impersonating a deity.

Sylvia had put her arm around Danielle and Danielle had put her head on Sylvia's shoulder. Sylvia looked at the stars and said, "They make you feel like dust."

Danielle laughed viciously. "The best way to ruin a cliché moment is to say the cliché out loud." She pulled the evergreen from behind her ear and flicked it away. It tumbled off the roof and out of sight.

"And anyway, I don't feel that." She turned to Sylvia. "People always say that about the night sky, but I've never felt that way when I've looked at it."

"How do you feel?" Sylvia asked.

"Empathetic," Danielle had said. "I feel like myself and each star are crossing these huge gulfs of time and distance, but there's this kinship." She rotated her head slightly, angling her gaze further upward. "I think it's how God feels about us."

Before Sylvia could say anything, rain began to fall. It came loudly and swiftly, and it fell out of a clear sky that stayed clear as they sat there. The rain soaked them, but when they looked up, they could still see the stars.

Later that week, Sylvia discovered that rain from a cloudless night sky is called *serein*, derived from the French word for "serene." All the mysterious processes of love had begun to work on her by then, and they were still working now.

Sylvia crossed the icy street, nearly home. She remembered that rain. It had come on too fast and too fully for Sylvia to say anything about the vast gulfs of time and distance, or kinship with the stars, or God. She would have said the wrong thing, probably, just as she had said the wrong thing about the stars. In that time, she'd had all the wrong ideas about herself, and the wrong ideas about herself had become the wrong ideas about everything else, about feeling like dust. But that night, Danielle's voice had lingered between the rain sounds, because the rain came on too fast for Sylvia to speak.

* * *

The next day was January sixth, known on the Catholic calendar as The Feast of the Epiphany of the Lord. The Feast of the Epiphany of the Lord marks the day on which Jesus was revealed to the gentiles, the first of whom are known as the three wise men.

It occurred to Sylvia, as she and Danielle walked through the snow toward St. Collette's, that they were acting out the same path, only without gifts, and with the wrong number of people.

They sat near the back of the church, and soon the entrance hymn began and the priest and the deacon processed to the tabernacle, where they stood overlooking the congregation until the music ended. Father Stephen let the ensuing silence settle along the pews, then shifted in his robe and said, "Good morning."

The congregation responded, "Good morning."

"I'm happy to see all of you here on this snow day, and rest assured that each of you will receive extra blessings."

The congregation laughed.

Again, Father Stephen let the sound run its full course, letting the silence settle before continuing. "As we prepare to celebrate these sacred mysteries, let us now call to mind our sins."

Sylvia and Danielle bowed their heads. As she did every Sunday, Sylvia considered whether or not to offer dressing as a woman up to the penitential act. She decided to offer it this week.

The deacon said, "Lord Jesus, you were sent to heal the contrite of heart. Lord, have mercy."

Sylvia and Danielle repeated, "Lord, have mercy."

The deacon said, "You came to call sinners. Christ, have mercy."

"Christ, have mercy."

"You are seated at the right hand of the Father to intercede for us. Lord, have mercy."

"Lord, have mercy."

"May almighty God have mercy on us, forgive us our sins, and bring us to everlasting life."

Sylvia and Danielle said, "Amen."

The psalms and readings progressed briskly, echoing in the vaults overhead. The deacon read the gospel, then Father Stephen took to the pulpit to discuss the significance of the three wise men.

"In today's gospel we see Herod, the closest thing at the time to an actual king of the Jews, as he is processing the apparent fulfillment of a prophecy," he said.

Sitting down now, Sylvia looked around the pews. She realized with dread that Father Stephen was right: most of the parish had taken a snow day. Plenty of the regulars knew who Sylvia was, and she assumed they had long since made their silent decisions about her. But she still feared that one day, someone who had never noticed before would see her walk by in the Communion line, and that person would have questions, and then louder questions. In a half-empty church, the risk seemed more acute.

"Let's hang back today," Danielle said, seeming to read her mind.

Father Stephen continued: "What terrifies Herod is not the fulfillment of a Jewish prophecy about a Jewish king. We must remember that the magi are gentiles, and they are stirred by a prophecy of their own. It is a pagan prophecy, in which a universal king—their king, they realize—is to be born among the Jews."

Father Stephen coughed, and even the cough's echo was allowed to run its course before he spoke again. "This is really quite remarkable. So what does Herod do? Mark tells us he was 'troubled.' Troubled how? Was Herod confused? Frightened? Threatened? Likely, all three. So he hatches this scheme: he will use these wise men as unwitting field agents in a conspiracy that will ultimately end in infanticide."

He paused as the word "infanticide" percolated through his congregation. Coughing again, he said, "It is difficult to overstate how sinister of a move he is making, how deep a betrayal—not only of his own people, but of others. These men have come to him in an act of great devotion, announcing their intention to pay homage to one whom they have recognized as their king, and he uses their devotion against them. He sees in them not piety but gullibility, not wisdom but usefulness, which he can ply into a disturbed, self-interested act.

"It is notable, then, that the revelation of Jesus triggers an abuse of power. This gestures toward an existing mode of kingship against which Jesus himself will arise. As we know, the wise men are not so gullible as they appear to Herod. They are warned in a dream not to return to him, and so they do not."

He shuffled his papers and placed them to the side of the pulpit, signaling a shift from the academic to a conversational tone. "If only all of our dreams were so dependable. Through Christ, we become free, and yet in that freedom there is fracture. There is instability, a sense of directionlessness. The Danish philosopher Kierkegaard called it dizziness. As we begin this liturgical year, let us recognize that in freeing all of humanity, Jesus has placed in our hands an unending responsibility to live according to him. The Herods of the world have not vanished. In choosing to turn toward or away from Christ, each of us chooses to walk the path of Herod or the path of the wise men. In our era we have no guiding stars, very few guiding dreams, and little sense of how close we are to the prophecies that have yet to be fulfilled. Instead, we have freedom. It must be used wisely."

He stepped away from the pulpit and took his seat behind the deacon. The congregation waited in silence while he looked at the floor. After a moment, he stood, and the Creed began.

When Communion arrived, Danielle tried to hang back with Sylvia, but Sylvia urged her to go. She watched Danielle approach the altar, then diverted her gaze as Danielle bowed.

On their way out, Sylvia noticed plastic sandwich bags stacked up next to the pile of used worship programs, each containing a pamphlet and a piece of chalk. She took one and handed it to Danielle, who leafed through the pamphlet while they walked home.

"Apparently the chalk is blessed," she said.

Sylvia loosened her scarf. The sun was strong today. "We'll have to be careful with it."

Danielle read on. "It's a house blessing. It says, 'The house blessing is a way of extending an invitation to Jesus to join us in our home lives.'"

Sylvia thought of that morning, when she had cut a spironolactone tablet in half. Maybe she could use help.

"'The traditional house blessing consists of writing XX + C + M + B + YY above the threshold of your home, where XX are the first two digits of the year, and YY are the last two.'"

Danielle held the pamphlet closer to her eyes and then laughed.

"I think it sounds nice," Sylvia said.

"That's not what I'm laughing at," Danielle said.

She handed the pamphlet to Sylvia, keeping her thumb pressed down on the text until Sylvia pulled it away. Sylvia read where the thumb had been. "'So, for example, the year 1996 will be blessed with nineteen + C + M + B + ninety-six.'"

Sylvia handed the pamphlet back to Danielle. "To be honest, I'm surprised it's not older than that."

Danielle stepped in a puddle, splashing slush onto Sylvia's boot. The same spot had been mostly ice on their walk to Mass. "Ooh, the letters have a dual meaning."

Sylvia held up her gloved hand. "Let me guess."

Danielle creased the pamphlet and held it up against her chest, turning her shoulders away and smiling a little. A sedan drifted through the intersection in front of them, running the stop sign. People were venturing out on the roads again.

Sylvia said, "All right, one of them has to be a Latin phrase."

"Christus mansionem benedicat. Sylvia gets an A-plus," Danielle said. "Translates to 'May Christ bless this house.'"

Sylvia put her finger up to her forehead like she was trying to open a telepathic channel. "The second meaning is something obvious too. I'll get it."

"You're going to kick yourself," Danielle said.

They had walked just over half a mile. The condition of the sidewalks worsened as they pushed farther into the purely residential part of the neighborhood, and long portions of the streets were still trapped underneath a layer of packed ice. It would be at least another day before they could drive anywhere.

"It's a trick question," Sylvia declared. "The second meaning is also a Latin phrase."

Danielle smiled and shook her head.

"I give up, then," Sylvia said. "What is it?"

The dream in which the three wise men are warned not to return to Herod is far from the only dream in the Bible. Scripture is heavy on dreams, and on people who listen to their dreams. Joseph is warned about Herod in a dream as well. Before that, he is told not to divorce Mary in a dream. When Herod dies, Joseph is told in a dream that he can come back to Nazareth. And before Jesus's trial, Pontius Pilate's wife has a nightmare that moves her to tell her husband, "Have nothing to do with that righteous Man."

There are dreams in the Old Testament too. King Abimelech takes Sarah to his harem, but in a dream, he is told not to touch her, for she is the wife of a prophet. Dreams come often to prophets, kings, and saints, but are not exclusive to them. The cupbearer and the baker who share a prison cell with Joseph each have a dream. The cupbearer's dream foretells his restoration to the pharaoh's court. The baker's dream foretells his beheading.

Sylvia had a dream years earlier, just weeks after her wedding. The modern Catholic Church views dreams as a vessel of private revelation. Dreams do not reveal truth that has not been revealed through scripture. The age of prophets has passed. Rather, dreams come to people to move them to actions that will expand their relationship with God.

In Sylvia's dream, she said, "I would prefer to be a woman." She woke up and remembered it. Later that morning she was making eggs for herself and said it aloud, softly, to the eggs. Immediately, she knew it was true. It was possible that she had thought of this on her own, and only within the silent walls of her dreamscape had she been courageous enough to express it. When Sylvia was being strictly rational, she saw it that way.

When she was being all of herself at once, though, she saw it differently. Rational Sylvia would never be so solipsistic as to believe that God himself had told her she was trans, yet Faithful Sylvia believed that help would be given to those who needed it. On the random, un-summonable, beautiful days on which she was easy with her faith, balanced in her rationality, and confident in her womanhood, she believed that she had been told about her gender by her guardian angel.

The Catholic Church is unambiguous on the subject of guardian angels. They exist, and they are universal. When she was being all of herself at once, Sylvia believed an angel had felt what she felt, had known what she knew, had witnessed her coming back to church, had believed in the sincerity of her desire to grow, had observed her becoming humble, and at precisely the right moment, had said, "Enough."

* * *

Sylvia fell asleep on the couch shortly after they made it home, and when she woke, the sun was already setting. She sat up and rubbed her eyes in disbelief. Out the window, she could see wispy snowflakes swirling in the golden light.

"Was it supposed to snow again tonight?" she called out. Danielle didn't answer.

Sylvia rolled over and picked up her phone. Her weather app still said it was sunny outside. She called out again: "Danielle?"

Still no answer. Sylvia stood and went into the kitchen, where the bottle of scotch from the night before was now empty. She looked out the kitchen window to see if Danielle was out front (she wasn't), then went upstairs to their room. Danielle wasn't in the house.

Sylvia went back to where she had fallen asleep and checked her phone again to make sure she had no missed calls. She turned the ringer on just in case. While she was thinking about where Danielle could have gone, her thoughts shifted laterally to the article about Danielle in *R-Home Magazine.* It occurred to her that the snow may have slowed down mail delivery a good bit. The article might be up on the website, though.

She had very little to do, having knocked out most of the nagging tasks on her mental to-do list during the previous snowbound week, and she had even less to do when Danielle wasn't around. She went to the *R-Home* website.

The article was up, and the time stamp indicated it had been published while Sylvia was sleeping. She would need to tell Danielle when she got back. In the meantime, she read, and as she read, she considered pretending she hadn't found the article. Sylvia could tell four paragraphs in that Danielle would hate it. She knew Danielle's thoughts and opinions on her interior design work, the reasons she did it and the deeper goals to which she connected each choice—to break the filters that normally made people overlook ordinary objects, pulling them toward the notion that nothing is insignificant. Those reasons weren't on the page beneath Danielle's photograph; she had been used as a watered-down example in what was really an article about local trends. She would hate it.

Sylvia finished the article and contemplated going back to sleep, but she was starting to worry about Danielle. She checked her phone again to make sure there were no calls, and after putting it down she picked it back up to check, once again, that the ringer was on. She paced around for a bit and ultimately landed in the kitchen. She was rifling through the pantry when the door opened, and Danielle came in carrying a paper grocery bag and a flat rectangular package. She was breathing hard.

Sylvia said, "Where were you?"

Danielle sat in a kitchen chair. She draped her shoulder over the back of it and tipped her head back too. She took in a deep breath and then pulled her head back up. "I saw a winter weather advisory for tonight, so I walked to Libbie Market to get some overpriced groceries for us tonight and tomorrow. And then on my way back I noticed the antique store was open, so I stopped in and I spotted a chalkboard from a turn-of-the-century schoolhouse. I felt like it would be perfect, plus they let me talk them down from fifty dollars to twenty-eight. And then when I got out, I realized I had to carry all that, and then it started snowing."

"You should've called me."

"I knew your ringer wouldn't be on. And you were asleep."

She had a point.

Danielle said, "And anyway, I've been feeling like a slug, so I thought a walk in the snow would be good for me if this is all going to continue into next week."

Sylvia nodded. She picked up the grocery bag and took a look at the contents: olive oil, white bread, tortillas, canned beans, mozzarella cheese, and cheddar cheese. "It's a good thing you didn't get wine. You might've passed out."

Danielle shrugged. She seemed embarrassed. Her cheeks were flushed from the walk, so it was hard to tell. "I thought we could brown the last chicken breast and make quesadillas with it."

Sylvia opened the refrigerator and removed the raw chicken breast. It was limp and slippery, and it made a slimy squelch as she put it on the cutting board. She drew the chef's knife from the block and held the chicken breast against the wood as she cut.

"My profile is up on the website," Danielle said.

Sylvia paused. "I saw it too."

"Did you like it?"

Sylvia put the knife down slowly. She put her hands on the edge of the counter and leaned on her shoulders, then hung her head and turned her gaze, upside down and sideways, toward Danielle.

"I'll sign on to whatever you thought."

Danielle smiled, laughing but not really laughing, sweeping her gaze near Sylvia but missing her face. "Sounds like you read it the same way I read it. I read it while you were asleep on the couch, and I got so mad that I came in here to calm myself down." She nodded toward the empty bottle of scotch. "But then I considered how far-gone I was acting."

Her eyes found Sylvia's eyes, and this time they stuck. They looked more open than open, and a little scared. She said, "Our fertility has been pretty hard on me, and I know that's nothing new. I know I've been egging you on to taper your hormones, and I haven't exactly been a beacon of self-control."

Sylvia took the knife in her hands again and resumed cutting. Raw, refrigerated chicken had a particular cold to it. The temperature started out mild, but the longer she held it, the more the cold seeped into her fingers. "I'm sorry I made us try everything else first."

"I'm not accusing you," Danielle said. "I'm not telling you you've done something wrong or that you've forced my bad habits on me. I'm not entirely sure what I'd even call my recent state; maybe a cold snap. I was holding that bottle of scotch up and I just thought about what you're doing, and I decided I need to clean things up."

The chicken was probably small enough to brown and fit into a quesadilla, but cutting each piece in half would nearly double the time it took to finish the task. Sylvia felt like the moment around her was playing out with a butterfly effect, like any change she introduced would set their whole marriage on a radically different course. She would have to take responsibility for whatever path they took from there, so she continued cutting the chicken smaller and smaller.

Danielle said, "But I was still fuming about that profile when I left. I think I made it halfway to Libbie Market in about a minute; I'm surprised I didn't get hit by a skidding truck. I was just livid about the whole thing, thinking I was going to clean things up to show them. I was going to clean things up, and think even better, and then they'd be sorry. I really wasn't making any sense, but I was mad enough to listen to myself." She laughed at that. It struck Sylvia as a defensive laugh, like she was laughing to convince herself this was a funny story and not one that made her feel completely bare. Danielle continued, "But then I guess I got a bit of runner's high going and that anger started to clear out and I thought, *Maybe it's fate for them to paint me as kind of bland and generic, just a young interior designer making things adorable.* The whole reason I did the profile—well, in addition to vanity—the main reason I did the profile was that I felt like it would age-proof my resumé. We're going to be pregnant soon"—Sylvia thought she heard a bit of insecurity enter Danielle's voice, but Danielle pushed through it—"and I've been thinking, I don't want to fit our baby into a career timeline. If I was working a job like yours, then maybe I'd have to. But I'm in a field where I can have a portfolio and an article about me in *R-Home*, and I can have those credentials in place to support me six months from now or six years from now. Right now it seems like I'll have to go back to work, but maybe we cut and skimp along and find that we don't hate it, and then maybe it'll turn out that it was better to be good and generic, instead of laced with strong opinions and born of the moment. Or maybe it turns out we get twins, and daycare costs so much that I can't even afford to go back to work until they're old enough for school. I'd see the vibes and trends changing around me and feel this pressure and anxiety to go back before they got too different. But in that profile, they say so little about me that's of any note that I could wait twenty-two years and it'd still hold up."

"I think that's a worldly approach," Sylvia said. She stopped cutting the chicken and tried to let her statement settle the way Father Stephen could—to let the silence give her statement weight and emphasis, instead of feeling how little she had offered in response to how much she was being told. Her hands felt like they had crystalized.

She added, "I'm proud of you," and went to wash her hands.

"I'm proud of you too," Danielle said.

Sylvia sniffed.

Danielle came over and rubbed the small of her back. "We can be together through this, like we were through other things."

The warm water came slowly. Sylvia rubbed her hands past the last of the soap, waiting for the water's steady warmth to bring the feeling back to her fingers. A draft came through the window, and she felt wet streaks on her face.

Danielle put her hands around Sylvia's waist and put her cheek against Sylvia's cheek. The line of her tear warmed between her skin and Danielle's. Danielle pushed herself closer. Sylvia felt her smile. "You've been really brave."

Sylvia nodded. "I feel like a coward."

She felt Danielle shake her head. "It's just a difficult time that's going to end and then be worth the difficulty."

Sylvia turned around in her arms and kissed her. She closed her eyes and drew Danielle closer to her. She cradled the back of Danielle's head and hummed a little. It sounded like a coo.

Danielle looked up from inside Sylvia's arms. "We still need to do the chalk blessing."

They left the raw chicken on the cutting board and went into the living room to get the pamphlet. Danielle opened it and began to read. She said, "Hmm. It says to incense each room of your house after the prayers are read."

"What happens if you don't incense the rooms?"

Danielle shrugged. "It also says you can have your priest come and do it."

The idea struck Sylvia in two potent but divergent ways. It would embolden her faith to have a priest come bless the house . . . unless Father Stephen took the occasion to reveal charges against Sylvia that he'd previously withheld. Before she had to decide which was more likely, Danielle said, "I don't feel good about asking him to come while it's snowing."

"Yes," Sylvia said.

Danielle went back to reading the pamphlet. "I was going to suggest we just read the prayers, but you're supposed to incense the room you're in while you're praying the Magnificat."

"I don't think I know the Magnificat," Sylvia said.

"That, we can fix." Danielle put the pamphlet down on the entryway table and headed back to the kitchen, taking the chalk with her. Sylvia followed and watched as she stripped the paper off her antique chalkboard. It was about eighteen inches by eighteen inches. The frame was light green copper, and the surface carried a billowy palimpsest from years of preceding chalk. Danielle laid the chalkboard flat on the kitchen table.

"I'll have to write small," she said. "Also," she paused with the chalk in her hand, "isn't this chalkboard cool? They must've had it hanging outside, or not had glass in the windows. Copper doesn't turn green inside. It doesn't turn green at all anymore, actually."

She didn't wait for a response. With the blessed chalk, she wrote at the top, "The Prayer of Mary."

"I'm immediately realizing how much of a shortfall this is," Sylvia said. The Catholic Church's partiality to Mary was well-known among Christians. It was one of the reasons Sylvia was partial to Catholicism over other, more outwardly trans-friendly denominations. She preferred not to speculate on how Mary would feel about her, but at least Mary had always seemed approachable. Her uneasy place in the faith offered so little to be sure about, but Sylvia felt sure that Mary would listen. She would listen when Sylvia told her that people spoke about trans women as though they were egomaniacs; as though they were so self-assured that they would correct God himself about their gender. Sylvia felt that Mary would listen patiently as she told her that she didn't see it that way. She could picture that anxious, caring face from all the paintings on their calendar, listening as Sylvia told her that trans people went down the social ladder when they came out, losing influence and voice as they engaged with themselves, becoming the meek. Trans people made the decision to be talked over endlessly, told what they meant by people who hadn't felt that eternal rattle, that hum, that noise. Mary would listen when Sylvia told her that transitioning was a humbling experience. Trans people knew their gender, and others didn't believe them. That created danger, danger just like the danger Mary had accepted the moment she was visited by the angel. Sylvia wasn't as brave or as faithful or as good as Mary, but Mary would listen, if ever they were to meet. Sylvia was sure she would.

Danielle said, "You're lucky I'm not making you memorize the Latin version." She had filled the left half of the chalkboard from top to bottom and now was writing more lines in a second column on the right.

"That's a bluff."

Danielle stopped. "Okay, you're right. But at least two members of my extended family could probably write the Latin version out with no notice."

Sylvia had no trouble believing that. Danielle's family had deep roots in the Massachusetts Catholic community. Two of her uncles had gone to divinity school, and one was a priest. Other relatives varied in their levels of dogma and rigidity, but there was no denying that each of them had been well educated. Danielle was one of the only members of her family who had spent time in a truly secular school, at any level.

"Done," Danielle said. She held the chalkboard up. It said:

My soul magnifies the Lord
And my spirit rejoices in God my savior;
Because He has regarded the lowliness of His handmaid;
For behold, henceforth all generations shall call me blessed;
Because He who is mighty has done great things for me;
and holy is His name;
And His mercy is from generation to generation
on those who fear Him.
He has shown might with His arm,
He has scattered the proud in the conceit of their heart.
He has put down the mighty from their thrones,
and has exalted the lowly
He has filled the hungry with good things,
and the rich He has sent away empty.

He has given help to Israel, his servant, mindful of His mercy
Even as He spoke to our fathers, to Abraham and his posterity forever.

"You look puzzled," Danielle said.

Sylvia blinked, then looked at Danielle. "Is this typically recited?"

"It's more of a hymn," Danielle said. "But!" She held up her index finger like an exclamation point. "It has the particular honor of being the longest string of words—spoken or sung—by a woman in the New Testament."

"Huh," Sylvia said. "Let's find a place for the chalkboard." She was reading it again. Something about it surprised her. She wanted to sit with the chalkboard and unpack her thoughts later. Maybe if she got up in the middle of the night again. . . .

"I'm thinking the wall behind the foot of the table," Danielle said. "It gets some really nice morning sunshine from the adjacent window."

Sylvia looked at the window to see what she meant, then remembered it wasn't morning, so the sunshine wouldn't be there. But even without the morning sun she could see that the snow appeared to be stopping.

* * *

Danielle had initiated Sylvia's spiritual convalescence, but she wasn't the one who finished it. At first, Sylvia's return to church was only a way of showing Danielle she was serious. Danielle was a serious Catholic, so Sylvia acted the part. She kept an open mind and enjoyed the academic quality of the campus priest's homilies, but she knew going in that there would be no answers for her. She was trapped in an incomprehensible matrix, where death was an ever-present hulking mass, capable of assuming any spooky form and of realizing itself through any vehicle. If Sylvia were to end up in heaven, she would be heaven's first depressed existentialist. She was sure of it.

At the time, she didn't perceive herself gradually opening up to the faith, though in retrospect she believed the cracks in her fears must have begun forming the minute she walked into a church with Danielle. She clung to Danielle as the one sure thing in her life, and to be with Danielle was to be with the faith. Danielle was forthcoming with both her love and her conditions: Outside of church, Sylvia couldn't hunch her shoulders and mope about mortality, or Danielle would be gone. She was also not allowed to unload her many burdens, nor was she allowed to close herself off. It was a rigid, uncomfortable balance.

On the days it came easily, Sylvia would give herself a moment to dis-associate and just watch herself, in disbelief at how well-adjusted she could appear.

At their wedding, a truly novel sensation had appeared before her, gleaming in contrast to all her dreary introspection. As she stood facing Danielle at the altar, everything seemed possible.

Sylvia's dream came to her a few weeks later. After she had come out to the eggs, she came out to Danielle. First, Danielle suggested that Sylvia speak to a priest. Sylvia agreed, once again to show she was serious. She made an appointment with the priest who had married them and told him she was transgender, and he asked lots of questions for which she had no answers. Did she plan to get any surgeries? She didn't know. Did she plan to have children? She didn't know. What did her wife think? She didn't know, not exactly. How did she plan to dress? She didn't know. Her only plan was to take hormones and go from there. The priest concluded that, while a number of things were off-limits—in particular, things that damaged her ability to pro-create—the rest of it seemed okay. He had used the word "okay," and he had suggested she gather a second opinion if possible.

Now Sylvia knew the answers to all of his questions, but the an-swers seemed tangential compared to what the hormones had actually done for her. Upon taking them, she had lost her existential fears. She'd since learned that people suffering from gender dysphoria were more likely to take high-risk jobs, not valuing their bodies enough to be cautious. After hormones, Sylvia became both less and more afraid of death than she had been before. Less afraid of an infinite life—even comforted by the notion of one. More afraid of a tidy, irreversible end-ing. She moved further into her faith. Her Catholicism became sincere at the same time she herself became unsatisfactory to it. She would never be able to explain to another person how her identity's contra-dictions didn't actually contradict. But if she were to have a baby, she believed, she would have fulfilled the church's requirements, and she would never have to explain herself at all.

* * *

The next three days were warm. The arc of the sun passed in long, flat strides across the neighborhood, methodically erasing the snow. By Wednesday Sylvia was back at the office. All that remained of the snowscape in which she had added up the days of her phaseout were the dirty icebergs in the office parking lot.

She drank lots of coffee, as she always did. And as she always did, Sylvia tried to determine whether or not she liked her job. On the one hand, she had chosen well in terms of companies. Hers was a company with high marks on the corporate equality index. The organization had accommodated and celebrated her transition. She felt safe there.

On the other hand, corporate life had a distinctly game-like quality that unnerved her. There were moments when she felt so perfectly suited to her role as a risk manager that she could tackle a black bear, the risks of doing so all appropriately managed. But when she tried to tell Danielle about these moments, they ceased to make any sense. While Danielle's hours of thought and labor resulted in beautiful restaurants, evocative photographs, and affecting textures, the hulking corporate risks that Sylvia's hard work kept at bay seemed to vanish as soon as she closed her laptop, like she had been hallucinating.

But there were other times, too, where the company's understanding of her psyche was so intimate, she wondered if this were the only place where she could know herself. Last fall, her whole team had taken a strengths assessment, paid for by the company, which was meant to tell them what they were good at. Sylvia's top strength came out as "intellection," and the description had made her tear up, she felt so understood.

To be strong in intellection is to generate a high quantity of thought. You enjoy thinking, and you likely enjoy the way that being alone enables you to think even more. During these times, you find yourself posing questions, looking at them from different angles, and trying out answers, weighing their sounds and tracing their edges before moving on to another question. Paradoxically, you may find yourself feeling the most burdened in times of the least stress, as the quiet allows you to generate question after question, and answer after answer.

Sylvia wafted through the early days of the week, preoccupied by the mistiness of it all. She knew she couldn't trust herself at the moment. She was thinking about sperm motility and soggy firewood, and about her marriage and risk management, and about cutting her pills and cutting an onion. She tried to remind herself that she had expected to drift a little during this period. But she had trouble thinking about any one thing for long enough to set it down, when so many things needed to be thought about.

Sylvia liked to go to work in the mornings with the lower half of her hair in a little fishtail braid, assembled while it was wet. This week, she found herself studying it on her trips to the ladies' room. This week, no matter what she did, her braids looked uneven, bumpy, and loose. Leaning toward her reflection, she could see all her trepidation woven into the rings of her hair, anxiety palpitating through her fingers as she wrapped strand after strand.

On Wednesday, her final meeting of the day ran long enough that the sun had set by the time she left. She didn't mind, though. The meeting had been with a group of coworkers she personally liked, and it had only dragged on because they had free rein of the conference room to chat, given that it was the last reservation of the day. On her way outside, Sylvia got to thinking about the personal aspect of a large office like hers. She was aware that her coworkers were not her friends, and she was equally aware that her bosses were not her parents, but her transition made the line more complicated. She had changed teams shortly after her transition, meaning her current coworkers—most of them young women within five years of her age—had only ever known her as Sylvia. Her friendships outside of work tended to predate her transition, and most now barely limped onward, if they still existed at all. Her friends had gotten the words of support right, but none had ever again managed the easy familiarity they'd once shared. Sylvia often felt like Danielle was her only friend. Her other friends were more like friends of a friend. They were friends with who she used to be—as was she—as were her brothers, her parents. Her interactions with them nowadays were more cautious than spontaneous, more layered than open. Her coworkers were not her friends, but the complications of an office dynamic paled beside the complications in her social orbit outside the office. Did Sylvia have friends? She wouldn't say no. But she would be more comfortable calling them acquaintances.

By Friday, Sylvia had let her inbox pile into the hundreds, and the volume of unread messages finally forced her to think about work and little else. She was almost relieved at her mental fatigue when she replied to the last of them and closed her laptop for the week. She walked to her car feeling emptied out, almost experiencing mindfulness. As she drove home, she wished she had drunk more water. Her coffee consumption had caught up to her and left her feeling like little spinning tops were twirling lightly in her bloodstream. A bit off-kilter behind the wheel, Sylvia was happy she had made it out of the parking lot before darkness had completely taken the road.

Her phone rang with a call from her parents' house, and she let it ring as she drove.

It was going to be okay. She had another week to go before cutting out another half-Spironolactone and half-Estradiol. Her thoughts and emotions felt like they were coming and going at oblique angles, but the thoughts and emotions themselves were familiar ones. She was going to be okay for the rest of this week and for the rest of next, and if the next step down had the same effect, then she would make it through that one okay too.

Harriet and Tyler were hosting a housewarming dinner party that evening. Sylvia's route home passed by a grocery store, and she had told Danielle she would pick up a bottle of wine on her way. She pulled into the parking lot as the sun sank below the trees, turning their spindly branches to dark lines within the weak orange circle, as if the sun itself were cracking.

The sliding doors opened for her, and Sylvia stepped into the fluorescent-soaked interior. Before her transition, before she knew she was trans, Sylvia had felt a hideous aversion to being seen. Grocery stores had been especially hard on her. They involved lots of close-quartered interaction, the carts making everyone bigger and more unwieldy in the narrow aisles. Navigating necessitated a litany of little courtesies: "Excuse me" as she snaked her way around another shopper to enter the bread aisle; "Could I just . . . ?" as she leaned across someone's line of sight to pick up a green pepper. Sylvia had never determined whether she hated to be seen back then because she'd suspected other people could see her secret (the secret she'd kept from herself) or if she had simply hated that people took her at face value. It wouldn't surprise her if both were somehow true. Before her transition, contradictory things had always seemed true. It had seemed true that she wanted to be a woman and it also seemed true that she despised the thought of being a woman. It seemed true that she felt kinship toward other women, and it also seemed true that she could hardly speak to them. It seemed true that all men wanted to be women, and it also seemed true that no one would understand if she spoke about her desire. It seemed true that she was trans, and it also seemed true that she wasn't. Grocery stores had brought all of it to the surface. They were something everyone had in common. Everyone shared the same basic need for food, everyone shopped with the same wiry metal carts, everyone offered the same banal apologies as they reached into each other's spaces. Sylvia fit as awkwardly into the entire world as carts fit into the crowded aisles, and supermarkets lay all her discomfort out before her. She had loathed them.

Now, she didn't mind them. Turning the corner into the wine aisle, Sylvia bit the fingertip of one of her gloves to pull her hand out. Holding the glove in her other hand, she reached for a bottle from Argentina that cost the right amount. It had mountains on the label and the font was classy. It seemed appropriate to bring to a housewarming. Carrying the bottle by the neck and still holding her glove with the other hand, she waited in line for the self-checkout behind a parade of other shoppers holding small purchases.

Sylvia's transition had made grocery shopping unremarkable for her, but before that, it was Danielle who had made grocery shopping bearable. She had even enjoyed it sometimes, particularly in the feminine aisles. Sylvia had hated buying shampoo by herself, with all the women's hair products standing between her and the tiny display of men's. It didn't matter if others were present in the aisle or not, it only mattered that someone could arrive at any point, could see her standing near the products for women and suspect her of being one—or see her continuing toward the products for men and suspect her of being one. Which would she have wanted at the time? Neither, easily. Not to be there at all, preferably; or for all the items on the shelves to be obscured so only she could ever know what she was looking at or not looking at. But when she was there with Danielle, Sylvia became anonymous, regardless of which gender the aisle catered to. She was just following her girlfriend around, looking idly at the shelves as they passed.

Sylvia paid for the wine, then put her glove back on and went out to her car. It was dark now, and the city was entering another cold snap. This one was supposed to be dry.

Starting the car, Sylvia decided she didn't like that thought about the aisles Danielle went down. She was selling Danielle short by focusing on that. She'd liked shopping with Danielle because Danielle didn't treat every tiny interaction like a threat. She didn't plan her routes to avoid where the crowds were heaviest, and she said, "Excuse me" with no apparent difficulty if she bumped into someone. Even in the most tightly packed sections, Danielle spoke easily, and Sylvia had found she could speak easily back to her. They talked about onions and cilantro, about wheat bread and heavy cream. She felt close to Danielle when they shopped together.

Introspection was still easy, she noted, or at least non-threatening. That was good. What was Sylvia really scared of, now that she was tapering off hormones? She was scared of the same idle thinking she'd been doing for the last few minutes, only darker. Scared of intellection working against her. Scared of her own mind creating that endless mechanical hum, spinning her thoughts in loops just to burn off energy.

Question after question, answer after answer. The answers would be confined to the scope of the questions, and the questions would descend into gloom. Before long, she wouldn't be asking herself why she felt so uncomfortable in the grocery store. No, that was the friendly kind of question she asked herself when she was steady, and when she was steady, she'd know the answer was that she felt like everyone was looking at her, at which point she would realize that no one was. But if things got bad enough, she wouldn't ask herself such open questions anymore. What was she scared of? The old feeling, disguised as a question: *Why are they all looking at you?*

Danielle was sitting in the center of the couch when Sylvia got home. She had started the fireplace and was staring into it. The flickering orange light gave her skin an effervescent glow. Sylvia wondered if she could persuade her to go to bed before the housewarming. Danielle turned her head and smiled. "I thought it would be good to heat the house up before we left."

Sylvia nodded. She took her gloves off and knelt in front of Danielle. She reached for her hand, but Danielle pulled it away. "Come sit with me," she said, patting the cushion beside her.

Sylvia sat down next to her and extended her arm to take Danielle under it. Danielle acquiesced. She leaned her head on Sylvia's shoulder and put her hand on Sylvia's stomach.

"What's on your mind?" Sylvia asked.

Danielle shook her head. "Just let me lie here for right now."

Sylvia obliged. She perceived the rhythm of Danielle's breathing through touch, not hearing her breaths but rather feeling the metered rise and fall against her side. She watched the fire.

"There's a bag of soap from Harriet on the vanity upstairs," Danielle said. "I've been talking to her a lot this week, since she's always home and my commute is so short. I don't like her, but she's interesting."

Sylvia nodded. "I thought 'interesting' was her word for us."

"You know how people project themselves," Danielle said. "I've realized that, if nothing else, she's a useful friend to make. She and Tyler are practically homesteaders. I'm not excited about their party tonight, not at all, but I'm excited to go around their house and see the whole pioneer setup they've got. Where they make the soap, where they're going to grow the peppers, where Harriet sews and repairs her arsenal of handmade dresses." She rubbed the heel of her hand in a circle on Sylvia's abdomen. "I think she'd make us dresses if we asked."

Sylvia pulled her tight. Danielle looked up at her. She was smiling. "I love you, you know," she said.

Sylvia picked up a strand of Danielle's hair that had fallen to the wrong side of her part. Without breaking eye contact, she moved it from one side to the other. "I love you too."

Danielle sighed. "I finally got around to reading Preston's Christmas card today."

The deep oranges and bright yellows of the fire went damp in Sylvia's eyes. The smoky smell dissipated, and the crackling sounds faded into dull, cottony ringing. "How was it?"

Her breaths were shallow now. The weight of Danielle's hand now seemed inhibiting.

Danielle said, "He's moving to Richmond in March. It seems he's very excited to see me."

Sylvia wanted to be surprised, but she was not. She was not surprised that Preston Ellridge IV was coming to Richmond, or that he would reach out to Danielle. She remembered the menacing way he had investigated and interrogated her after she proposed to Danielle. How he was suddenly everywhere, talking to everyone, asking pointed, probing questions about her. *Tell me about this* exciting *fiancé; interests? Likes? Dislikes?* First pestering Danielle, then other people he knew through Danielle, periodically circling back to Sylvia herself when secondhand sources grew weary: *How do you and your brothers get along? How about you and your mother?* Obsessive to his molten core, Preston had never struck Sylvia as the kind of person who would change.

"How do you feel about seeing him?" she asked.

Danielle lifted herself from Sylvia's shoulder and pulled her legs inward. She crossed them underneath her and assumed a straight back, as if she was about to meditate. "He's a friend I've had for a long time, and I'd like to talk to him if it'll be straightforward. I'm also worried about what it would mean not to see him, with him coming to Richmond."

Sylvia nodded.

Danielle said, "We could both go see him together."

Sylvia shook her head. "I have a sneaking suspicion that's the worst option."

She was trying not to have any relevant thoughts. If she didn't allow her reaction to solidify into concrete thoughts, then she wouldn't have to keep them to herself. She sat as still as she could manage and thought about the snow—how only a week before, everything had been covered in rolling, glistening, blinding white.

Danielle reached out to put her hand on Sylvia's knee. She had been sitting so straight that the forward motion startled Sylvia, like the hand had reached out of a painting. "I don't think he would try anything, or even say anything. I really do think he feels bad about before. I know I'm being a little generous with him, but I don't think he realized how long I'd known you or how long we'd been serious. We just didn't talk about our love lives, you know? We talked about love some—just love in the abstract, though. Not between two people like us. He never really talked about dating at all, and so I guess I didn't really talk about you much either. I mentioned you of course, I'm sure I did. But until he met you, my relationship never seemed to come up. I know that's hard to believe, with how frequently it came up after then. But it didn't."

Sylvia turned her head slightly to look at Danielle's hand, then at the fire. She closed her eyes to gather herself, but the imprint of the fire remained, a series of fluorescent-blue scratches against the blackness of her eyelids. "If his moving here hasn't become important already," she said, opening her eyes again, "then I don't want to continue talking about it long enough for it to become important." She turned to look at Danielle, who was still leaning forward. "Does that make sense?"

Danielle smiled and nodded twice.

Sylvia felt dizzy.

"I'll just go see him once or twice. I'll keep my distance, and meanwhile you won't overthink it."

The word "overthink" brought Sylvia back to the snow. It seemed like a word on which snow had fallen for an entire year. She was surprised it hadn't collapsed in on itself, feeble little word that it was. "I won't overthink it," she said.

Danielle rubbed her thumb along Sylvia's knee, then pulled her hand away and gave it a slap. "Let's go to Harriet's."

"Yes," Sylvia said. "Just give me a second to run a brush through my hair."

She walked up the stairs, keeping her footfalls soft but gripping the handrail tightly. The key was not to think about it at all. If she could just not think about it at all, then no thoughts would fester. Sylvia shut the bathroom door and took her hair down, turning away from the mirror. Head bent toward the floor, she linked her fingers together and spoke quietly, so quietly she couldn't be sure that there was sound, and there may only have been simple, formless, useless breath.

"Angel of God, my guardian dear

To whom God's love entrusts me here
Ever this night be at my side
To light and to guard,
To rule and to guide."

2

What's it like on your planet, where all the seasons are Spring?

Preston Ellridge felt there couldn't be a more beautiful externalization of his current state of mind than the farmers market. Yes, the farmers market, that irrepressible nexus of the small business world, the format and pattern of which could be found in any town in the United States, but the particulars of which were as singular as the bloom of a galaxy petunia. The characteristic electricity that marked his better periods unfurled before him, pulsing through the air. He was happy to be here in Richmond, happy to be an entrepreneur, and most of all happy to be entering the farmers market on a dewy spring Sunday morning, searching for his friend among the other go-getters who had arrived early to beat the rush.

It had been a long time since Preston had seen her. Years, in fact. He'd been traveling around Europe for most of the last twenty-four months, with short stints in Oregon and California speckled among his transient engagements. Not that he was a transient by any stretch of the imagination. His travels revolved around research and mastery. Where other people of resources simply used those resources to bully potential competitors out of their chosen field, Preston had used his resources for the purpose of gaining commercial knowledge typically inaccessible to people of comparatively smaller financial assets.

As each of the three previous Preston Ellridges had done, Preston Ellridge IV thought in terms of competitive advantages. His bloodline had acquired their wealth through this particular power of perception, on which his grandfather had once written a venerated essay. Each of them could seemingly interview any market and draw out its leverage points in friendly, direct tones. If one possessed either the means of leverage or the means to obtain the means of leverage, then the remaining steps to success quickly became academic.

Preston weaved around other shoppers, surprised at how dense the crowd was at so early an hour, even when he adjusted for typical farmers market standards. The entrepreneurs at each stand were still drafting off the initial burst of energy that accompanied opening time, vigorously hailing passersby. At least two stands were selling local pickles, another was selling kimchi, and one was selling microgreens, which were arranged in crates around the owner like patches of grass. Several stands selling local honey were advertising its alleged allergy benefits, a timely commodity as cities across the region took on their yearly yellow-green coating. Soon commuters would be stopping at gas stations to wash the pollen off their windshields after failing to whisk it away with wiper fluid, periodically pausing their work to stop for a sneeze—unless, of course, they had ingested local honey. The commercial nearly wrote itself.

To complement this hubbub, food trucks and coffee trucks had also pulled in, a true testament to the idea that the success of any eatery was merely a byproduct of location. It came down to more than that, of course, but these trucks cleverly avoided direct competition with restaurants by sneaking into spaces where the only alternative was another truck. A gimmick, albeit a brilliant one. It was by a coffee truck that Preston spotted her.

She had just been handed an iced coffee, or perhaps a cold brew, and was taking her initial sip with her eyes closed. She would probably spit it out—or bring it up through her nose—if he tapped her right at that moment. Instead, Preston watched her take in the sip, looking immensely satisfied as she did so. He couldn't help but think of how, if she were the type of person who would rather have nothing than have something of sub-par quality, she would have taken that first sip warily, almost pecking at it, as if to make the coffee prove itself. Preston pegged that thought as one to come back to. He was sure there was an angle there, in the different ways a person takes a first sip.

He approached in muted bounds, landing softly on his toes, then tapped her on the shoulder. Harriet's face showed alarm as she turned, recoiling, to see who had touched her, then relaxed into a look of delight.

"Hi there!" she said.

She stepped to the side to let another customer pass, then leaned toward him with her free hand extended to draw him into a half-hug. Preston held her hug for the appropriate amount of time (more than one second but less than two), then asked, "Did Tyler come as well?"

Harriet sipped her coffee and shook her head. "Not this time," she said, swallowing. "He couldn't get a Friday afternoon flight, and he didn't want to wake up for an early morning flight either. I have until three p.m. today before I have to go get him."

"I'm sad that I missed him. Give him my regards," Preston said. Only the second statement was sincere.

"I'm not entirely sure what he's done with your regards from the last time," Harriet said.

Preston laughed. It was true that he and Tyler always seemed to be a missed connection, having only met once before during a week in which both Harriet and Preston had visited their families at the same time. Harriet's parents lived close to Preston's family's summer home, and even after each of them had moved away, they nevertheless encountered one another on a near-annual basis, their family obligations always managing to overlap for one holiday or another. Curiously, many of these encounters had happened after Preston and Tyler's first meeting, but Tyler was never present for them. He was, according to Harriet, perpetually on the road for his job, but it had always seemed to Preston that no job short of a presidential campaign could require so much travel. Apparently, not much had changed between them, though Preston understood a seismic change had occurred within their shared circle of acquaintances: in an odd twist of fate, Harriet and Tyler had become friends with Danielle.

"In either case, I'm delighted you were able to join me for this week's jaunt," Harriet said.

He had always liked the variety of words Harriet employed. Her sentences always had the feel of a home garden. "I wouldn't miss it," he said. He swept his hand around to indicate the farmers market as a whole. "This is such an exciting way to begin the Richmond chapter of my journey." Preston clenched his fists as he said the word "exciting," as if he were squeezing the excitement into the air.

"I forgot you talk like that," Harriet said.

Preston laughed, although he didn't find the comment as funny as the lack of self-awareness behind it. Preston considered his speech patterns lightly energetic at their furthest extreme, but it was likely everyone who ever met Harriet had been struck—or worse, off-put—by how she talked.

"It sounded on the phone like you've been spending lots of time with my friends," he said.

They had moved away from the coffee truck and were now walking along the perimeter of the market, where they could be hailed by stand owners.

"I'm quite partial to Sylvia," Harriet said. "Danielle, not so much."

This remark both puzzled and troubled Preston. "Why not Danielle?" he said.

Harriet sipped more of her coffee before answering. For now, Preston contained his impatience. If past observations of Harriet's caffeine intake were any indicator, he knew the pace and candor of her speech would elevate continuously over the next twenty minutes or so. He would get what he needed.

"For one, she's not very consistent. I spent the last month making her a dress, and when I showed it to her almost done, she adored it. In fact, she was really kind of saccharine. And then when I finished and brought it to her, she called me a hippie bitch."

Preston was even more puzzled now. Did Danielle dislike Harriet, or was she just unhappy? Harriet stopped to sip her coffee again. Preston waited for her to elaborate.

Harriet said, "Sylvia's very sweet, though. She sniffled a little when I finished her dress."

"I think I missed something," Preston said. "When did Danielle call you a hippie bitch?"

"Just about a week ago," Harriet said. "But for context, a lot happened to lead up to it. We had a housewarming in January that they came to—both of them were there—and before that I'd been worrying we offended Danielle somehow when we went to their house for dinner."

"You've been in their house?" Preston asked.

Harriet turned to lead them under the canopy of a stand selling elderberry syrups. "Can I ask you something?" she said to the proprietor.

"Of course," said the proprietor, a waifish woman in her mid forties with long, straight gray hair and a youthful face. Preston wondered if she had let herself go gray as a branding mechanism—a way of riffing on the name "elderberry."

"Is it true that elderberry gets rid of allergies?"

"It boosts your immune system, which fights allergies, so some people make the connection. For just allergies, though, I'd recommend local honey." She gestured to some jars labeled "With Raw Honey." "It puts the allergens into your system so it can train to fight them."

"I see," Harriet said. "My husband is just a sneezing mess around this time of year. I'm thinking I need to bring him around here."

The proprietor smiled, although Preston could see she was disappointed that a sale was not imminent.

"Thank you so much," Harriet said, drifting out from under the stand's roof. Once they were clear of earshot, she leaned toward Preston. "So disheartening."

"At least she didn't call you a hippie bitch," Preston said, hoping to point things back toward that topic.

"I need to get over this childish phobia of bees," Harriet said, speaking quicker now. "Bees are just amazing. They make honey that cures your nose and wax you can use for practically anything. Plus, urban beekeeping is hot right now, but I just quake at the thought of all those stingers in my backyard."

She downed a big sip of her coffee. "Even right now I'm shuddering inside just picturing it, and I'm worried I'll have a dream about bees later, but they're so amazing! They would make great friends if I could just calm down, but I can't seem to do it. I was hoping we could just grow elderberries because those are good little plants that don't fly around and sting you, but it always comes back to bees when I try to do something. I've bought more beeswax than any other substance, I think, all because I'm too scared of bees to try beekeeping."

"You were saying something about a housewarming," Preston said.

"Can I ask you a question?" Harriet had stopped in front of an organic pickle stand this time. She glanced up at Preston, who was trying to keep his face blank. "Actually, I'll ask when the cucumbers come up," she said.

They walked away. "The housewarming," Harriet said. "This is what I mean by saying Danielle's not very consistent: It was a few months ago, a little after we moved in. They showed up looking cute together like they always do, although I didn't know then that they always look cute together, since we had only just met them; but they did, and Danielle was so bright and gregarious. She was pulling Sylvia along most of the night, telling people nice things about her and smiling at her. She was bordering on uxorious for the majority of the evening, like the only thing she cared about at all was making sure Sylvia was having a fun time. I remember talking to them on and off—I was playing hostess, so I didn't talk to them the whole time—and thinking, 'Wow, Danielle is such a good partner.' The only time I saw them apart the whole night was when she pulled me aside—" Harriet made a pulling motion and took a horizontal half-step, "—and she said, 'Those dresses you showed me the other day are just beautiful.' I specifically remember that she used the word 'beautiful,' which I liked, because it's a word that people usually hold on to, like a super old wine they're keeping for the right occasion. I was flattered and a little bit flustered. I always get kind of embarrassed when someone mentions my sewing, I'm not sure why. But she told me they were beautiful and asked, Would I be able to make one for Sylvia and her? I remember that she said Sylvia's name first, and really the whole conversation seemed like it revolved around getting something for Sylvia; she just seemed so enamored and devoted to Sylvia."

Preston shoved his hands in his pockets. He reminded himself that this story ended with Danielle supposedly flying off the handle, although he'd had his doubts about that even before hearing the circumstances.

"Microgreens!" Harriet said. She'd moved six feet away while he was lost in thought.

Preston decided to stay put. He already knew about microgreens from his research. They were more flavorful, easier to grow, and healthier than most roughage, great for cultivating an eco-friendly health food vibe. They would probably have a place in his third or fourth restaurant, but not his first.

Harriet came back with a cardboard box that resembled a takeout container. "I'm sorry. Tyler and I are trying to grow microgreens this year, but we've never done it before, so I wanted to buy some as a reference. I'm going to buy them until we get them right."

"That's a good system," Preston said. He had never been able to reconcile Harriet's drive to master farming and handicraft skills with her baffling lack of initiative to monetize them. She'd been that way when they were growing up together too. Back when they were sixteen and Etsy was still exciting, he had once suggested she make an account to sell the trinkets she made out of seashells. She had laughed at him for the rest of the day.

"What was I talking about a second ago?"

"Danielle being in love," Preston said.

"Right. Hold on." Harriet lifted her coffee to dramatically drain the last of it. "Well, I said yes, I would make dresses for them if they would reimburse me for fabric. I didn't see much of them until we all went to the fabric store, and then that day it was the complete opposite. Danielle was kind of snappy and had her arms crossed a lot, and Sylvia was the one trying so hard to make sure Danielle had a good time. She was showing Danielle different colors, running her hands through things, making jokes, holding her hand. . . . I suspect that they're a smidge codependent, to be honest. They drove in their own car, though, and when we got back to my house to take measurements, they were both bustling around and having fun again. Although I did make us all gin and tonics, so maybe that was why."

"Wait," Preston said. "You've seen them both naked?"

"Perv, no," Harriet said. "What do you think women do when we're alone?"

Preston tried to contemplate this question, but he couldn't shake the image that had come into his head. Harriet and Danielle in there together. . . .

"We had fun, though," Harriet went on, walking slowly and scanning for other booths that interested her. "And I had fun making the dresses. I finished Danielle's first, and I was going to take both of them over when I was done, but I was so excited about how Danielle's turned out that I took it right over to her the minute I finished. I happened to finish it right at the time of day when Danielle is home but Sylvia's still out." She stopped walking for a moment. "I feel strange knowing their schedules. Is that strange?"

"You do live across the street," Preston said.

Harriet still seemed shaken by the realization. "Come to think of it, I know their weekend schedules too. I could probably predict who's going to be where at what times today and get it mostly right. I guess I spend so much time painting, drawing, making candles, sewing, planting, watering, and leatherworking in various parts of the house that I've just absorbed things. I do have a fairly spongy brain in some ways; Tyler says it's like a pancake. Excuse me, can I ask you a question?"

Preston nearly put his face in his hands, but he caught himself. Instead, he opened and closed his fists while Harriet accosted a man selling "award-winning" olive oil.

The market crowd was becoming more dense. The large open space had acquired the murmuring background hum that accompanies large crowds. It was a sound that Preston had detested growing up, with his parents' extensive social circle invading the house on a regular basis, crowding him out in his own home. Now he cherished it, primed as he was to enter the restaurant business. One day soon, Preston would hear that hum in a place of his own making.

"Apparently all you need to make olive oil is a bucket and an oil press," Harriet said, sidling back up to him. "I honestly don't know why anyone buys anything."

"Especially not when they live across the street from you," Preston said.

"Okay, so like I said, Danielle had gotten home but Sylvia hadn't yet, which seemed perfect because I didn't want Sylvia to feel slighted, so I folded the dress in some parchment paper to make it seem, I don't know, concocted? And I brought it over to Danielle, but she must've been stewing in one of her discordant moods. She and I talked some, and she invited me in and everything, and she did seem grateful, or at least impressed. But then a couple minutes after I'd gotten there, she made some excuse about needing to finish something or other, and as she was closing the door, I distinctly heard her say, 'Hippie bitch.'"

"So she didn't say it *to* you?" Preston asked.

"Well, no, not exactly," Harriet said. "But I don't really see how saying it away from me is better, especially since she was slamming the door in my face. Like I said, you just can't reconcile one moment to the next with her. She was plenty inviting when I first showed up, and then frostbite personified by the time I left, and this right after I told her about how I'm—*yeow!*"

She jumped sideways in a flail, nearly strewing her microgreens across the parking lot. Arms drawn in close around herself, she frantically scanned the area, then relaxed an instant later. "False alarm. Not a bee," she said.

"Told her about what?" Preston asked.

"Told her? Danielle, right. She just seemed to turn on a dime after I told her I'm pregnant. Doesn't that seem odd?"

Preston's mouth opened involuntarily. His eyes dropped to her abdomen. "You're having a baby?"

"Shoot," Harriet said, "I forgot I hadn't told you."

Preston opened his eyes and his arms both wide and took her in for a hug. Harriet held her microgreens out away from his shoulders. "Congratulations!" he said.

"Thank you," Harriet told him. "Tyler and I are both excited. We've been rather laissez-faire about trying to set a timeline or monitor cycles or anything like that, but now that now is the time, it seems right enough."

"When are you due?" Preston asked.

Harriet looked down at her abdomen and rubbed in a circle. "Mid-November."

"Just incredible," Preston said. "And Danielle seemed to get angry when you told her?"

Harriet looked at the clouds. "Not angry, really. More just sort of like, we were friends, and then we weren't. But she was like that the night I met her too, and I do like her some of the time, and she is my neighbor, so what is there to do, really? And Sylvia's very sweet. She almost teared up when I gave her her dress, and she asked a lot of questions about the baby, like how long had I known, how was I feeling, all sorts of things. She was very interested. I like Sylvia a lot."

Preston said, "Let me ask you one other thing. Have you and Danielle, or you and Sylvia, ever talked about me?"

Harriet seemed confused. "I don't see how we would've. You didn't even tell me you knew them until the day before yesterday."

"Of course. That was a silly question."

Harriet nodded.

"One thing, though," Preston said. "Could you avoid mentioning me, if it's possible?"

Harriet seemed even more confused at that. "I suppose so," she said. "I really don't think I'm going to see them for a while, unless Danielle comes over."

"Right, right. Well, I'm sure it was a misunderstanding," he said, stepping away from her. "And give Tyler my regards. I mean it. Tell him next time I see him, I'll be expecting my regards back."

Harriet inspected her microgreens. "He'll hold on to your regards till then."

Preston walked quicker now, building toward escape velocity, because he wanted to be in his car. He wanted to be by himself, driving fast on a sleepy Richmond highway, zooming around the city. Ellridge men thought in terms of competitive advantages. It seemed to Preston that he currently had them in spades.

Everywhere he went, Preston carried a leather backpack that contained, among other things, a vintage copy of the *Harvard Business Review*, in which his grandfather had captured the theory of the market that persisted through all his family's subsequent endeavors. The magazine lay peacefully in the laptop slot, insulated from all variants of weather and light, as well as the other objects Preston kept on hand for inspiration: a Burberry scarf purchased in London, England; an Opinel No. 8 folding knife purchased in Savoie, France; and one of the original collection of two thousand copper mugs brought to America in 1941, spurring the invention of the Moscow Mule.

Preston was captivated by iconic products—by the guaranteed disruption induced by design, by the exogenous design shocks that rocked old industries and birthed new markets. Certain products seemed to attain an inescapable gravity by combining the functional and the beautiful so seamlessly that other products became awkward by comparison, as if built by aliens. He felt that the modern restaurant had not yet been defined in such a way, and he was going to define it.

And where better to do so than Richmond, Virginia? This was a city so fervently in love with its restaurants that it nearly defied the market. Sixth in the United States in restaurants per capita, competing on the level of some of the most visited cities in the country. Unless Richmond had secretly become a travel destination rivaling Miami or Las Vegas, all those restaurants were living by the steady devotion of local foodies.

The first competitor that Preston went to visit after the farmers market was Sapphire's Café. It was a corner café across the street from Meadow Park, and he had heard people talk about it in cultish tones. He arrived just after noon to find every seat taken, which was not much of a feat, given that there were only four—no, five tables in the establishment, plus four seats at the bar, one of which shared territory with a pie stand.

A couple stood behind the row of occupied bar seats, either waiting for a table or waiting for takeout. Preston stood at the door, not yet noticed by the bartender-host, and pondered the value of a constrained space. Constant business; a sense of unattainability; an exclusive vibe that didn't come across as contrived. . . . It was an angle to consider. The spaces he'd looked at so far were all big; maybe he needed to go small.

The bartender handed a picnic basket and a bottle of wine to the waiting couple.

The man took the basket and led the way out, holding it above his head as he slid around chairs and shoulders. Preston stepped outside and held the door.

"Thank you," the man said, followed wordlessly by the woman, who was holding the open wine bottle by the neck. Preston lingered long enough to see the couple look both ways, then jaywalk across Meadow Street and into the park. While he was lingering there, one of the patrons at the bar got up and paid, leaving a seat for him.

Just brilliant, Preston mused as he sat down. He could picture Meadow Park on spring evenings, stocked with picnicking groups, young women wearing their boyfriends' fleeces, their skin lit up with fading sunlight while the men sat chivalrously between their dates and the sidewalk, none of them realizing they had done so. The image straddled a line between advertisement and performance art.

While he perused the menu, Preston's thoughts moved laterally from Sapphire's to himself. Working toward a concrete goal, thinking about the ways small decisions came together to form the big picture, searching for structural disadvantages in his competition—this was when he was at his best. The past few years of his life had only felt dire and bleak because he hadn't oriented himself fully toward a goal. If he'd felt alien to the three Preston Ellridges who preceded him (each of them so poignantly insightful), it was only because he hadn't defined the problem. Preston's great-grandfather had recognized in the Great Depression an opportunity to subdivide the grand houses of the twenties into multi-unit buildings, and so made his fortune in renovations. His grandfather added to that money by manufacturing standardized shipping containers at a time when most considered them a niche improvement. And then, of course, there was his own father, who had understood the potential of the internet before most major brands did, generating an incredible return on investment through domain name speculation. But what Preston now realized about the stories he'd grown up hearing was they started with his predecessors already building on their ideas. Yet for all that every story was underpinned by the brilliance of those ideas, he had never heard about the years of wandering that must have inspired the ideas themselves. He had never seen himself in the previous Prestons because he had only just reached the part of their stories he knew. At last it was his turn to build something, and he felt just like them.

Preston's electric blue Audi A8 gleamed so exuberantly from the packs of drearier vehicles that he felt others could see his energy as he drove around town to re-evaluate the spaces he was considering, mentally shrinking and expanding them to better weigh what he had learned through Sapphire's. There was also the matter of public spaces like Meadow Park. The spot in Church Hill was easily the closest to any sort of public space, being almost two blocks from Chimborazo Park. But the one in Oregon Hill was a straight, uphill shot from the James River overlook. It was possible the sight lines could work well enough in his favor to pull customers down to the overlook in a way similar to how Meadow Park pulled visitors out of Sapphire's, if perhaps more subtle.

"This is weird," Preston said to no one, standing outside of a sushi bar that was decidedly not the premier Italian restaurant in the city, triple checking the address and looking like a tourist with his leather backpack on his shoulders.

A passing VCU student asked him if he was looking for Guido's

Octopus. "Yes," he said, and started to ask a question before the student interrupted.

"Up there," she said, pointing through a glass door that Preston had mistaken for the entrance to an apartment above the sushi bar.

He followed her advice, worrying he'd just fallen victim to an undergrad tradition—maybe "Misdirect a tourist" was written somewhere on a list of things to do before graduating. The stairs were carpet, stained and narrow. A mop and a broom stood leaning on the wall opposite a wooden door. As he opened the door, Preston was already mentally preparing his excuse, certain he was about to be mistaken for a burglar. Then he stepped into a brick-lined space with vertical windows and dramatic sunlight like a church.

Was every restaurant in this city an insider gimmick?

Preston was seated at a table near the center of the room, where he pulled out his notebook and began jotting down impressions a couple lines below where he had stopped writing about Sapphire's. He listed a couple obvious takeaways, but he was having trouble focusing. Every table was full, despite the restaurant's odd location, and the tables were so close together that he had to sit up to keep his shoulders from touching either of the men nearest to him. The room smelled impossibly good, some indecipherable mesh of garlic, wine, sausage, basil, parmesan, and—seemingly—perfume. His lunch at Sapphire's had been relatively light. Preston ordered a glass of wine. It came in a stemless glass with a conical shape, a weird form, something he should note. He wrote down, "pared-down aesthetic on the micro scale," and felt the phrase would be inscrutable if he looked at it again. He started drinking the wine and crossed it out.

For the last few years, Preston had been in Bordeaux, Napa Valley, Rioja, Tuscany, Burgundy, Mendoza, Willamette Valley—cultivating his taste, enlarging his cultural sense, experiencing the old winemaking traditions, the foods that generational knowledge had placed next to each glass. Mastery of the old led to mastery of the new. All innovation stemmed from radical intimacy with tradition. His lunch at Sapphire's had been light; he was drinking wine out of a pared-down aesthetic; sunlight was streaming in through the tall windows, set against the darkness of the bricks. Outside, he could see the tops of buildings. People spent so little time looking at the tops of buildings. Edward Hopper had painted the tops of buildings. He often painted from the windows of hotels, or from the window of his car while looking at hotels. Maybe Preston could hang an Edward Hopper painting in one of his restaurants. Weird to be thinking about Edward Hopper right now. He was feeling a bit dizzy.

Strange, he thought, the way drunkenness could act as a probabilistic function. Drinking a lot, drinking on an empty stomach—or cultivating a tolerance, drinking on a full stomach—these things influenced the probability of feeling the way he was feeling right now, but they weren't hard cuts, were they? The feeling he was feeling right now only came when things lined up a certain way—some of which were perceptible and controllable, while others were invisible guitar strings plucking softly in the background. He was going to found a place that could reliably induce this feeling, this moment—but in this moment, he felt overmatched. He'd been in Guido's Octopus for ten minutes, and already he was feeling like the space had left the earth. He'd come up those stairs, the ladder into the shuttle; he'd blasted off; he was drifting out. *Liminality: The process of using symbolism to lift a person out of the limitations they unknowingly place upon their own perception.* There was a section about that in his grandfather's essay. He couldn't remember how it came up, but in context it made sense. Religion was good at liminality. Preston wasn't religious, but Danielle was.

Actually, it was Danielle who had told him about liminality. It wasn't in his grandfather's essay at all; his mind had jumped there by mistake. Danielle had discussed it with him years ago, that night when he had called her so late. She had answered, talked to him as though it were the middle of the afternoon. She was designing a . . . something. He couldn't hear her, he could only hear the fact that she was talking to him, about something that mattered to her, opening up to him like an evening primrose. Preston was feeling very odd now. Hopefully the waiter wouldn't come back until he was through with this train of thought.

Danielle was the reason he knew about Hopper too. Danielle was inspired by Hopper. She liked how he painted interiors, riffed on arrangements of objects, prioritized the viewpoints induced by windows. Twilight. That was what she had been talking about when liminality came up. She was designing the waiting room of a massage therapy center; she had wanted to imbue it with a sense of twilight. Twilight was important to her.

As he thought about twilight in the context of Danielle's values, Preston became conscious of a vision taking shape. He suddenly felt positive that he knew what she was doing at this moment, as if the scene were projected on each of the dramatic vertical windows. She was standing on a chair, unscrewing a lightbulb, changing a lightbulb, exasperated at the act, having asked her spouse to do it many times in the preceding days. The electric socket hung just beyond the tips of her fingers, and she had to stretch. She had just taken a shower and her hair was wet, cascading down her back in dark coils. She turned her eyes upward as she screwed in the new bulb, and they shone with delight as it flickered on.

He was meeting her tomorrow. It occurred to Preston that he had suggested meeting for dinner, and she had said no, they had to meet for lunch. Avoiding spending the twilight with him; keeping it for Sylvia. He had suggested Sapphire's and again, she had said no, they had to meet somewhere else. Making it hard. He was meeting her tomorrow. He would have plenty of time to spend with her in different spaces, at different times of day, after he hired her. After he hired her, he would have all the time he needed.

Danielle had come straight from church, and she was apologizing to Preston for being late. There had been baptisms and a lot of announcements, she was telling him. Little Sisters of the Poor had come to speak, and those were always the longest announcements, but you couldn't leave. An old nun was up there talking about how Little Sisters of the Poor's mission was to make old people feel wanted. She couldn't walk out early, literally expressing to an old person that she didn't want to listen, and it just went on and on, and then parking around Empire Sandwiches had been more of a struggle than she remembered downtown being, and, anyway, she was telling him that she was sorry. And the whole time she was telling him she was sorry, Preston was grateful, because she hadn't had time to stop at home and change, so she was still wearing the dress she had worn to church. It was a light purple dress with delicate floral touches. She looked like a preacher's daughter in a 1960s period piece.

"—and then after all that, I got almost all the way here before I realized that I hadn't locked the car, so I had to walk all the way back," she said.

"It's really okay," Preston told her. "I have all the time in the world."

Especially on a day like this one. Their table was out on the patio under the awning, the sun just barely touching his shoulders.

She smiled. "I guess it's a little slower here than you're used to."

Preston leaned back and looked around the patio. He had chosen well. After Danielle had rejected Sapphire's and the park, this place had been one of two he considered next. The runner up, Charleston 1925, more transparently reflected his dreams. It had a warm and sultry atmosphere, with swooping strings of white lights hanging from the ceiling between rows of French flags. The logo above the door portrayed a turn-of-the-century chorine lifting up her skirt. But when Preston tried to picture Danielle with him there, he realized that she appeared uncomfortable, embarrassed, even in an image he'd concocted. It was too forward, too suggestive, too lavish a place to meet the real Danielle, with whom he needed to discuss business before moving on to anything else.

"I don't know if it's a fast or slow thing," Preston said. "More of a thing where I know where I'm headed, and I have the steps laid out. Some of them are immediate, and it would be a waste of time not to take them, while others require patience. During those times, I try to relax and let myself think organically." He leaned forward. "I'm getting into the restaurant business here, and I'm self-funding."

Danielle laughed, bringing her hands to her mouth as she did it, like she wanted to catch the laugh and push it back in. "I'm sorry. It's just the way you said 'self-funding.'"

Preston enjoyed being laughed at by Danielle and no one else. He enjoyed being lightly chastised by her for his gestures and proclamations; he had enjoyed it since the day they met. Danielle had shown up as a plus-one at his sister's wedding, tagging along with one of the bohemian grad students his sister liked to slum around with. She had listened while he and her date talked at length about future travel plans, growing visibly annoyed at the way Preston's plans always sounded a little better than her date's, although Preston wasn't trying to show off. The conversation had trailed off for a moment following a stark exchange about accommodations (Moroccan hostel vs. Neapolitan resort), and then Danielle leaned over the table, away from her date and toward Preston instead, looking at him from under him, expression bewildered. Just before he could ask what she was looking at, she said, "What's it like on your planet, where all the seasons are spring?" And Preston had felt something then. He felt certain no one else could have asked him a question like that and stirred the same reaction. They'd spent the rest of the evening talking, long after Danielle's date drifted away, and exchanged numbers at the end of the night.

Since that day, Danielle had functioned as an on/off switch in Preston's life. An exogenous electric current had enveloped him for days after that wedding, driving him forward with ecstatic momentum. He had discovered the current that evening, riding back from the wedding with his parents, so ebullient that he had out-talked his own father, saying nothing of note and yet unable to stop himself. The current had coursed through him all night, and by morning he believed he would no longer be able to function without it. It would last for days, weeks, months at a time, always triggered by Danielle in some way, triggered by something as simple as a text, until it was revoked—always, again, in a manner of or pertaining to Danielle—revoked by something as simple as a text withheld.

Across the table from him, Danielle held up her hands like a banner and pulled the thread of her joke a little further. "Preston's Diner: A Self-Funded Establishment."

He shook his head. "It's got to be, 'Self-Funded Since 1978.'"

"1843," Danielle said.

"And it's not a diner," he said.

She held up the imaginary banner again. Her gold-plated bracelet briefly caught the sun. "Preston's Eatery: Self-Funded Since 1843."

"You've done this before," he said.

"Self-funded?" Danielle asked. "Oh no, I always have investors."

The current Danielle had sparked in Preston was overflowing now, lifting him up. He sat straighter, smiled without effort. How could he give up on her when she could trigger this surge of confidence? But Danielle was married to Sylvia, influenced by Sylvia. That meant he was transitively influenced by Sylvia. Whether she knew or not, Sylvia had possession of Preston's on/off switch. How could Preston let that continue?

He pictured himself leaning forward then. He could almost feel his imaginary body doing it, leaning forward to nimbly touch her hand and say, "Speaking of that . . ." But he couldn't bring his physical self to move. Not yet. *In a moment*, he told himself. The opportunity had come and gone too quickly, and now the timing was off. He would need to wait until the next opening.

"It does sound exciting," Danielle said. "So then what *are* you going to call your restaurant?"

Our restaurant, he found himself thinking.

"I haven't selected a name yet, nor finalized the concept. I've been all around the city doing market research these last few days."

"I can help with that," Danielle said.

Preston's pulse accelerated.

Danielle gestured to her side. "Near where we live, you have Luna's Market and Libby's Market, depending on which direction you go.

Then in the Fan there's Ward's Market, Mulberry Street Market, Robertson Market, and Ramboldy Market."

Preston forced himself to laugh, feeling like it came out backward. It wasn't solely the letdown of her joke. It was also the way she had said, "where we live." She said "we" so casually.

"What about foreign markets?" he asked, stretching the wire to spark the next opportunity.

Danielle craned her long neck. "There's a bodega somewhat close to here, I think in the direction I'm facing. Il Mercato Richmond is the name." She leaned forward and lowered her voice. "But between you and me, it's more of a ristorante."

She was having fun with him. Danielle had fun with everybody, though.

A waitress came to take their order. Danielle said, "I have a lot of questions."

To calm himself down, Preston thought about market dynamics. The sign of a healthy market was that the best offer consistently won out: the business that made the best offer to customers would make the best sales; the manager that made the best offer to prospective employees would have the most hiring success.

("And do the mixed greens have any cilantro in them?" Danielle asked.)

When they were healthy enough, markets became pedagogical. Each person's choices represented the advantages of every business they gave patronage to. Successes and failures in healthy markets revealed psychological undercurrents that could, when properly interpreted, explain all of society.

"Is the blue cheese spread more of a spread," Danielle made a spreading motion, "or a crumble?" She made a crumbling motion.

Watching her hands, Preston was reminded of Harriet's interrogations at the farmers market. It was funny—not in the way that would make him laugh, but conceptually funny—to see the two of them act so similarly with neither knowing it. He could see why they didn't like each other. In Harriet's case, the questions stemmed from a neutered competitive instinct. She wanted to replicate things that others did and then do them better, without actually competing. In Danielle's case, she asked questions because she was so exquisitely female.

"In that case . . ." Danielle said. She held out her hand, pointing at the waitress with all five fingers. "I will have . . ." she jabbed her hand downward with each word, "the . . ." she pointed up, lingered, then slapped her finger down on the menu, "Napoleon!" She handed the menu back.

"The Direwolf for me," Preston said.

Danielle laughed at him again. "I'm so sorry," she said. "I just pictured you asking people to call you The Direwolf."

Preston looked around to see how close the other tables were. They were closer than he would have liked, but he had a chance to show Danielle his spontaneity, and he thought she would like it. He grinned wide enough to feel the muscles in his face flex, then softly howled.

Danielle was laughing harder now. "I'm sure you make a tremendous businessman."

A second opportunity for his pitch had arrived. All he had to do was say, "I wanted to ask you something about that," and then the first words would be out, spades would be broken, and the crux of his plan would fall into place. The chance was right there, right in front of him, just eight words away.

He couldn't do it.

Danielle stood. "I'm going to run to the ladies' room before our food comes."

Her hand brushed his shoulder as she walked by. Almost like she was consoling him with her touch, saying, *You'll get it next time.* She had taken her bag with her, so Preston now sat alone, with no evidence he was here with someone else. He looked around at the other tables to see if their occupants were watching him. He felt conspicuous. He wished he hadn't howled.

Preston looked down at the table. In unhealthy markets, the best offer had only a minor chance of winning out. This condition almost always resulted from widespread coercion, whether by unscrupulous competitors or by various forms of social pressure, most of which amounted to simple inertia: people were compelled to do what others did, and usually, others did what the generations before them had done.

Relationships were an example of an unhealthy market. Women entered into abusive relationships every day. They stayed in marriages with husbands who let their bodies go. Coercion was rampant. Women had broken free of the economic binds that once justified their clinging to a failed marriage, but they had so thoroughly internalized the inertia of generation after generation of women before them that they could no longer detect the coercion at work.

"I'm glad you got a table outside," Danielle said, smoothing her dress as she sat back down. "Your restaurant should have a patio."

Preston's imaginary self returned, showing him the motions. It wasn't even his imaginary self, really. It was his usual self, the bold and decisive person he was in every moment but this one. All he had to do was follow his usual instincts, and then he could carry things forward. *"I'm more interested in the interior,"* his instinctive self coached, but the sentence felt too jagged for Preston's actual throat. Instead, he said, "Patios are a nice feature, but they're inherently seasonal." Then his instinctive self chimed in: "I'm more interested in the interior."

Preston almost didn't realize the words had been said out loud. Danielle's eyes sparkled. "Are you working with any of the designers around here?"

Preston thought of Caesar crossing the Rubicon. Caesar hadn't backtracked. He hadn't said, "Whoops." No, he had said, "The die is cast."

"There's one that I'm reaching out to," he said. He reached down into his leather backpack. His hand brushed aside the *Harvard Business Review* and pulled the January issue of *R-Home* from the laptop slot. He held it up. "I read a profile of her in this magazine." Preston looked into her eyes. The contact was so pure that he felt like she could see his skeleton. "Do you know her?"

Danielle reached one of her hands across her chest and pulled the opposite shoulder inward. Again, her gold-plated bracelet caught the sun, keeping it this time. "I'm . . ." she looked at the building across the street, then back to him, "flattered. I really am."

He was in range. This was the part Preston was good at: selling, networking, recruiting. He was a dynamo in business settings. All Ellridge men were. Danielle was standing at the door. He only had to bring her in.

"I'll pay you double your normal rate, and I'll work around your schedule," he said. "If you want to meet at your office, I'll go there; if you want to meet at the site, I'll be there; if you want to meet at your house, I'll go there. And you'll have complete creative freedom," he added.

Danielle was still holding her shoulder. "That's generous," she said.

"On top of that, I can offer you a stake in the restaurant, which will position you to see a direct return on the investment of your time and energy."

"I don't need complete creative freedom," Danielle said. "I like the push and pull."

"I'll push you and I'll pull you, then."

"Preston—" Danielle started, but she didn't appear to have anything else planned. She sat there, still holding her shoulder. The yellow glare from her bracelet filled his eyes with splotches, but he couldn't avert his gaze. He couldn't look away, or she wouldn't know he was serious. The splotches grew, crowding out Danielle's shoulder and portions of her face, displacing her with bright, ugly blue-green blobs.

Preston said, "I don't think you've done your best work yet."

The portion of Danielle's face that he could still see went from disheveled to vexed and was headed toward angry, but Preston continued: "I view design as the single least replicable advantage in a restaurant. That sense of function and appeal, coming together so plainly that they seem to have sprung into being fully intertwined—that's what I'm after. It's what makes an instant classic, makes even the established competitors into imitators."

He was in his wheelhouse now. He reached toward the middle of the table, not touching her hand or even approaching it, just putting a part of himself closer to her. "You'll never find another client who's starting from design like I am. Others see it as decoration, or they see it as one of many important factors. I see it as the top of the pyramid, and that's why I'm hiring you."

He continued to hold her in his gaze, feeling like this time, he could see her skeleton. It didn't matter that she was looking away. She knew where his focus was. He said, "I'm convinced there's no better partner for a talent like yours, here or anywhere else."

Danielle stayed silent for a long time. Preston let her. People took jobs for three reasons: fulfillment, money, and status. He had done his part. He had given her the best offer on all dimensions. His offer would dwarf others in terms of money. His commitment to design ensured fulfillment. And if she believed in him enough as an entrepreneur to feel that his restaurant would succeed in a city ruled by food, then his offer ensured status as well.

"I can't," said Danielle. She stood. "It was nice seeing you, and I hope things go well."

Preston saw her putting on her sunglasses in the shade as she walked away. She looked at the ground and walked with a hunch, then rounded the corner and disappeared from view. Preston remained in his seat, looking at the darkened windows of the other buildings. A few seconds later their food arrived, like a prank.

* * *

Preston had failed once before.

His first serious idea had come to him suddenly, almost accidentally, in the manner such ideas preferred to materialize. It was at the time of his and Danielle's original dalliance, years after their initial meeting, after she had graduated and he had traveled and their respective lives had slowed, when their contact became easier and more frequent. She was close to him and seemingly drifting closer, yet still unavailable, perpetually "with someone" in whom Preston had so little interest that he was unsure if she had been with a single unimportant person the whole time or a revolving door of unimportant people. He was at his family's beach house, sipping espresso by the window while his three sisters and their husbands sat talking around the coffee table. They were talking about sandals.

At first, he'd tried to ignore the conversation, uninterested in the topic and deep in a series of thoughts about espresso that felt important. But he couldn't suppress his ears, and eventually the name "Jackie Kennedy" caught his attention.

He turned slightly, just in time to catch the narrative. The current trend in women's sandals, it seemed, stemmed from a pair that Jackie Kennedy had once brought back from Italy for a Florida-based cobbler to recreate for her. That cobbler began to produce and sell them en masse, and they soon became popular throughout the area. A different company quickly caught on, made a near-identical version of the sandals, and began to market them nationwide.

That company was Jack Rogers, and they had been so successful that the style of sandal itself had become known as "Jacks." Meanwhile the original company, now known as Palm Beach Sandals, enjoyed a fraction of that same popularity and was more often than not confused for a knockoff.

His sisters were in agreement that this was an injustice. One of the husbands offered a few tepid words of agreement, and the conversation moved on.

The story inspired little sympathy in Preston, to whom the Florida cobbler seemed like a small business owner who had failed to sense the nationwide opportunity in time to seize it. That was the cruel reality of markets. Without sustained execution, good ideas were comets, streaking across the sky and then disappearing.

He'd finished his espresso and headed out toward the beach, hoping to restore his previous train of thought. Such a lively little drink, espresso. Stimulating and arresting, and the backbone of so many possibilities. But hardly anyone drank it in America, so different from what he'd experienced in Italy.

Italy. He paused.

Atop the wooden staircase that climbed over the dune, Preston realized who the real victim of his sisters' story was. Not the cobbler in Florida, but the one in Italy, who had sold the original pair to the store that sold it to Jackie Kennedy. He would've been two knockoffs behind before he even realized he'd started a sensation, and how was he to compete? Who would even believe him? Preston could practically hear the eye rolls. *"Yes of course, Uncle Luigi, you really invented Jack Rogers. Mmhmm, now let's just take a quick peek at that pill organizer."*

That thought had opened a channel that insight now rushed to fill. It was like a lucid dream. *Do nothing,* he told himself. *Don't push it too hard, or you'll wake up. Go out to the ocean and wade, and let the tide come to you.*

He knew he had it when he caught himself practicing his pitch an hour later, speaking easily and confidently as he ran his feet under the outdoor shower. "It's an online marketplace dedicated to identifying, venerating, and distributing the select few products capable of calling themselves the Original. The staff is equal parts technologists and researchers. The former work on algorithms to detect objects of significance, both for their design and for the longevity of their appeal. Clothes are an obvious focus, but any original concept that sparked a trend could fit. Espresso makers, notebooks, rifles, lamps, kayaks, umbrellas—if it's a product for which there is an original design, the algorithm will identify it. The researchers will find the true original, and the new marketplace will list it."

It was a good problem to solve, and an Ellridge problem to solve, at ease among the magnificent problems of urban space, international shipping, and digital brand identity that his predecessors had solved. Bigger even than a problem that flowed from the market, it was a problem with the market itself; innovators were being suppressed by the entity that should have enriched them. He continued his pitch: "It will be the go-to website for consumers in search of style and truth, consumers who are being preyed upon by shameless imitation. And it will empower the true innovators to reap their just rewards and innovate even more."

Investors would be the eventual audience, but in this imaginary discussion, he was speaking to Danielle.

He needed to tell her. He could call her, but what if she didn't answer? And what if she called back at a time when his energy had waned? She would not fully understand unless he could capture and transmit the whirling energy of this precise moment.

He went to his room. His hands outpaced his mind. Before the idea of writing a letter occurred to him, he had already found a pen and a legal pad, torn a page out, and written "Dear Danielle" at the top. Surely this was the most romantic form of communication, a way of bottling the moment of inspiration and sealing it, letting it ferment and settle before it is finally uncorked.

In the days that followed, he developed his business plan. Every day while his father drove to the golf course and his sisters readied themselves to sunbathe, he worked through the morning until the mail arrived, at which time he would bound out the door and down the driveway, his heart thumping as he approached the mailbox.

For five days, he opened the metal door to disappointment. With no hope that today would be the day Danielle wrote back, his inspiration would dwindle, only to return the following morning. It was during this time that the idea of working with Danielle first began to take shape in Preston's mind. He felt as though he was working with her already. She was there with him every morning, responding to ideas as he had them, sometimes propping him up, sometimes knocking him down, whichever he needed more. Who else could he talk to? His father would be chatting up cart girls until midafternoon then napping until dinner. His sisters and their husbands thought he had developed a habit of sleeping late, unaware that he was waking up earlier than ever before, writing things down, drawing things out, researching instances of displaced originality, modeling financial scenarios, all of it in continuous discussion with his imaginary business partner. She would be perfect to run the research department, he thought. He would broach the idea a little further on.

When the time was right, he'd recruit her, and from that spark the rest would flow.

On the last day before his family was to leave, Preston went out to the mailbox one final time, full of excitement and dread, his heart pumping and receding. He pulled the metal door open slowly, squinting in, too anxious to open it all the way. He thought he saw the shape of an envelope and opened the box farther, letting in more light. It landed on the surface of a letter, addressed to him, with Danielle's name in the top left corner.

Preston didn't make it to his room. He didn't even make it indoors. He stood there in the lacerating North Carolina sun, opening his envelope. His sisters and their husbands may have been watching him. He didn't care.

The first thing he noticed about her letter was its length. Not one page but two. Not two pages but three, counting the back of the first page. She had written him a long, thoughtful letter in pen, and almost certainly in solitude, accompanied only by the sound of her pen against the paper. The ink was slightly smudged, and he realized she was left-handed.

She had written wonderful things about his idea, and about her support, and her belief in how he could bring it to life, and she had also written about her own life. She was happy lately, falling in love with Richmond in a way that surprised her, building a career that satisfied her, doing her best to recognize that she was content and to not feel impatient for more (but he would give her more regardless, he thought). She considered the idea of corresponding by letter to be "so thoroughly Preston."

He read the first two and a half pages in rhapsody, but his euphoria deserted him as he approached the end. Yes, she thought his idea was excellent. And yes, she hoped they would be able to correspond by letter more often in the future, maybe even make it their "thing." And yes, she thought it would be great if he could stop by Richmond sometime soon, but not because she so badly needed to see him. No, that wasn't why. She wanted Preston to come to Richmond so she could introduce him to her fiancé, who had proposed only four days earlier.

He walked heavily back to the house, picturing his letter sitting on her floor, pushed in through the mail slot moments after she left to go see this mysterious person, who was waiting with a ring.

* * *

After the disastrous lunch, Preston didn't see Danielle again until May. By then, both the Church Hill space and the Oregon Hill space had fallen into different hands, and he hadn't written a line in his notebook since the couple of scribbles he'd made about Empire Sandwiches while waiting for Danielle.

He was at Ellwood Thompson's that morning, trying to decide between iceberg lettuce and romaine (ostensibly to learn more about salads for his restaurant, which didn't have a home, name, or concept yet). In reality, he was loitering in the produce section because he'd read somewhere that eating lots of vegetables and drinking lots of tea could get one out of a rut. But he had chosen to count that as an incidental benefit.

He was holding two heads of lettuce when Harriet came around the end of the nearest aisle. They made eye contact, and she waved and came over. She had gained a noticeable amount of weight from her pregnancy, though the bump was not yet showing.

"Facing a lettuce conundrum?" she asked.

"I'm trying to decide which one looks healthier," Preston said.

Harriet pulled the iceberg lettuce from his hand and put it back on its shelf. "Romaine lettuce has more fiber," she said. "Anything else I can help you with?"

"Point me to the tea section, if you will."

She pointed up over the lettuce shelf. "Over that way. You can say hi to Sylvia."

Preston felt like he had licked a car battery. "Sylvia's here?"

"Yes indeed. She and Danielle have been helping Tyler and I get things together for our Derby party today. I mentioned I was going to Ellwood Thompson's to get meat for Kentucky Burgoo, and Sylvia offered to keep me company. She said she was interested in perusing the tea selection. She was really sweet about it, like she is about a lot of things, just mentioning how she was interested in the tea selection at Ellwood Thompson's, trying so hard to make sure I knew she wouldn't be in the way of my shopping."

Preston started to put some distance between himself and Harriet, moving in the direction she had pointed him but planning to go the opposite way as soon as she turned around. He was sure Sylvia had been told about what happened at Empire Sandwiches.

"You should come today," Harriet said.

Preston considered the suggestion.

Harriet continued, "I've never made Kentucky Burgoo, but I read online that people eat it at the Derby. It's basically a pile of meat simmered to mush. I don't really get the appeal, but tradition is tradition I suppose."

"Who's going to be there?" Preston asked. He looked behind him as he spoke. Sylvia could come around the corner at any moment.

"Tyler and I, and Danielle and Sylvia, some of our friends from Westover Hills, and some of the other neighbors we've befriended so far. Not anyone you know, that I'm aware of, although given the odds that we would've ended up living next to Sylvia and Danielle, maybe that's not a good bet."

Preston looked behind himself again.

Harriet said, "Mostly couples, anyway, and some kids I think. Some people will probably be in Derby attire, but we assured everyone it's not a costume party, per se. We're starting around four-thirty if you want to swing by."

It seemed that Harriet, at least, had not been told about Preston's failed attempt to hire Danielle, but he still assumed Sylvia had. "It sounds like you and Danielle have made up," he said.

Harriet shrugged. "I like Danielle just fine when she's not smoldering about something. And it's good to have neighbor friends. This party was Danielle's idea, actually, although Tyler was the one who really latched on to it. We can't get him to stop doing his Southern accent."

Preston said, "I'll consider it," and turned to leave.

Sylvia was there.

She was holding a box of tea and standing at the edge of the bell peppers, positioned between him and the checkout lines. Upon seeing her, Preston realized he had never fully believed that she had gone through with the whole thing. Like most people connected to her or Danielle, he had heard the rumors and agreed that her sudden and total departure from social media did lend them credence, but it had seemed so far-fetched. The possibility taunted him. That Danielle's spouse had become a woman seemed entirely too unlikely, precisely because it seemed entirely too ideal. Certainly, he'd thought when he'd heard—certainly if this were indeed happening, they would divorce?

He was milling around London at the time, feeling as though he had been unwittingly cast in a Shakespearean comedy, one in which the hero loses out to another man only for it to later come to light that the man in question is a woman. The marriage thus invalidated, the way becomes clear for true love to conquer all. Everyone gets what they want and ends up happy, including Sylvia, who (why not?) marries a rather eligible baron. But news of their divorce never came, and for a long time Preston assumed that meant the rumors had been unfounded, just another laugh between his sister and her artsy friend, the one who'd disliked Preston ever since he lost his wedding date to Preston and Danielle's first conversation. When Preston heard the rumors were true after all, that only his assumption that the couple would divorce had been inaccurate, he knew coercion had once again set the course of people's lives. Planetary orbits were askew. The universe needed a catalyst to reroute everything to the proper channels.

That was only his theory at the time, but it was enough to finally jolt Preston from the waking slumber in which he had been living ever since he read Danielle's letter. He had continued his slumber through his first introduction to her quiet fiancé, the appeal of whom he tried in vain to understand; and he had slumbered through their wedding, a family-only affair that rolled onward as he sat on a bench outside the church, uninvited, listening to the faint organ music to confirm to himself it was happening, even as the last of his coveted electricity flickered and deserted him, never to be summoned by Danielle again. He had slumbered through that argument when the hotel manager told him he needed to vacate his room, saying they were booked and that his time was up. He had slumbered through picking up one or two of the airplane bottles and wine-stained plastic cups from the floor before deciding he could leave it, all of it, including the luggage he'd brought with him, all but his leather backpack. He had slumbered his way across the Atlantic and remained there, still deep in slumber, until the rumors of Sylvia's transition reached his ears and woke him, his plan forming rapidly as he processed the implications.

And even after his plan emerged, Preston hadn't brought himself to believe that Sylvia's transition, the foundation of all he was to enact, had truly happened. Even when Harriet was at the farmers market telling him she had made a dress for Danielle's spouse, he hadn't believed it. As Danielle had walked away from him several weeks ago, his mind had gone to the possibility that Sylvia had expressed a desire to be a woman but had failed to become one, and that her failure had stifled the rest of Preston's plans. But clearly she hadn't failed, so why had he?

Sylvia took a few steps forward and stopped, farther away from Preston than Preston was from Harriet. "You two know each other?" she asked.

She was a good bit smaller than him now, the opposite of how it had been before.

"Harriet's family used to live in the Outer Banks," Preston said. His tone bothered him as it unwound. He sounded guilty. "My family spent summers there, and we got to know each other that way."

Sylvia nodded. "I never pegged you for a surfer."

Harriet's father had worked at a surf shop near Preston's family's house. Preston was unnerved to hear Sylvia express such casual knowledge about Harriet. In the short time since they'd met, Sylvia had rapidly gained ground, undercutting him even further than he could have guessed. Unsatisfied with the future she had already taken from Preston, she was now moving to displace Preston from the past as well. For a hideous moment, he questioned his competitive advantage. In becoming a woman, Sylvia had allowed herself access to thoroughfares between herself and Harriet—and herself and Danielle—that Preston could not access. For the first time, he was forced to admit she had a strategy, maybe even a good one.

"I wasn't exactly a natural, but I was well taught," Preston said with a glance at Harriet. He still had the past, if he could hold on to it.

Instead, Harriet said to Sylvia, "I haven't gotten to the meat yet."

"I'll come with you," Sylvia said. She walked in front of Preston and joined Harriet.

Harriet leaned toward Preston. "You really should stop by if you have time. This burgoo is going to be celestial."

Sylvia smiled and added, "Like a Kentucky night sky."

They walked away together.

Preston became aware again of the romaine lettuce, still in his hand and getting wilty from the warmth. He drove home, formulating an epiphany about why Harriet had acted distant toward him as soon as Sylvia showed up. It was the same reason Danielle had turned down his offer. This was what Sylvia did. She came into situations and drew invisible lines around people, cut them off from everyone she didn't approve of. She cultivated loyalty to herself through risks and institutions and then behaved on impulse. The people around her were ensnared in a textile of coercion. She did things that made no sense, then manipulated others into inverting themselves to offset her. She was a trickster goddess, floating through walls, redrawing boundaries, exploiting intimacy for vanity.

Crossing the threshold of his downtown condo, Preston was so energized by the depth of his realization that he became abruptly aware of the state of his home: takeout containers on every horizontal surface, fruit flies laying eggs in the sink, spoiled milk in the fridge, milk on the verge of spoiling next to it, dust particles floating in the slits of light coming through the half-open blinds.

His awareness continued to expand. As he checked the time on his phone, he noticed that he had no missed calls, recalling the impulsive voicemail he'd left with a private investigation agency in the small hours of the morning. It was no wonder they hadn't called him back. He must've sounded insane.

Once again, the electricity crackled to life. He would go to the party. Danielle and Harriet deserved better.

* * *

"You didn't have to knock," Harriet said as she stepped aside to let Preston come through the door. The ice in her mint julep shifted as she moved, and around eight different smells struck him at once as he crossed the threshold.

"If you want a drink, you can follow me into the kitchen," she added, "and if you want a cigar, you can join Tyler and the rest in the parlor."

Realizing that cigar smoke was one of the smells that had struck him—and was growing stronger now as he followed Harriet farther into the house—Preston thought again of liminality and how Danielle had once told him the Catholic Church used incense to induce the same phenomenon.

The kitchen was thick with smells of meat and vegetables, the savory scent shot through with a heavy strand of mint. A tall, stainless-steel pot sat atop a live burner, its contents simmering to mush. In a line along the counter sat a salad bowl full of mint sprigs, an ice crusher, and a saucepan of simple syrup, leading up to several bottles of bourbon.

"This is the burgoo you found me scavenging after today," Harriet said, giving the pot a stir with the wooden spoon. "I'm holding my breath around it as much as I can, given the strength of my nose right now." She gave her glass a little shake, making the ice sing out. "I'm making my own drinks virgin, of course, but you can make yours as strong as you like. There's still some crushed ice in the bucket on top of the refrigerator, and the muddler is—" she spun around with her finger in the air, "—somewhere, but if you can't find it you can use the other end of the wooden spoon. It's quite accustomed to that. Now I'm going to get away from the smoke-and-meat smell in this house and finish my drink in the garden."

"Thanks," Preston said. She didn't acknowledge it. Through the kitchen window, he watched her reenter the garden, where she joined three women he didn't recognize, standing in the shade of a magnolia that protruded from the other side of the fence. Farther back, on a wooden bench, he spotted Danielle and Sylvia sitting with another woman he didn't recognize, all three of them in bright floral dresses. Two young blond boys were showing them some sticks; Danielle was saying something while Sylvia sat with her drink in her hand and smiled.

Preston retrieved a mason jar from one of the cabinets, hoping it was intended for use as a drinking vessel and not one of Harriet and Tyler's home projects. The simple syrup stuck to the edge of the pot as he poured it. A couple drops landed in a puddle on the floor, which seemed to have been sticky already. Preston added mint leaves to his mason jar and looked around for the muddler.

While he was looking, a man he didn't know came in holding a mostly full drink. He poured bourbon over the top and said, "Didn't make it strong enough this time around. Tastes like toothpaste if you don't cut it right." He extended his hand to Preston. "I'm Rick."

"Preston."

"Well, Preston, finish up that julep and join us in the next room over here. We've got a heated debate going, and I think some country club perspective would do us good."

Preston wanted to ask Rick where the muddler was, but he was gone too quickly. What had he meant with that crack about "country club perspective"?

A rumble of laughter came from the next room. Preston followed the sound, his julep still unfinished in his hand, and immediately felt like he had entered a courtroom. Tyler was sitting on the windowsill next to a box fan, flanked by three men closely bunched on either side, all of them smoking cigars. Every man in the room was looking at Preston.

"Preston Ellridge the Fourth, as I live and breathe," Tyler said in a mock-Southern accent that made Preston want to drink bleach. "I do declare, you appear to stand in *disregahd* of each and every rule of the parlor."

"Nailing the accent," one of the men at his side said. Another leaned behind Tyler to exhale smoke into the box fan.

"What rules would those be?"

"Parlor rule number one: One cigar minimum for entry." Tyler slid a wooden box across the hardwood with his foot. It landed just short of Preston. "Hand-rolled by none other than yours truly."

Preston was beginning to understand. He looked at the box but didn't reach down. "I'd expect nothing less."

"Parlor rule number two," Tyler said, holding two fingers up and out in front of him. "Drinks need to be so stiff you could hit a baseball with them."

"That would be easier if you could keep track of your muddler," Preston said.

A couple of scattered *ooh*s came from the men at Tyler's sides. "Simmer down," Tyler said. "He's new."

Despite the insular facade they collectively presented, Preston guessed that at least half the people in this room had never met before. Preston had seen Harriet use her strangeness to make unconnected people forget their unfamiliarity before. She was personable enough to be weird and weird enough to loosen people up. And from their single previous meeting, Preston knew Tyler could amplify her strangeness further. Still, it was jarring to see them take it to this extent.

Tyler held up three fingers. "Rule number three, and the most important rule of the parlor: to enter the parlor, you must place a bet on a horse."

He gestured to the far corner of the room, where the names of the horses and their respective odds had been written on an eighteen-by-eighteen-inch chalkboard with an oxidized copper frame. Preston squinted.

"Who's everybody got right now?"

Rick said, "The good money's on Sam Brown Came to Town. Myself, Toby, and Charles are all riding." He pointed to each person as he named them.

Tyler topped off his mint julep with a flask. "The only town Sam Brown is headed to is Loser Town."

The man named Charles said, "Not your best work."

Tyler waved him off. "Good money's on Sam, but the smart money's on Westchester Desperado."

Preston pointed to the window. "What's the consensus out there?"

"We don't make the ladies bet," Tyler said. "Things get pretty rough and tumble as it is."

The man named Charles said, "With the exception of Danielle."

Tyler nodded. "Danielle insisted."

Preston looked into his mason jar of mint leaves, then at the chalkboard. "Unsurprising. I'm going to take a long shot and bet on The Loosest Goose."

The Loosest Goose's odds were 48-1.

Tyler leaned back to exhale into the box fan, depositing the smoke into the garden. "I don't get the sense you've done this before."

"What gives you that impression?"

"Well," Tyler said, leaning so far forward that he seemed he would fall, his free hand cupped over the side of his mouth like he was revealing a trade secret that couldn't be overheard. "For one thing, you're betting on a goose in a horse race."

He let the silence smolder around them, still leaning in with his cigar held near his crotch. Then his face widened into a smile and the room rumbled with guffawing laughter. Preston joined in, though his own laugh was more nasal.

"Thanks for being a sport," Tyler said. "Now head over to TwoStee-ple-dot-com and place that bet, then get yourself a cigar! We're about to get the projector set up."

Preston nodded and exited the room, still unsure where the mud-dler was. He had his in now, though. He went through the motions of setting up a TwoSteeple account and placed a five-hundred-dollar bet, then took his unfinished drink toward the door to the garden, figuring he would ask Danielle which horse she had. From there, he had it. He opened the door.

"Did you need something?" Harriet asked.

Voices had immediately ceased as Preston stepped outside. The two blond boys were standing still. All seven of the women in the garden were looking at him, their eyes eerily blank, even Danielle's. Harriet's impatiens lined either side of the patio, deferring to a taller row of irises farther back. At the end of the irises sat Sylvia, petting a pure-white cat like a kingpin.

"Still can't find the muddler," Preston said.

Sylvia said, "Try the ice bucket."

Preston nodded and went back inside. He lifted the top from the ice bucket and found it sitting right there on top of the remaining ice. Attempting to go out there had been foolish. He thumped the muddler against his mint sprigs, trying to think of a new plan.

He needed to get Danielle and Sylvia both in a conversation. Just the two of them, but not in private. Another wave of laughter came from the parlor, where he assumed Tyler had chosen another guest to hound.

"We still need your help settling this debate," Rick said, appearing with three half-full mint juleps balanced against his chest. He placed them all in a line and uncorked a bottle of bourbon, then poured it over all three.

Preston wanted to ask him what had set off the country club remark earlier. It was true, of course, that his family had belonged to a club, and that he was familiar with it, and even that he could go back there right now and be welcomed in, because he and his family still belonged to it, but he was almost certain none of that was relevant to whatever they supposedly needed him for. "Not sure I'll be much help," he said.

Rick put his chest against the counter and drew the three mint juleps to himself. He rose again, taking them with him. "I think you'll find it's right up your alley."

What did he mean by that?

His drink at last mixed, Preston followed Rick into the parlor, where the man named Charles was trying to focus the projector.

"Tiny bit more," Tyler said.

"I got it," the man named Charles said.

"Tiiiny bit more," Tyler said.

The box of cigars was still in the middle of the floor where Tyler had slid them earlier. Preston crouched down to pick one up. As he stood, he heard Tyler say, "Let me cut one of those for you."

Tyler took the cigar from him and pulled a small black object from his pocket. It looked like a cross between a bottle opener and a guillotine. "Kevin over there cut his too far down earlier and just about ruined it for himself. There."

He handed the cut cigar back to Preston, with the cut end facing him. "Lighter's over there by the fan; when you're blowing out, aim it toward the blades. Harriet doesn't hate the smell of smoke, but she's got the nose of a bear right now." Then he looked back at the screen and said, "Too far."

Preston walked over to the fan, where a lighter sat next to the cord. A huge spider with a bulging orange back watched him from the upper corner of the window. Preston sat on the windowsill where Tyler had been earlier and lit the cigar, still trying to think of a plan.

The garden door opened and someone went into the kitchen. Preston slid back onto his feet and ducked under the projector to see who it was.

Harriet had come back in to stir the burgoo. "Smoke by the fan," she said, then went back outside. A simple tug of the string; Sylvia's invisible lines remained at work.

Preston turned around.

Tyler was adjusting the projector himself now. "I told you," he said.

Preston went back to the windowsill. Over the top of the fan, he had a partial view of the garden. Harriet had left her original group and joined Sylvia and Danielle on the bench. The three of them were laughing at something together.

Markets revolved around information. Efficient market hypothesis dictated that the market was unbeatable due to the speed at which it could adjust to public information—information that formed speculation on the stock's future behavior. All that had happened to the stock—and ever would happen to the stock, within the bounds set by available information—had already been priced in. It was foolish to buy a stock on the assumption it would rise. It had already risen.

The direction of the market changed when new information contradicted consensus predictions. Danielle had turned down Preston's offer on a consensus prediction that Sylvia would disapprove. If Danielle were led to believe that Sylvia would approve, then her decision would adjust, perhaps enough for her to come on board with him.

"That's a clear picture," Tyler said, walking away from the projector with his hands held high in triumph. "Preston, look at that picture quality."

Preston turned away from the window and looked at the image. They were showing highlights from a previous Derby, in which a horse facing dramatic odds made a late pass to secure the win. "Crystal clear," Preston said.

He turned back to the window. Sylvia and Danielle were standing now, saying something to Harriet. At this distance, they looked small enough to be devoured by the spider in the window frame. Harriet nodded and said something back. Sylvia and Danielle walked away. He braced himself. They could be coming in.

Behind him Tyler said, "As clear as a crystal. You only get that kind of dexterity from hand-rolling cigars."

"I'll give you a call next time I need my projector adjusted," the man named Charles said. "Or a cigar rolled."

"Can't promise either of those," Tyler said. "Start winding those cigars down, everybody. Race is in twenty minutes, so we've got fifteen to clear the smoke out before the ladies come in. Now if you'll excuse me, I've got a bowl of burgoo to secure."

He went into the kitchen. Preston watched the window to see whether Sylvia and Danielle were coming in. Instead, they walked out of the backyard and around the side door. Had they gone home?

Rick said, "Somebody needs to get a video of that accent."

Hearing that, Preston realized what had been bothering him since he arrived. It wasn't the accent, but the atmosphere of parody: the way that Tyler spoke of calling in the ladies, as though each person in the garden were a charming little hothouse orchid; the way they had divided the party into men and women, as though they were abiding by a bygone value system; the way their actions pretended to reflect wealth and influence, as though anyone present had experienced either. Preston had experienced both. Wealth and influence came with crushing responsibility, and the people who had it wriggled under the hammer of that responsibility. Only people who hadn't experienced that responsibility mistook it for something to pretend at and undercut.

Wealth came with the requirement that you pursued things, did things, made things, had things. Everything you did was high-profile. Your failures made their way into circles that most people didn't know existed. Success meant dignity. You had to be dignified with wealth or you would spiral. These people didn't know about it, how it pulverized and debilitated you.

The men had all put out their cigars, and Tyler was waving the chalkboard around to blow the lingering smoke toward the box fan. Eight minutes had passed since Tyler announced the twenty-minute warning. The ladies would be in soon. Preston put out his own cigar and breathed in to steady himself. Coercion was at work right now, and he would have to work with it.

Tyler continued waving the chalkboard around to clear the smoke. His shadow created a hole in the projected image, as though his silhouette was fanning the crowd. A couple of the other men in the room were topping off their drinks, in which the mint sprigs had long since disintegrated. From the projector's speaker came the chorus hum of the spectators drunkenly singing "My Old Kentucky Home."

The horses were heading for the starting gates, and Tyler was unplugging the box fan while Rick and the man named Charles brought in chairs from the living room. Preston stood still, sipping his drink with his new friend the spider and steadying his thoughts. He stood there, not moving chairs or fanning smoke or unplugging fans, but providing authenticity. He was the bridge between this party and the world it imitated. Eventually he would take Danielle to that world and she would see how misguided this whole act was, how deeply uninformed these people were.

"All right," Tyler said, "here they come."

A parade of women entered, led by Harriet and, to Preston's relief, ended by Sylvia and Danielle. They streamed in and dispersed about the room, eyes turned expectantly toward the race. Danielle stood in the back corner with Sylvia, away from Preston.

He went over to her. She acknowledged him with an airy smile and then turned away, indicating that their interaction need not go any further, but Preston disagreed. "I hear you have skin in the game," he said.

She turned and looked at him with her mouth slightly open, as though he had spoken French. She seemed distant. "You mean the race? They were making a big dumb show out of ladies not betting, even though none of us wanted to. So I put down twenty on West-chester Desperado."

"I bet on The Loosest Goose myself," Preston said, smiling. "What about you, Sylvia?"

Sylvia looked at him for a moment, apparently caught off guard. He was surprised at how disheveled she looked up close. Her braid had mostly fallen out, and she was missing an earring. "Danielle's bet was enough for both of us."

The projector was now displaying a countdown to the race. The remaining time ticked under three minutes, and Preston said, "You'll have to buy yourself something if it pays out."

"You will too," Danielle said. She still seemed far away, discon-nected from the room and the race.

"You know, I think you could buy yourself a lot more things with the stake in the restaurant I offered you."

Danielle smiled, and Preston could see it was out of frustration. "I just want to watch the race."

Two and a half minutes to go now.

"What stake?" Sylvia asked.

She hadn't been told.

Preston's mind recalculated rapidly. If Sylvia didn't know about the stake, then Danielle hadn't mentioned the stake. If Danielle hadn't mentioned the stake, then there had to be a reason why she hadn't mentioned the stake. The reason had to do, specifically, with Sylvia, and how Sylvia would react; if he could find the reason, perhaps he could convince Sylvia; and if Sylvia was convinced, then the swiftest, loftiest, shiftiest barrier to convincing Danielle would have fallen.

He said, "It's a self-funded venture, and I'm offering fifteen per-cent of whatever ROI we generate." He turned to Danielle. "And fol-lowing design, you don't have to lift a finger."

Two minutes now.

Danielle and Sylvia looked at each other. They wanted to seem like they were speaking without words, exchanging opinions through eye twitches, but Preston could tell they were reading each other, try-ing to infer the other's thoughts. To withhold was to distrust, and

Danielle had withheld the stake. Where they seemed to be looking into each other, so deeply connected that the slightest gesture amounted to a paragraph, they must have been mystified by one another and afraid to display it. They looked at each other that way for thirteen seconds, the countdown clock measuring their silence, and then Danielle said, "And I get this for as long as the restaurant stays open? And profitable?"

Fulfillment, money, status. Preston's sense of their relative importance was correcting in real time. He had wrongly assumed status would be the core of Danielle's acceptance, but it didn't matter that he had been wrong when all three would be present. He had done his research. Richmond's modern identity flowed forth from its food. The match was perfect. He was perfect for this place, as Danielle was perfect for this place—as he was perfect for her—as this place was perfect for them together.

Sylvia put her hand on Danielle's knee. Her tacit approval had been granted.

"That's correct," Preston said.

It was happening.

One minute and fifteen seconds left now.

Why did the stake matter so much? The rate at which he had offered to pay her upfront easily dwarfed the money she would receive from the ongoing investment. He had thought of that as a kicker, but they didn't seem to be taking it that way.

"What if the restaurant goes out of business?" Danielle asked.

It was happening. He had it. Just had to close it. "It won't," Preston said. The clock was inside of one minute. He added, "I went across the ocean and then across the equator, to every significant food destination in the world. I've read six different books on running a successful restaurant, and that's just in the last year. And I've run my initial slate of ideas past multiple restaurant group owners in the States to get feedback. Everything is solid."

Danielle and Sylvia looked at each other again, anxiously this time, now plainly searching each other for answers. Preston unnerved them. He understood that. His past behavior had raised suspicions. That made sense. Sylvia hated him. And yet, they didn't know what to do. His intentions weren't pure. He knew he was only thinly concealing them. They were deciding to ignore that, but why?

Then his epiphany came: Whatever unique value the stake may hold for Sylvia was irrelevant. What mattered was that Danielle had protected her. She had left out the part of his offer that would have made the decision difficult. Now the decision was in front of them, and Sylvia was unprepared. Just as Danielle must have known she would be.

Even now, Sylvia could speak up, say no, walk away, and set him back for good. He watched her. She wasn't going to speak up. She wasn't even going to lift her hand from Danielle's knee. He could see her relaxing, settling. She was cocky. She was overconfident. She thought she had Danielle so spun around that she could just sit back. Her line was sliding. He kept watching her. He watched her face. She knew the offer was good. Danielle knew it too. They were afraid of each other. Afraid to be the one to say no. Afraid the other wanted to say yes. Sylvia's tricks didn't work in front of Preston. She couldn't walk away and distort everything. Without manipulation, Sylvia had nothing. Preston had her figured out. Soon Danielle would see it, too. Sylvia would act weak. She would play at vulnerability. She would cry big crocodile tears out of her big puppy eyes. But this time, Danielle would see through it all. Even a shapeshifter could run out of shapes. Preston didn't need any tricks, though. He had the truth underneath his feet: his was the best offer, and the best offer would win out.

Fifteen seconds. He had it.

Danielle said, "I want twenty-five percent."

"Done."

"And I set when we meet."

It was happening.

"No problem."

Ten seconds.

Danielle craned her neck so she was as close to his eye level as she could manage. "And you need to assure me this will take no longer than ten months."

"I can put it in a contract."

Five seconds.

Sylvia linked her fingers in Danielle's and squeezed. Across the room, a starter's pistol pointed up toward the cloudless Kentucky sky. "Okay," Danielle said. "I'll work with you."

With that, they were off.

* * *

Preston couldn't entirely discount the general public's antipathy toward country clubs. Though he considered it misinformed, he had felt some version of that distaste a decade earlier at an unfamiliar club outside Charlottesville. It was his sister's rehearsal dinner, and Preston was seated at his family's table, trying and failing to get a word in. All the Ellridges besides him had gathered crowds around themselves, each of their seats at the circular table surrounded by guests who had drifted over to stand around them.

Closest to Preston, his father was telling the snake story to an old neighbor. "So Preston walks in, no idea what's been going on, and as soon as he sees the hamster running around under the blanket he assumes it's a snake, and next thing we know—"

"It was Abigail who thought it was a snake," Preston said, but he didn't speak loud enough, and his father was already past it.

At the other compass points of the circular table sat his three older sisters, each orbited by their own cultivated cliques. There was Julia, the athletic eldest, talking to a group of her former soccer teammates and their husbands, all of them laughing about something he hadn't heard. Julia's college GPA had never climbed above a three, but it never fell low enough for her to lose her soccer scholarship, and so no one seemed to mind—despite the fact that she never needed a scholarship to begin with. She was a graduate assistant coach now, and every day she parked the Cadillac purchased through her trust fund right next to the head coach's Corolla.

Preston was unsure how her soccer teammates, who hardly knew him or his sisters, had all been invited. How was it that, at every family gathering, everyone else always seemed to have their own kin?

"And anyway," his father was saying, "the only three reasons somebody's going to take a job are money, status, and—honey what's the third one I'm always saying?"

"Fulfillment," Preston said, but again, no one heard.

The ballroom was loud, packed with easily two hundred people, maybe more. They had extended the rehearsal dinner invitation to wedding party members and travelers, a nominal designation that every guest had applied to themselves.

Next around the table from Julia was Abigail—the artistic one and the bride—sitting next to her husband-to-be and talking to a smattering of bridesmaids and groomsmen. Of his sisters, she was the only who had even attempted a traditional job, though it had been arranged for her. She had soldiered through a little more than four years (miserable ones, to hear her tell it), before declaring that such work stymied her creative spirit. Now she was finishing up a graduate degree in architecture from nearby UVA, their parents happily paying tuition in addition to the cost of her wedding.

That she had managed to plan a wedding while also attending grad school was apparently impressive. Preston rolled his eyes to no one.

"Now, when you're traveling," his father was saying, "the key is to have a hotel brand you know is going to live up to your standards. We've always liked the Ritz for that."

Preston didn't even try.

Rounding out the table was Cassandra, the homely sister, currently pregnant with her first child. She was the closest to him in age, though she was much closer to the other two sisters than to him. Cassandra Preston Ellridge, the sister who had nearly absorbed the family's expectations—who occasionally seemed as though she might venture into understanding Preston—before pulling herself back to her rooms of padded walls. If she had ever faced the wide-open world, she might've realized how frightening her middle name could be. Instead, she had married an investment banker and now seemed unaware there existed meals other than brunch.

It was with some surprise that Preston realized Cassandra was talking to people he knew better than her. Harriet's parents were here, and he felt a brief wisp of hope that meant Harriet was here too. She would probably be game to sneak outside with him, where they could just drink a bit and pretend they were at the beach. He stood to move closer.

"Preston, my guy!" Harriet's dad said as he approached. "How's it hanging?"

"Loose like always," Preston said, his hope increasing. "Is Harriet around somewhere?"

Harriet's mom shook her head. "She did tell us to say hi to you, though, so, hi!"

Preston lingered a bit longer but soon found himself drifting away. His father had begun to offer his opinions on artificial intelligence, and the room felt hot. Preston walked outside onto the grounds of the club. A long, flat field stretched out before him, and he felt it mirrored his life ahead.

Saturn was supposed to be visible that night—or was it Venus? He searched the sky for a brighter star than the rest, but none stood out except Polaris, twinkling at the top of the Little Dipper.

Headed nowhere but away, Preston stepped onto the smooth grass, then kept walking. When he had gone far enough to feel far away, he looked for Mercury or Mars in the clear sky and thought about how much he had never asked for.

He did not know that in less than twenty-four hours, he would meet Danielle and become dizzy as the lights inside his mind all came on for the first time. He did not yet know how he would spend the years to follow, chasing the power source of those lights like he was trying to wrap his arms around a sunbeam.

As if to complete his misery, rain began to fall just then, swiftly and heavily out of a cloudless night sky. Preston hurried back toward the ballroom at first, but he wasn't even halfway there before he realized he was soaked. He slowed down, and his walk became a trudge over the soggy ground. Just about right, he thought. Just perfect. Exactly what he needed. He sighed. Maybe one day, something great would happen to him, and it would all turn around. But until then, he was stuck in the rain.

3

Danielle walked around to the side of the gas station that marked the state border just to be alone with her hopes. Her period was now two days late, with no sign of appearing as they entered the afternoon of a third. Her hopes blossomed as she rounded the corner, overtaking the multitude of reasons to be frustrated. The area smelled like trash and cigarette smoke, and Harriet had mentioned her pregnancy at least ten times, and she was worried her sunscreen was leaking in her suitcase, and Sylvia was clearly carsick, and Tyler's music choices were suspect at best, and Preston kept "thinking of" things he "forgot" to mention about their accommodations. Danielle was encircled by delightful reasons to be upset, but all of them lacked the power to bother her right now, small as they were beside her hopes.

She loitered for a few more seconds. Two days late was medically normal, she knew, and she had been two days late before, and she could be setting herself up to be crushed right now; and she would hate to be crushed, and Sylvia would take it hard if she was crushed. Being crushed would be crushing, but if Danielle couldn't stay hopeful on the way to the beach, with the whole uneasy equilibrium of her life holding fast against so much uncertainty, then she would just have to never be hopeful again, and that wouldn't come easy to her.

Tyler was getting into the car as she came back around. "Duck out to smoke?" he asked.

She shook her head. "Just wanted to be away from people for a second."

Tyler laughed as he started the car, leaving the door open. The others were all still inside. "We're a crew here, all right."

Preston came out of the convenience store, looking down and walking quickly in the wrong direction. "Over here," Tyler called, leaning out the door. Preston corrected course toward the car while Tyler put on his sunglasses. As Preston neared them, Tyler tilted his head at the plastic bag dangling from Preston's index finger and asked, "Get enough for everybody?"

Preston sneered. "I think I've contributed in other ways."

"Whoa now," Tyler said. "Let's not forget who's paying for gas."

Danielle smiled at them, bemused at their theatrics with no one in the audience but her. She looked around the hood of Tyler's Highlander to see if Harriet and Sylvia were out of the ladies' room yet.

"Real budget hit to pay for gas in a hybrid," Preston said.

"Sorry, couldn't hear you over the sound of all the hacking and wheezing you're not doing, because of how clean this air is."

Danielle said, "Now, now."

They both looked at her as if she had said something gratifying.

Just then, Sylvia and Harriet emerged from the convenience store, laughing about something. Danielle wished she could like Harriet the way Sylvia liked Harriet, just brushing off the commentary and editing out the smugness. Harriet was pleasant enough, and welcoming enough, and engaging enough, and caring enough—if you could get past that total confidence she had in all of her opinions and that fake way she was humble about them.

Sylvia had been sitting in the middle row with Danielle, and Harriet had been sitting in the front to keep her legs stretched, and Preston had been sitting in the third row by himself, with that leather backpack of his, leaning an elbow on the windowsill and watching the cornfields roll by. When Sylvia and Harriet got back in the car, they switched seats. They must have agreed to switch while they were inside together, with Danielle outside and un-consulted about sitting next to Harriet; and not for the first time Danielle caught herself feeling excluded from their deepening bond, which had started as neighborly kindness, then moved on to friendship, then moved on to whatever came one level after friendship.

"All right folks," Tyler said, plugging the aux cable back into his phone. "We're entering rural North Carolina. Local laws stipulate that we now have to listen to Americana until we see the ocean."

Harriet said, "Just drive the car."

"Sylvia's on my side," Tyler said. "Aren't you, Sylvia?"

Sylvia glanced behind her. "Technically, I'm on the passenger's side."

"Diplomatic as always," Tyler said.

He backed the car out of its space, and as he pulled back onto the road, Johnny Cash's voice came dribbling out from the speakers, singing:

Delia's gone, one more round
Delia's gone

Danielle tapped Sylvia's shoulder with her finger, and Sylvia turned her face toward the window, and Danielle leaned forward so her lips were close to Sylvia's ear and quietly said, "I love you."

Because she had such a haphazard menu of feelings before her, loving Sylvia was the one Danielle wanted to select. Because she was grateful to Sylvia, grateful that Sylvia had been so brave about going off hormones for her, and grateful that all of their sex had been mind-warping, animal glee since the hormones went away, and grateful that this was the month that Sylvia had told her the healthy sperm would start coming through, and grateful that Sylvia was even handling this beach trip well. It had been Preston's suggestion that they all go down to his family's house, and to take Harriet and Tyler, because Harriet's family was from down here; and Preston felt that both he and Danielle needed a change of scenery to unlock their mutual creativity; and she was enjoying working with Preston. He was keeping their interactions professional, and he was being polite to Sylvia too.

Sylvia curled her arm around her shoulder and stroked Danielle's cheek. "I love you too."

Johnny Cash sang on quietly about what had driven him to kill the low-down, trifling Delia.

"Can we listen to something else?" Harriet said.

Tyler huffed. "Fine." He grabbed his phone and scrolled with one hand, alternating between looking at the road and looking at the screen.

Harriet said, "You could have Sylvia do it."

"I got it," Tyler said, flicking his thumb. Then he looked up and said, "There it is!" He pointed so frantically that the car veered.

Danielle looked in the direction he was pointing and saw a billboard depicting Jesus on the cross, pictured from behind with the sun shining in one corner. It said, "Freedom: Paid for by the blood of Jesus Christ."

Tyler finished switching the music and put his phone down. "Best billboard of the trip. It used to be facing the other way so that you'd see it on the way back, but it went down in a hurricane. Now, though, it's been—" he paused, leaned in toward the center of the car, turned his head as much as he could while still looking at the road, and tapped his sunglasses, "—resurrected."

"I think I'm offended?" Sylvia said. "Danielle, are we offended?"

"We are definitely offended," Danielle said.

She could hear Preston snickering behind her, and Tyler was laughing at his own joke and at the way it had gone over. Danielle felt light, like she was one story above the smog of an industrial city, close to the muck and the darkness but still breathing easy. The equilibrium was holding. If she was still late by the end of this trip, then it would hold forever.

All around her, Johnny Cash sang:
I got sheep, I got mules
I got, all livestock

Preston's beach house turned out to be a perfect specimen of rich-person taste. The top floor had an open plan, with a marble-surfaced kitchen and big wrought iron pendant lights, while the furnishings in the dining and sitting areas were as mahogany and beige as money could buy. It reminded Danielle of a fawning celebrity apartment tour she'd once read and mocked, only bigger and realer.

Beyond the showy wood and boring hues lay a rolling view of the ocean, though, and that was hard to ruin. A pair of binoculars sat on the windowsill, creating a moment of invitation. It was the only artful touch in the house, maybe the only artful touch on the block.

"It's not how I remember it," Harriet said, coming upstairs from the room she and Tyler had claimed.

Danielle realized she had been taking in the scene without considering how visible she was.

"How so?" Preston asked.

Harriet took a few more steps toward the center of the room— space that often went curiously wasted in open-plan arrangements like this one. She put her hand on the edge of the couch. "It's cleaner."

Preston took a Corona from the fridge and twisted the cap off. "My sister made a big thing of hosting Memorial Day this year, so nobody's been here since New Year's."

Harriet said, "That Corona must be nice and aged, then. Can I smell it?"

Preston was sitting at the dining table now. He held his bottle out toward her. Harriet put her ski-jump nose toward it and inhaled.

"I'm sorry," she said. "I know beer doesn't age, but now that I can't drink this is all I have."

Danielle went downstairs, where Sylvia was unpacking her suitcase. "I can't take more of the pregnancy chatter."

Sylvia smiled but continued unpacking.

"I mean it," Danielle said. "She twists every moment around to bring it up."

"She just feels like everybody's looking at her," Sylvia said.

"You could tell her that she doesn't have to."

Sylvia's face twitched with a dismissive laugh. "I think you'd have more success with that. She's kind of afraid of you."

Danielle was mad now, and Sylvia wasn't recognizing it, and she didn't want to be mad at the beach. But Danielle couldn't stop herself from being mad without a reason to not be mad, and she couldn't come up with a reason right now. She went into the bathroom alone and looked at herself. She braided her hair for an excuse to be in there longer.

"Here's how you can think of it," Sylvia said, leaning on the door and tying on the top of her bathing suit. "You guys will probably overlap."

Danielle twisted her braid slowly, considering.

Sylvia said, "It'll be good to have somebody to talk to about it, and if you spend this whole period getting mad, then . . ."

"What if she's not who I want to share it with?"

Sylvia breathed in, looking indecisive about whether to reply or not. "I think—" she grimaced a bit, then breathed again "—she would be hurt by that."

Danielle walked out of the bathroom and sat on the bed. Sylvia was right, and hurting Harriet was unfair, and she was supposed to be maintaining the equilibrium, and this beach trip could go a long way toward setting up the kind of bond that would help her through a pregnancy; and she hadn't let herself think of the actual pregnancy very much because it seemed so wraith-like—so fleeting—as a possibility; and she should acknowledge that Sylvia was right. And she would, if she could only let herself think beyond the uncertain part.

"We should put on sunscreen in here," Sylvia said.

Danielle almost laughed at her. It was so obvious. She wanted to put on sunscreen down here in the room where Preston wasn't allowed, and Preston wouldn't be able to maneuver either of them into rubbing his back. He never would, but Sylvia had imagined it regardless when they packed the night before, and now that she had imagined it she had to prevent it. "Good idea," Danielle said.

Sylvia swept her hair forward. "Can you do me first?"

"Of course," Danielle said. Thinking about Sylvia's insecurities instead of her own was helping her mood. That was a positive aspect of marriage. Marriage involved lots of shared burdens and mutual issues, carrying troubles together like pallbearers. It didn't always work out that way, though. Sometimes marriage involved two people with problems so disparate they were a joy to soothe for each other. She was feeling better now.

"Cold," Sylvia said.

"You're fine," Danielle said.

She could feel Sylvia's shoulders quaking.

Someone knocked on their door. "Who is it?" Danielle asked.

"We're heading to the beach in a minute," Preston said through the door.

"We'll be out in a bit," Danielle said.

She heard Preston drag his feet away from the door. He was being generous by letting them come here, and stay here, and it was true that the two of them had made a lot of progress on the restaurant in the six weeks since the Derby party. And it was just as true that they seemed to be stalling out—and working by the ocean had always been a romantic ideal of hers—and that was not something she was going to say out loud to Sylvia, she realized.

"All right," she said. "Finish up and do me."

She pulled her tank-top over her head while Sylvia rubbed sunscreen into her legs.

It wasn't necessarily a *romantic* ideal of working by the ocean, Danielle amended. It was really just that the ocean itself was romantic, and the work she did was romantic too, and it was hard to combine the two and not get the same thing. She did love the ocean, though. Aquatic creatures had so little to do with humans and human things. Most of them would be befuddled by the most basic human experiences. Deep-sea fish would be confused by cycles of daytime and nighttime, and bottom dwellers would be overwhelmed and panicked by the speed at which things fell outside of water, or by how many things fell down at all; and, actually, most fish would feel completely imprisoned by gravity as land dwellers experienced it. Actually, if a person could put a fish in outer space and ask, "How similar to your regular life does this feel," the fish might say, "Not all that different." And really the cycles of the tide were connected to the moon, so in truth the ocean had more to do with the moon and space than it did with the Earth beyond the beach.

"Cold," she said as Sylvia rubbed circles over her back.

"Don't mock me," Sylvia said.

Danielle turned around to face Sylvia, leaving her standing with her sun-screened palm suspended in front of her. "You're right about Harriet," Danielle said.

Sylvia nodded. "I figured I was."

Danielle turned away again, then shuddered as Sylvia's hand returned to her back. "I think we did it this time."

"I think so too," Sylvia said.

Whenever Danielle felt worried about their fertility—as she had felt for most of the last year now—she was inclined to rip things up. That included her friendships, and Sylvia's friendships, and her own body. Sylvia had taken care of her through her struggle. Danielle knew that pregnancy would be hard, but it would be a path, a defined and certain path that she could walk and adjust to, and not a suspended state of wondering. And she could adjust, and she wanted to because Sylvia had been holding her up for a while now, and she wanted to return some of the favor. When she was done worrying about her fertility, Danielle could go back to her natural state, where she could look at her life and her friends and her relationship and see what all of them needed, and improve them, and repair them.

Sylvia handed back the bottle of sunscreen, looked at her hair, and said, "I'm going to copy you and braid mine too."

She went into the bathroom. Danielle squirted more sunscreen onto her hand, nearly depleting the bottle. They had underestimated how much they would need.

A clamor of footsteps rolled above them. A door slammed, then through their private screen door, she saw Harriet's and Preston's and Tyler's feet all pass over the walkway that led to the dune. She liked that this house was inverted, with the living area on the top and the bedrooms down below, such that comings and goings were so oddly framed.

Sylvia's head popped back out. Her braid was half-finished. "Did they just leave?"

Danielle smiled. "We haven't even been here an hour."

Sylvia continued to stand there, her hair in her hands, waiting for a different answer.

"Tonight," Danielle said.

"Fine," Sylvia said, and moped back into the bathroom.

Danielle finished up and began loading beach towels into their tote bag.

"What if it's really fast?" Sylvia said, again stepping out of the bathroom, her hair now three-quarters braided.

"Tonight. I promise."

"Fine," Sylvia said again, and again moped back into the bathroom.

Danielle dug around in a suitcase until she found the Boston Red Sox cap she'd brought. She called out, "Do you want your sun hat?"

"No," Sylvia said from the bathroom. "It's not actually that functional."

Danielle adjusted her hat in the mirror. She looked like a Boston Red Sock.

Sylvia emerged from the bathroom, braid finished. "I'm ready."

They headed up the stairs to the top floor, and as the room came into focus, Danielle realized what she would do with the space if given the chance. She would replace the beige couches with blue couches, and between them she would put an ovular coffee table to gently evoke fish and waves, and she would replace the wrought iron pendant lights with hanging globes of various sizes, and she would extend the kitchen island so long that it became a table, and she would put captain's chairs all around it, and she would put a big campy steering wheel by the row of windows facing the ocean; and people would get up from the blue couches and the captain's chairs to put their hands on that campy wheel and just look out at the ocean, and soon they'd find themselves steering.

Preston and Tyler were throwing a frisbee on the beach when they arrived, while Harriet sat in a folding chair under an umbrella, reading a book.

"Is this seat taken?" Sylvia asked, rolling her beach towel out on the sand next to Harriet.

"I was saving that, actually, for a very important visitor," Harriet said.

Sylvia lowered herself onto her knees. "I'll get up when she arrives." She stretched out onto her stomach.

Danielle rolled her own beach towel out next to Sylvia's. She sat on it, hugging her knees, and watched Preston and Tyler throw the frisbee. Their game had moved into the ocean now, and they were diving to catch the frisbee, making a big show of coming up with it whenever they caught it. They reminded Danielle of Sylvia as she had first seen her years and years ago, diving for a frisbee on Lambeth Field.

"Is it just me, or does Preston seem different here?" Danielle asked, not really speaking to Harriet but not really speaking to anyone else.

"It's not just you," Harriet said, closing her book. "The couple of times I've seen him in Richmond, I've been incredulous at how little I like him. His family used to come down for about a month every summer when I was growing up here, and we all thought he and his sisters were the nicest, most relaxed of the seasonal crowd."

Sylvia fidgeted and turned her head. Danielle put her hand on Sylvia's back, listening to the waves. Preston and Tyler had moved farther into the water, and they were whooping about something.

Danielle said, "I wouldn't say I don't like him in Richmond. After we crossed the state line, though, as we got farther into North Carolina, he just seemed to—" she scratched her nose "—uncoil a bit."

Harriet was watching them too now. They were coming back in with the surf. "It's probably good for everyone."

"The jellyfish are out," Tyler said, reaching under Harriet's chair for his beer.

Preston said, "And we think we saw a stingray."

There was something arresting about the way he said "We."

Sylvia hummed a bit to let everyone know she wasn't sleeping.

Tyler pointed the frisbee at Harriet. "Come throw with us?"

Harriet put her hand on the baby bump and laughed.

"What about you, Danielle?" Preston asked.

"I have to make sure no one makes off with Sylvia."

Sylvia hummed again.

Tyler crouched down, his head about a foot from Sylvia's. "How about you?"

Sylvia lifted her head and looked at him, then put it back down. Like a cat.

Tyler lifted his beer up high and downed it with his elbow extended, posing like he was in a commercial, then tossed the bottle into the shade. "Looks like the wet blanket patrol needs some more time in the sun."

He and Preston went back out onto the flat, damp sand.

Danielle put her hand on Sylvia's back again. "You should go out there with them."

Sylvia raised her chest off the ground and scanned the horizon. She shook her head. "No, no, I don't think that would be good."

Danielle rubbed her back. "I just want you to acknowledge that you could."

Sylvia shifted her neck some. Danielle chose to interpret it as a nod.

The next morning, Sylvia and Danielle woke early to get ready for church. Danielle showered first and dressed hastily, then went upstairs by herself to have breakfast. On the mahogany table was a local newspaper open to a halfway-done crossword puzzle from months ago, and she worked on it in her head while she ate her bagel, halfheartedly looking for a pen.

Harriet came upstairs a few minutes later, bleary-eyed and beach-haired, and said, "And I thought I was getting up early."

Danielle looked up for a moment, then went back to the cross-word puzzle. She was trying to remember the name of the actor who played Big Daddy in *Cat on a Hot Tin Roof.* "We're going to the early Mass. We didn't want to hog the car later in the day."

"Ah, that makes sense," Harriet said, walking to the binoculars. "That explains why you two scampered off to bed so early last night too."

She glanced over with that smug, wry look she had on her face all the time.

"Yep," Danielle said.

Sylvia came up the stairs, wearing her sun hat and fastening a bracelet. "Good morning," she said.

Danielle had always liked the way Sylvia said *good morning*—and she knew that was odd, and that it was trivial, and she didn't mind that it was odd and trivial. Sylvia had said it the same way since they met. She said good morning like she was speaking to the morning itself; like the morning was a little dog she was training, and she was telling it to be good, warmly but sternly. People often observed Sylvia's distaste for confrontation and mistook it for passiveness, though Danielle didn't know how they could; perhaps they had simply never heard her say good morning.

Danielle checked her watch. "We probably need to go."

"Let me just get a bagel toasted."

Harriet was looking out through the binoculars. "I'm impressed you two are going. I assumed you got a pass when you were some-where else."

Sylvia pressed the toaster's lever down and laughed. "My family certainly thought that way. You also got a pass if you had allergies. Or if it was raining. Or if it was too sunny."

"Don't forget traffic," Danielle said. "You didn't have to go if there was traffic."

Sylvia drifted over to the table and put her hand on Danielle's shoulder. "Danielle brought me around. It's actually fun to go to church out of your usual habitat. The basics are the same, but every church has a different feel." Her bagel popped out. "Want to come with us?"

Danielle's jaw nearly dropped.

Harriet's face flushed. "I'm not Christian."

Sylvia was undeterred. "You can come for the human interest of it. Maybe some folks there can show you how to make stained glass."

Harriet was really red now. "I appreciate it, but I looked at the tide chart last night and low tide is in—" she looked over at the clock "—one minute. I'm going to go out and gather shells. I haven't made a really good shell necklace in a long time. I thought my parents would get a kick out of it too, if I showed up wearing one of the necklaces I used to make obsessively when I was an elementary schooler. They were the first thing I learned how to make, actually."

Sylvia was smiling. "Well, if you find a lot, I wouldn't mind learning how."

She lifted her bagel out and wrapped it in a paper towel, then grabbed Tyler's keys off the island. Danielle followed her out to Tyler's car.

As they walked down the stairs, Danielle again considered the room they had just left. On second thought, she wouldn't put a big captain's wheel in it, because it was too much; and she didn't like the idea of varying sizes of globe lights either, since the variance in size would convey a constant playfulness, exciting some of the time but unwelcome in moments of nautical contemplation; she would actually make them hanging globes of the same size, and she would stripe the wall behind the island-table, all lines and circles, the island-table and its globe-light beacons pressing out of the harbor of the kitchen and into the ocean of stripes, subtly.

Sylvia started the car and backed out of the driveway without a word, leaving it to Danielle to ask.

Danielle said, "What was going on with Harriet back there?"

Sylvia's composure deserted her. She seemed sheepish now. "You're going to hate this."

"What was it?"

"Let me make this turn," Sylvia said.

Danielle listened to the click of the turn signal and waited for the road to clear. The cars drove close together on the single-lane road that went up and down the peninsula. The plant life here struck Danielle with how different it was, with the oleanders and the mimosas growing wild in between the houses, and even palm trees and cacti along the side of the road; and all of those were visible just in the small swath of road and neighborhood she could see right now, and it all struck her as belonging to a lush tropical paradise or a dangerous desert island far off in the sea, and the moon was visible in the bright morning sky.

Sylvia completed the turn. "All right, so like I said, you're going to hate it, but I can't get this out of my mind. You know I'm a little—" she adjusted her hat "—insecure about my place at church."

"I do," Danielle said.

Sylvia bit her lip. "Sometime in the last, I don't know, six months, I got it in my head that if I can convert somebody, just literally one person, then I'll have made up for any invisible lines I've stepped across."

Danielle didn't hate it, not necessarily, but she was unnerved by the sincerity. "Of all people, though. Harriet?"

Sylvia smiled. "She's pretty atheist, but I don't think her heart's really in it."

"I don't know," Danielle said.

"About Harriet? Or about the whole plan?"

"Both," Danielle said.

Sylvia said, "Maybe it's just a feeling in search of a justification. I've always been pretty grateful to you for converting me."

"I was trying to make you marriageable," Danielle said.

"I know, and I was already Catholic, and all that. I just . . ." She bit her lip on the other side. "I enjoy being a religious person. I like driving to Mass right now. I like pondering the readings. I like listening to Tyler's Johnny Cash albums and not having to—" she made an air quote with one hand on the steering wheel "—'Get past all the Christian stuff.' And all of that is on top of me feeling that nagging insecurity too. I think people see me out here being trans and they say, 'That's real; that's her identity, who she really is at the center.' And they don't understand that I feel like religion is just as central for me, and that it's done a lot for me, especially in these last few months. So if you want, you can just think of it as passing that along."

Danielle looked at her, unsure whether to continue talking about this or not. She hadn't liked the idea of converting to offset something. She was of the opinion that God didn't deal in bargains, and that bargains were associated with the devil for a reason, and that overall, Sylvia would be happier if she could focus on her personal relationship with God and not her political relationship with God. There were lots of occasions where she felt sorry for Sylvia; where Danielle could watch her trying to develop her own theology and almost see her eyes pointing in different directions, feel her headache radiating into the room. Sylvia sometimes got into this grandiose, political, dogmatic, inauthentic, and even sinful way of thinking that only led to miserable dead ends, and she tended to indulge that kind of thinking in her lowest periods, and sometimes it just funneled her further and further down. Danielle understood the roots of that feeling: The Church wasn't entirely hostile to people like Sylvia, but it was quiet and opaque in the small assurances it offered, and Sylvia was constantly tempted to pick at what was and was not said; and there was much more left not said than was said, which left a lot of silence for Sylvia to dissect, because Sylvia couldn't let silence be silence. Danielle, on the other hand, felt that letting silence be silence was a way of expressing and nurturing faith; and she felt it was important for Sylvia to discover authentic ways of growing in her faith; and she respected Sylvia for continuing to try and engage with her faith amid the forces compelling her not to.

Still, though, it bothered her to think of Sylvia converting Harriet.

"I'm sorry," Sylvia said. "I didn't mean to put everybody on edge."

Danielle put her hand on Sylvia's forearm. "Let's enjoy Mass."

The church was enormous. Judging by the oblique aisle angles and abstract stained glass in the windows, worked in bright colors, Danielle gathered it had been built sometime in the middle of the twentieth century. They arrived, and sat, and prayed, and listened, and both received Communion. As they waited in the line of cars turning out of the parking lot, Danielle asked if they could run to the grocery store before they went back to the house.

Sylvia obliged, and when she unbuckled her seatbelt Danielle put her hand on Sylvia's abdomen and said, "I'll go in by myself."

Sylvia looked at her for a moment, bewildered.

"I want to get you something," Danielle said.

She walked alone into the grocery store and veered over toward the pharmacy section. Not even a full day had gone by, and she had intended to wait until after the trip to buy a test, but Danielle's cycle still hadn't come, and she already felt like she would burst if she didn't get something concrete soon. She picked up a two-pack of the expensive tests with the really high accuracy rate, elated at the idea of finding out for certain and spending this whole week sketching out design ideas in the mornings and lying on the beach in the afternoons, sunbathing and picturing her and Sylvia's budding family; and she would find a goofy way to tell Sylvia they had finally done it; and she almost walked out of the store with just the pregnancy tests in hand until she remembered she needed something to throw Sylvia off the trail; she turned around to get a bouquet of sunflowers.

The rest of the day drifted away from Danielle like a kite. Plans rushed along and Sylvia stuck by her side. She tried twice to manufacture an opportunity to sneak off and take a test, and twice Sylvia interpreted her excuse as an invitation to follow. Later, Danielle tried just sneaking away when everyone was busy, but when it came time to open the tests, she was petrified.

Harriet's parents had insisted that everyone come to visit that night for dinner, not just Harriet and Tyler. At six o'clock they piled into Tyler's car and drove into a neighborhood Danielle didn't know could exist on a strip of land like this. It was neither ritzy nor derelict. It could've been a neighborhood outside any city in the country, save for the scattered palm trees and cacti that implied the ocean was close at hand.

Harriet's mother was young, and she looked exactly like Harriet. Something about having a sisterly mother suited Harriet, although Danielle couldn't pin down what.

She gave Harriet an enthusiastic hug and glanced worriedly at her abdomen. "How are you feeling?"

"It's day to day," Harriet said.

She was playing it up, playing the part, playing the pregnant sufferer. Danielle breathed in. She was supposed to be practicing charitability.

"And of course, I have a hug on hand for the esteemed Preston Ellridge the Fourth," Harriet's mother said, drawing Preston in.

"So nice to see you, Mrs. Coriander."

Tyler tilted his head toward Sylvia. "You see how a son-in-law gets treated around here?"

"Hush," Mrs. Coriander said, drawing Tyler in for his turn.

"So nice to see you, Mrs. Coriander," Tyler said.

Mrs. Coriander drew back and put her hands on her hips. "That's Henrietta to you and you know it."

Tyler smirked.

Henrietta turned to Danielle and Sylvia, who were standing in the doorframe, pushed together by the small space. "One of you is Danielle, and one of you is Sylvia."

Tyler whispered, "This is your chance to switch places."

Henrietta waved him off.

"I'm Danielle," Danielle said.

"Nice to meet you," Henrietta said, shaking her hand.

She turned to Sylvia. "And that would make you Danielle's wife Sylvia."

The comment made Danielle feel naked, and guilty, and like something was wrong with her, and confused at how hard it was for her to say "wife" when even Harriet's mother could say it without gathering herself.

"Nice to meet you," Sylvia said.

Henrietta led them into the garage. "Pardon the carboys everywhere. Harriet's father is brewing as usual."

In the garage, Harriet's father was laying down newspaper on the floor. Two folding card tables were leaned up against the wall, and a gallon jug of Old Bay sat on the floor next to the stack of newspaper, and on the other side of the newspaper was a bucket of crabs.

Harriet's father lifted himself from his newspaper and straightened his spine, his eyes landing on Danielle. "Zane Coriander."

Danielle shook his hand. "Danielle."

Sylvia waved. "Sylvia."

Preston said, "I was doing my best not to get my hopes up for crabs, but I have to admit I'm relieved."

"You ought to know we don't skimp around here," Zane said. "Help me set up this card table."

"I'll take the other one," Tyler said.

They got the card tables set up and spread more newspaper over them, then brought in chairs for everyone. Zane brought in a cooler of beer bottles with no labels. Danielle took it all in with a studious slant. She was in a garage, with the walls of a garage and the vibe of a garage; and the table was junky and the cooler was old, with a beat-down vibe rivaled only by the chairs; and yet it all quivered with such energy, and her job was to capture that energy and bottle it, and somehow she still couldn't compete with a layer of newspaper and a two bare lightbulbs.

Soon the table was covered in Old Bay, and crabs, and unmarked bottles, and little mallets; and everyone was ripping apart crabs, and Sylvia and Danielle were just sitting there looking at their freaky eyes.

"Do you know how to eat crabs?" Preston asked.

Danielle shook her head.

"I'm so sorry," Henrietta said. "That never occurred to me."

"It's okay. I just need some help getting started," Danielle said, making herself smile.

Preston picked up a crab. He was sitting directly across from her. "First, you're going to pull the claws off." He picked the claws and legs off, holding his fingers away from the pointy spots. "And you want to be careful here, because one little prick from the claw and you're going to be getting Old Bay in that open wound for the rest of the meal."

Henrietta said, "Not that that's ever happened to anyone we know."

"Nobody at all," Preston said. He picked up the mallet. "To get the meat out of the claw, you're going to give it a good whack."

"The key to the whack is to be polite, but firm," Tyler added.

"Then you pull it apart," Preston whacked the claw with the mallet and turned the claw over in his hands in a way Danielle couldn't entirely follow. "And that's how you expose the claw meat, which is succulent, yet scarce."

"Stick to the crabs," Zane said in a mock-warning tone.

The others laughed, and that included Sylvia, who laughed a little.

"The rest of the good stuff is in the underbelly, under this thing shaped like a capital T."

Danielle saw something different.

Preston pulled the capital T out and opened up the crab's belly like he was performing a C-section. "And here we arrive at the feast. You pick this part clean and then move on to the next one." He held out the crab for her to take.

"Keep it," Danielle said.

"Really. I can pick another one."

"You worked hard," Danielle said.

He moved the crab slightly to the left. "Sylvia?"

"I've almost got this one done," Sylvia said.

Preston shrugged. He took the crab back and began pulling the meat out of the underbelly and took a sip of his beer.

Zane said, "How'd the beer come out?"

"Tremendous as always, and it's not just the nostalgia."

Zane pointed at Preston with his thumb and said to Danielle, "This kid's first drink was one of my homebrews. I came back from giving lessons and caught him and Harriet red-handed."

"You're going to embarrass him," Henrietta said.

Harriet said, "I was the one that put him up to it."

Zane finished a sip of his drink and continued. "I was mad stirred up, wanting to know whatever else was going on here, ready to drag him back to his father, when Preston looks me right in the eye and says, 'Sir, I wanted my first beer to be a good one.'"

They were talking about Preston in such a different way than Danielle would have talked about him. And the way Danielle would have talked about Preston was so different from the way Sylvia would have talked about Preston. And the way that Sylvia talked about Preston would surely bother Harriet's parents; they wouldn't believe a word of it. Was it just a matter of word choice, or did Preston really appear so differently to everyone?

"What did you do?" Tyler asked.

The question made Danielle feel more comfortable. That Tyler didn't know the story meant that the story was being told because Preston was here, and not because she and Sylvia were here.

"I just thought back to the only other time Preston called me sir, that day his parents signed him up for lessons."

Preston put his nose in his hands. Just beyond his thumbs, Danielle could see that his cheek muscles were flexed. He was smiling.

"You should've seen him when he and his dad walked up to me that first day. I didn't know his name yet, but I doubted I'd remember it for long anyway. I mean, he had no chance. I'm supposed to teach lessons to this kid whose dad's wearing Gucci swim trunks, while the kid himself looks like a cartoon surfer: shark-tooth necklace, long blond hair—backward hat, if you can picture it knowing what he looks like today. His father's saying this is his first surfing lesson, and he's going to take them all month. I guess he was eleven years old then."

If you can picture it, Danielle thought. She could picture almost all of it. The hair and the hat were easy, but she couldn't picture Preston small.

"Ten," Preston said.

"Ten years old, and I was thinking, 'This kid's going to give it a shake for a hot second and get disillusioned the third time he falls off.' It was just how perfect the whole image was. It didn't seem like he needed surfing."

Henrietta swirled her wine glass, which she had filled with Zane's beer. "You have to consider that he had been giving lessons long enough to be past those kinds of jejune presumptions."

Oh my, Danielle thought. *She talks like that too.*

"Right," Zane said. "The only thing that didn't fit in—that gave me any sense that this had a chance to work out, weirdly—was what he said when I asked him if he'd ever balanced on a surfboard before, and he said, 'No, sir.' It was just so unexpected from somebody trying so hard to be the opposite of somebody who'd say, 'No, sir.'"

Zane stopped to survey his audience. From the way his eyes jumped between Sylvia and Danielle, Danielle could see that one of them was supposed to ask a question, either about how Preston surfed or what happened with the beer.

Danielle debated which track she wanted to follow. She didn't really want to direct the story because she had started to like the perspective Zane and Henrietta had on Preston. It was softer than the perspective she assumed others would have on him—so much softer that she wondered why she had assumed a family like Harriet's would regard him with at least some contempt—softer, even, than the perspective Preston usually had on himself. Maybe that was why he had loosened up so much when they crossed into North Carolina.

"How did he surf?" Sylvia asked.

Danielle glanced over at her, surprised.

"Like he was born for it," Zane said. "I hardly had to teach him anything, and even the things I taught him, he did better than I'd shown him. I still think he was the most natural surfer I've ever come across."

In glancing over, Danielle had expected to see Sylvia at ease. Instead, she saw her upset, though she was sure no one else knew her well enough to see it. But Danielle could. Sylvia was picking at her crab slowly, and her eyes were drifting down away from Zane, and she had her elbows down at her sides; and Danielle was confused for a moment, wondering why Sylvia would feel despondent. But then she realized that Sylvia had been looking forward to this dinner, and she had been preparing herself, and she had assumed that as Harriet's new friend, she would be the center of things, and instead they were telling stories about Preston; and she felt overlooked, and she felt displaced, and she was wondering if Harriet cared about her or if she was just convenient; and she was having a hard time with that, because she cared a lot for Harriet. She had found something in Harriet, and Danielle didn't understand what; but looking at Sylvia right now she could see how intense whatever it was, was.

"He's giving me too much credit," Preston said.

Under the table, Danielle reached for Sylvia's knee, even though she didn't understand. Sylvia's disappointment in the moment made a little sense to her, but on the whole she didn't understand. This was a problem that existed in the region of Sylvia's headspace that sat farthest away from their communal territory; but Sylvia was upset by it, and Sylvia needed her. Sylvia's hand came down, and she linked her fingers in Danielle's, and Danielle realized what the problem was, as if she'd been told through Sylvia's fingers; and she felt exposed by realizing what it was; and she wanted to tell Sylvia that no, it wasn't what she had let herself think, and she didn't need to be worried about the Corianders having an issue with trans people; she was just letting her disappointment take other hurtful shapes. And she tried to tell Sylvia that by squeezing her hand back, aware that she had no way to squeeze her hand in such a way that Sylvia would receive exactly what she wanted to say; but she trusted what she had been told through Sylvia's hand, so she had to trust that she could reply through her own.

"And you thought of all that while he was drinking your beer?" Sylvia asked. The tremble in her voice gave her away.

Zane put his hands up near his ears. "The 'sir' just put it all in my head at once, and I'm not sure what about that exactly made me so mellow, but I just kind of chilled out. I talked to him and Harriet about how sixteen seems old, but it's just early for a lot of things."

It was strange. Danielle could picture the scene. She could picture Preston here with Harriet, the two of them standing there looking guilty, and she could picture Zane—even though she'd just met him, she could picture him putting his hand on Preston, telling him it was all right, that he understood. But she couldn't picture the same scene happening in Preston's house. She couldn't picture any of his sisters, or his mother, or his father, or Harriet, or even the house, even though she'd been staying there for two days.

"He's underselling it," Harriet said. "That lecture was unambiguously A-plus parental discourse."

"I still don't drink," Preston said, holding up his beer bottle.

Zane and Henrietta laughed.

Henrietta turned to Harriet and Tyler. "Unfortunately, the two of you have several years to go before lectures will work."

Danielle tightened her grip on Sylvia's hand. Neither of them were getting many crabs picked.

"We're trying to be Zen about it all," Harriet said.

Tyler nodded. "Plenty of our friends have had kids, and they've spent the whole pregnancy cramming themselves full of all this information. They're tired before it even starts."

"And the gear," Harriet said. "We know people who tell you they aren't worried at all, that it'll be fine. Meanwhile they're panic-buying baby gadgets, and it's just so transparently desperate."

Sylvia yanked her hand away. She put it back on the table and leaned over to Danielle and whispered, "Too tight."

That night everyone made drinks in the blender and went out to the pool. They started playing music out of a Bluetooth speaker and got into a heated debate over whether it would be better to be an astronaut or a sea captain. Even Harriet was acting drunk to fit in. Sylvia and Danielle got cagey about where they were headed and went to the hot tub, and they did some things to each other that could be stopped if someone came looking. The moon was full and the equilibrium seemed endemic. Danielle felt like she could say anything to anyone, and it would be fine, and nothing would reverberate into the future.

She was drunk, and she was enjoying it, and she was feeling drunk in the lucid way; living in the world was usually a big, beautiful scatter plot, but Danielle felt drunk in the way that made it seem like a nice smooth curve instead; and the full moon was visible like it had been visible that morning.

Danielle and Sylvia got a little out of hand with each other, and Danielle was worried she'd been too loud about it, but the fact that the speaker was still playing gave her a lot of comfort; and the fact that Tyler and Harriet and Preston were now arguing over whether it was better to be a polar bear or a panda bear made her feel like she hadn't been too loud; she felt like they wouldn't be arguing so loud if they had noticed she and Sylvia sneaking away; and she decided to ask Sylvia, "Are you in love with Harriet?"

Sylvia was just as drunk as she was, and maybe she was even drunker; and she had been arguing passionately with Preston earlier that astronaut was the superior career, where usually she treated Preston like a bad dream she had to get through; and Sylvia said, "No. Are you in love with Preston?"

And Danielle didn't mind being asked, and she should have expected the question, because she knew it had been on Sylvia's mind; and really, she relished the opportunity to put it to bed with her; and she said, "No. Is Harriet in love with you?"

And that thought must have taken Sylvia completely by surprise; and her surprise made Danielle feel better, because if you love someone, you've thought at least a little about whether or not they love you; but Sylvia said, "Not that I can imagine. Is Preston in love with you?"

And Danielle hung her head some, and she considered what her answer should be, and she considered what her answer actually was, and she considered whether the answer she would give would be the same as the answer she thought was correct, and she said, "Probably."

And Sylvia nodded and said, "Are you in love with me?"

And Danielle touched Sylvia again, and she kissed her under that big full moon, and she was doing it for Sylvia's benefit but also for the benefit of that big full moon, because it had been following them around all day.

* * *

The next morning, Danielle worked with Preston while everyone else went to the beach. She was happy to be back at a pursuit, and this one was coming together nicely. Preston had kept his promise to put design at the forefront of everything he wanted to do with the restaurant, and they were working in a kind of abstract telephone, where Preston would talk about something he wanted to do with the menu or the concept or the atmosphere and ask her, "What does that bring to mind for you?" Or she would think of something she wanted to do with the materials or the lighting or the layout or the fixtures and ask him, "Does that fit with what you want to do?"

They had a good working rapport already, and it was even better at the beach. Preston had a lot of frenetic energy about his life as a whole, and his energy became even more frenetic with use; and it was the opposite of how he turned when he wasn't interested in something, just checking out and declaring everything "fine" or "okay" or "no problem" until something else worth thinking about came along; and she appreciated that about him, because she could always tell what he was thinking. He had a hard time being honest with her when he didn't like something; and Danielle liked criticism, and she liked feedback, and she liked collaboration; and without his energy level swaying around and exposing his real feelings she would have gotten bored by now.

She and Preston had agreed to work from nine a.m. to noon throughout the trip. Anything more than that, and they'd have to stay multiple weeks to get the requisite beach time in, and Danielle was uneasy about being in someone else's house, driven here in someone else's car, and Sylvia didn't have the vacation time to stay more than a few weekdays, so they had to make some allotment for beach time where Danielle wasn't in anyone else's house or car, where instead she was simply on the long open edge of a big open continent; but Danielle could only relax on the beach after she had walled herself inside long enough to accomplish something, and spending anything less than three hours working would leave her with too little time to get into a rhythm with Preston and thus make enough progress that she could go out to the sand and let herself go blank.

She and Preston were starting to hit their mid-morning stride when Harriet came up the stairs and asked if there was a tire pump anywhere in the house. "Sylvia and I want to take those bikes out, but both of the front tires are flat," she said.

"We've got one," Preston said. His eyes drifted up to the ceiling fan while he thought. "There are a couple of places it could be. Let me find it for you."

"Thank you," Harriet said.

She went back down the stairs with Preston, leaving Danielle by herself in the beige top-floor sitting area. At first, she went on doing what she had been doing; but Harriet and Preston were taking a while, and Tyler was still at the beach (at least, she guessed he was), and after they'd been gone a couple minutes, Danielle realized this was the opportunity she needed. She left her laptop open and unlocked to give the impression that she had only left for a moment, then went downstairs.

She had hidden the pregnancy tests underneath some towels in her and Sylvia's bathroom vanity. She took them out and read the instructions over again. It was good she had been drinking water all morning. She had everything she needed, and she went ahead and followed the instructions. They said the test took two minutes to work. It had a horizontal line in a little window on the dry end, and if a second vertical line appeared within two minutes—no matter how faint—then she was pregnant. She put the test down on the counter and set a two-minute timer on her phone, then lay on the bed and waited.

She managed ten seconds before she checked the timer again, thinking at least a minute had gone by. The next time she checked, an additional fifteen seconds had elapsed. She put her phone out of reach and walked to the window, hands on her hips. Forty more seconds went by while she stood there, and at one minute, she went to check if the test had developed a line early. It hadn't.

Danielle went back out into the bedroom. Pregnancy hormones supposedly shot up fast, and they doubled quickly, and they doubled again quickly after that, and she was several days late, and she would have expected the test to pick up on that faster than two minutes. But she was an optimist, and she believed things would work out until the odds hit zero; and she could concede the odds were dropping fast, and they were being cut in half quickly, and their half-life was running out again just as fast. She was watching the test and the timer both now, holding the little window up to the light, squinting hard. There was nothing there.

She stopped the timer at two seconds remaining, counted to two on her own, and then threw the test into the trash. It hit the side wall of the aluminum can and echoed loudly, like she had thrown an object as big and loud as her despair into a dry well. Danielle was about to walk out when she realized that the test was visible in the trash, and she didn't want to be part of that kind of sitcom revelation; and she was wearing shorts with pockets, and the test fit nicely into her back pocket, and she could keep it there until she decided what to do with it.

She didn't feel crushed. She felt okay. She was taking it well, really. She didn't feel squeezed out and hung in the wind; and she didn't feel shattered; and she didn't feel like her shoes were full of broken glass; and she didn't feel like she wanted to go downstairs and push Harriet off that bike and take it and ride up into the sun; and she didn't feel like her and Sylvia's marriage had begun to teeter and tip over; and she didn't feel like everything around her was disappearing inside of violent, breaking waves. She was taking it well.

"You're crying," Preston said.

She had wandered back upstairs; she wasn't sure how long she had been downstairs; her laptop screen was dark; Preston looked concerned; she wasn't trying to cry; she didn't want to explain it to him, not when Sylvia didn't even know yet.

"It's nothing," she heard herself saying. "What were we working on?"

Preston said, "You don't have to tell me what's wrong, but we should take a break."

No, Danielle didn't feel like Orpheus at the edge of the underworld; no, she didn't feel like she had violated some spiritual agreement by checking before she got back home; no, she didn't feel like if she had been able to hold on and keep her impatience at bay, then she would have checked when she got home and the test would have been positive; no, she didn't feel like she had made it to the edge of the underworld and looked back at her wife like Orpheus and watched her baby get whisked back down to the ash; no, she wasn't feeling anything dramatic; no, she didn't need Preston's help; no, she wasn't taking it poorly; she was taking it well, and taking it well enough that she could just wait for Sylvia to come back and then at the right moment, tell her.

Preston said, "Just say something, even if it's not related. Just start talking and see where it goes."

"I need to talk to Sylvia," she said.

And no, she didn't feel resentful toward Sylvia for holding on to that last half-pill of estradiol each day, just putting it down her throat instead of realizing that she could do whatever she needed after this era was over, because she was too scared and kept insisting things would work out in June; and Danielle wasn't thinking about how she hated the way Sylvia feared returning to how things had been before, as if

How Things Had Been Before was some terrible horrorscape, when for Danielle that had been an easier time, when that past self Sylvia so detested was the person for whom Danielle had fallen. No, no, she wasn't thinking—no, she didn't resent the six months Sylvia had spent repeating that things would work out in June, when it was June now, and that hadn't happened.

Preston pointed at the counter. "Her phone is right there, and Harriet's is on the table. We can just sit until they get back."

Danielle nodded.

"If you need me," Preston said, leaning toward her, "I'm right here."

"I need to talk to Sylvia," Danielle repeated.

"She'll be back," Preston said. "I know it'll be good for her to come and help you this time, when you've helped her so much. And if it's the kind of thing you can only talk about with another girl, then I get that. But how about I take a crack at it while we wait?"

Danielle could only shake her head.

"Well," Preston said, "how about I tell you about my lowest point, and maybe that'll make you feel like you can handle this, whatever it is?"

They were sitting on the couches now, and he was leaning toward her and looking at her with concern, and holding himself up with his ab muscles while his hands sat linked below him, floating. She took in the way he was gazing at her, in disbelief at his audacity.

"I was institutionalized for a period in England," Preston said when she didn't answer. "For multiple months, in fact."

He was making it about himself instead of asking questions, and Danielle was surprised, because she felt offended by him making it about himself; and at the same time, she felt relieved, and she felt like she could listen to him while her other thoughts ran their course in the background.

"Hospital?" she asked.

He shook his head. "Guess again."

Danielle was settling down now, and she was sure he could see her settling down, and now she was the one tipping her hand with her energy level; and her face felt numb, and she hated to think what that looked like, and she hated to think what impression he was getting from her numb face; and she also hated to think about anything else that was on her mind.

"You mean you were in a mental institution?"

Preston looked up at the ceiling, laughing. "Amazingly, that would have been better."

"You mean," she said, and then she paused, speaking the question in her head before she said it out loud, as if to confirm the words were really the right words; and she marveled that they could possibly be the question she needed to ask now, right now. "You were in prison?"

"Three months," he said.

She started to ask, *What did you do?* But before she asked, she caught herself. She was alone with this man, in his house, on an island, with water on either side.

"Don't look so threatened," Preston told her, lowering his head to be below hers. "I wasn't myself at the time, by a long shot. That's why I had to laugh when you guessed it was a mental institution. If I'd had any pragmatism at the time, I would've come back across the ocean and checked myself in to one. Instead, I pulled a knife on a cop—or a bobby—whatever stupid name they call them in England. I don't exactly remember why I did it, but I remember the fallout. I wound up in a Brighton jail, festering over the fact that I'd caused an international incident. Except . . ." He lowered his head even further. With his head where it was and his hands linked, he almost looked like he was in prayer. "Except I wasn't important enough to cause an international incident, and the police holding me didn't see much reason to notify anyone in a hurry—consulate, family, or otherwise. Things crawled along at this impossible rate. The days didn't so much run together as stop passing."

"How did you get out?" Danielle asked.

"Word finally got to my family," Preston said. "I'd been going progressively darker on them in the time leading up to all this, and evidently I'd been so unreliable that it took more than a month for them to get suspicious."

Preston took a deep breath, then continued. "They kicked up some dust and got me moved to the embassy in London for a few additional weeks while everything got sorted out. In the end, there was a mutual agreement to act like none of it happened. It was really the model of international cooperation, with a nice dose of English restraint thrown in." Another breath, and he turned toward the ocean. "Unfortunately for me, though, I'm not an English bureaucrat, so my family doesn't feel obligated to treat me so diplomatically. Most of my sisters have frozen me out, and my father won't talk to me until he's satisfied I've turned a corner."

Preston turned away from the ocean, back toward her. He spoke so softly she almost couldn't hear, like he thought the room was bugged. "He doesn't technically know we're here."

"Are we . . ." Danielle said.

Preston nodded. "Yes, we're technically trespassing. But I'm not worried about it. I realized after I got out that I had been living out a death wish, not for myself but for my potential. I thought I had killed most of it off after I scrapped the originality marketplace idea, and figured my breakdown in England would take care of the rest of it. But what I actually did was prove how tough it was. I've got my potential and my confidence lined up now, and if my father were to walk in here right now, he'd see it."

Danielle was still tilling through her thoughts about the baby, and she was still gobsmacked that Preston was telling her this right now; and she was still internally wobbly, and now she was conflicted over whether to be charitable—because he didn't know what he was doing—or wary, because he could be up to exactly what Sylvia would think he was up to right now; and she was trying to sort out what she thought from what others wanted her to think; and she was neither charitable nor suspicious, she realized, but angry; because everything she thought had to be influenced by someone, and no one would let her just think, even though everyone had something they wanted her to think.

Preston put his hand on her knee, and Danielle's shoulders shivered. "Thanks for working with me. I've been feeling so much pressure to keep my momentum up. Having you around has helped with that."

Perhaps the footsteps behind her were lost in Preston's voice, or maybe she heard them and wished them away, aware of what they meant. But Danielle saw Preston's expression change, and his eyes move, and when she turned, she saw Sylvia looking straight at Preston's hand on Danielle's knee.

"We bought a kite," she said, then went back down the stairs.

Danielle stood and went after her. She didn't look back at Preston. As her head dropped out of his line of sight, she was struck by an icy realization, colder than bottom of the ocean: that she was stuck here until Preston, Harriet, and Tyler all agreed it was time to go home.

"Sylvia!" she called. Quietly, because she didn't want Preston or the others to hear the tremors in her voice.

"Sylvia!"

From their bedroom, she heard a sliding door open. Danielle darted inside and saw Sylvia with the kite; and she was already outside, and she was sliding the door closed behind her.

"Sylvia, wait."

Sylvia paused. Danielle walked toward her and put her hand on the door. She slid it back open and reached for Sylvia's hand, and she just looked at her and realized she didn't know what to tell her first.

"The two of you were something to behold," Sylvia said.

"He put his hand on my knee. I didn't ask him to, and I didn't like it."

Sylvia looked down. "I trust you."

"Come back in."

Sylvia shook her head. "I believe you, but that's not the problem."

"What's the problem?"

Sylvia continued looking down, then she loosened her arms and let the kite fall to the deck as she unleashed a long sigh. "Let me show you."

She came in through the door and grabbed Danielle's elbow. She tugged at it, pulling her into the bathroom. They stood in front of the mirror together. Danielle was wearing one of her old, faded Christian sorority T-shirts, and Sylvia was in her black bikini top. "We don't look like you and Preston do," she said.

"I don't want to look like Preston and I do," Danielle said.

Sylvia shook her head. "I've made myself ignore it for so long, but I feel so good and true to myself when I think about how we look to me, and so distorted and disappointing when I think about how we look to you."

Danielle understood. She had considered the way they looked as a couple when Sylvia decided to transition; and she disliked it when strangers mistook them for sisters; and she had a distinct memory of being on top of a building with Sylvia under a clear night sky and thinking about what someone would see if they came up behind them: their silhouettes perched on the gable in the clear night rain, looking exactly like her idea of love; and she had struggled to contain her misgivings about that all changing; and she had pictured them as those silhouettes many times, thinking about how they still looked exactly like her idea of love; and she wanted the matter to stay settled the way she had settled it.

She said, "I think you look content. I like being married to someone who's content."

Sylvia shook her head again. "I love you for staying with me, and you know that. But it's only been a couple years, and when I see a pairing like you two, I just think, 'What's going to happen as all this stretches on?'"

Too many lines were crossing at once. Danielle couldn't soothe Sylvia, and spurn Preston, and stay quiet on Harriet, and handle the test result all at once; and she felt herself backsliding into the stupor—back into the shock—back into the aftershock after Sylvia came out; she was backsliding into her lonely room in their first apartment, and her lonely room brought her into their old neighborhood, and their old neighborhood brought her back to those ponderous walks she had taken, and on those walks she had considered herself a Catholic, as she had all her life; and she had considered their marriage a Catholic marriage, and Catholic marriages are immutable; and she considered how horrible it would be to put herself through an annulment, and how humiliated she would feel, and how humiliated Sylvia would feel; and she considered that such humiliation didn't seem warranted for what she had been told, no matter how difficult it was to process; and she considered that God had always had her trust, and she had internalized her trust in God so deeply, and while others sought out moments of pure religious experience and abandoned their faith when such moments proved elusive, Danielle had always understood that religious experiences occur where they are needed and not where they are desired; and yet that faith had been challenged by Sylvia's announcement, and Danielle had found herself hunting around for signs and omens that were not there; and she must have walked ninety miles in the channels of her thoughts, down those shimmering autumn city blocks, back when Sylvia was just starting her hormones; and she sometimes felt as though Sylvia had purposely come out to her in their neighborhood's best season, because to remain with Sylvia was to remain in Richmond, and to leave Sylvia was to leave Richmond—this city to which Sylvia had brought her—this city that had once seemed so off-putting and self-impressed, so grimy and pretentious; insular, foreboding, and narcissistic—where Danielle had strained to find the essence of the place and eventually found it, and eventually created a place for herself inside of it, hard-won from the beginning—and every stop sign had struck her like a plea, every building like a taunt, endless rows of taunts; and she despised the whole conspiracy of buildings; buildings so uniform in period and so different in personality, with the promise of so much more personality in their interiors, with her whole professional life dedicated to interiors; and she believed there would be buildings anywhere she went, but Danielle had suddenly cared about *these* buildings, all of which taunted her so continuously, multiplying in front of her as she thought; and she sometimes felt like she was walking out of everything: out of her city, her life, her faith, crossing through the void, only to make a circle, circling back into the buildings, with Sylvia among them; until she decided abruptly on one of those walks that no, she wouldn't leave, and she would trust her feelings, even though logically she found it easy to argue that she needed to leave, because her arguments appeared so small in contrast to her feelings, and her feelings told her that she still loved her spouse, and this too would somehow pass; and soon enough Sylvia began to change. And the changes were mental at first, and Sylvia seemed to change in such a tender way; and the hormones seemed to bring her into such a healthier way of seeing, and hearing, and speaking, and touching, and absorbing, and processing, and observing, and deciding, and even loving; and Sylvia was open with Danielle in a way that she had never been; and Danielle had not realized how closed-off Sylvia was until she was no longer closed-off, and that sense of how open Sylvia could become had bolstered Danielle against the coming wave, against all the waves; against the wave of changes to Sylvia's shape, against the wave of changes to her smell, against the wave of changes to her skin, against the waves of horrible things that Sylvia would say, explaining herself in terms of clothes, measuring herself by the length of her hair, living and dying by the greetings of strangers; and Danielle held on, and gripped herself and said, "This too shall pass," and she repeated it to herself many times, and each time their marriage approached the event horizon of collapse, that openness would reappear; and as Sylvia began to understand the true nature of being female, her interpretation of herself became less and less superficial; and with that change the tide began to ebb, and the openness began to supplant the fear, and miraculously the temperature of the whole thing seemed to cool; and Danielle felt so justified sometimes; and she hadn't become perfect, or enlightened, and that didn't bother her; and only she and Sylvia understood how all this had come to pass, and that was enough, and they didn't need to understand anything else, and they lived together in that mysterious empathy, and they grew as a couple, and now only one piece remained; and Danielle felt that a baby would bolster them, and that a baby would emerge as a whole, single, unified person, invulnerable to all the interpretation and dissection that their marriage had undergone, all of it to produce this baby: unencumbered, real, with real skin and real eyes and real hair; and she felt that every diaper change would erase a little of the intermittent doubt, and that every bedtime story would obliterate more of the erratic self-questioning; and over time it could finally all go away.

Danielle said, "Let me show you how I want to look. It's simple."

She left Sylvia in the bathroom and went to the bed. She took a pillow off the headboard and slid it under her Christian sorority T-shirt. "Touch it," she told Sylvia.

Sylvia looked at her solemnly. "I get it."

Danielle pointed to the pillow under her shirt. "Touch it."

Sylvia touched it.

"Leave your hand there." Danielle pointed to the mirror. "This is what I want to look like. This is what I need you to make happen."

Sylvia looked into her face, and whatever molten frustration had been in her eyes before turned to steam. "You're crying."

Danielle looked away. She put her hand in her back pocket and removed the pregnancy test. She brought it out in a balled-up fist, and at first it was invisible; and she held her fist out to Sylvia's face and opened it. "It was negative," she said.

Sylvia put her arms around her, and pulled her in, and Danielle put her head in Sylvia's chest, and she cried; and her crying was active this time, and it was mournful, and long, and overwrought, and unknowing, and Sylvia held her close; and waves were breaking in the distance, and jellyfish were floating in the shallows, and Sylvia said, "Next month," and Danielle wanted her to say it, and she was happy that she said it, and she was happy that Sylvia could say it, and not only say it but proclaim it, and proclaim it with such faith; and she didn't believe her.

* * *

Danielle and Preston stopped working together at the beach after that. Danielle told him she preferred to use the rest of their time as an actual vacation, and he agreed that it seemed they both had a lot on their minds. She tried to stay close to Sylvia for the remainder of the trip. She felt like things had begun to splinter in their first days here, and if she could stay close to Sylvia, then she could plug the cracks that had opened up, and they could return home with things mostly unchanged, without any explosive developments in any direction.

She and Sylvia had lots of time to conceive. It was typical for couples to take two to three attempts. With Sylvia totally clear of hormones, mostly clear of hormones, they had only tried once. Danielle felt like she could hold them both together, and she could keep the cracks between them from widening the way they had in the winter, and she could turn their marriage back to what it had been in the spring. The spring had been lovely. Sylvia was heading downhill, but she was being brave, and Danielle was coming back from that cold snap she had endured over Christmas and into New Year's; and they were meeting each other, and the fact that they were meeting each other mattered more than either of their burdens, and the days had been so tinged with sunlit possibility; and for the rest of the time they were at the beach she spent every minute she could with Sylvia, thinking she could get both of them back there. Back to the dazzling peak they had reached in May, when they were at that party in Harriet's garden, and Harriet said the race was soon; and Sylvia said the race was soon, and she was feeling frisky, and she wanted to know if Danielle was feeling frisky too; and Danielle was, and Danielle was feeling so hopeful that it seemed like nothing about their physical selves had any bearing, and they lied to Harriet, and they went home, and they took each other's dresses off.

And normally Danielle had trouble with that; and normally she preferred to initiate sex at times when Sylvia wasn't all coifed, like when Sylvia was just coming out of the shower, or when she had changed into her T-shirt for the night; and Sylvia knew that, and it bothered her some; and Danielle disliked the fact that the clothing she was taking Sylvia out of mattered to her; but this time it all went by so easily, and she had felt free, and she knew it wouldn't last, and she was letting herself feel free while she could; and naked together on that day, she had felt like they were barer than they'd ever been, and in their bareness they had become decipherable, and when she looked at Sylvia she saw all the eras of Sylvia accumulated; all her layers were there and visible, and Sylvia lay her down on their bed, and she was moving slow, and she was so patient, and she had said to Danielle, "I'm going to use every minute left before the race." And she was true to her word, and Danielle felt like they had been transported to a deep trench in the ocean, and the trench obscured everything but their two souls, and it seemed impossible and unfathomable that everything wouldn't work out.

They were trading places now. Through her cold snap, Danielle had needed Sylvia to be with her, and listen to her, and make sacrifices for her; and now the sacrifice had been made and Sylvia needed her. She needed her more now. Sylvia seemed to mostly brush off what had happened, but not entirely, and Danielle knew how Sylvia thought. Sylvia couldn't stop herself from repeating things. Her mind jogged in wide, constricted circles, and it didn't matter how little something was. If a thought was in the circle, then Sylvia would encounter it, and she would encounter it over and over again until it wilted, and if it didn't wilt on its own then Sylvia would just keep encountering it, over and over and over. Danielle could sense the gears clicking into place, beginning to turn.

Sylvia stopped going out alone with Harriet. She drew Danielle into things. She spent her remaining time in groups of odd numbers. Either alone, or with Danielle and Harriet, or with all four of the others. She talked to Preston only when something transactional arose.

When they finally packed their things and piled into Tyler's Highlander, Johnny Cash singing about the gospel all around them, Danielle felt triumphant. She had seen the typhoon coming and adjusted her course accordingly, and when they got back home to Richmond, she could redraw the bounds between herself and Preston, and between her and Sylvia and everyone else, and between Harriet and Sylvia; and she could redraw them in a way that gave her and Sylvia all the control over whether or not their bounds could be crossed. Those bounds would hold for two to three more cycles, and then she would be pregnant; and once she was pregnant her pregnancy would draw its own invincible lines around them. It would happen, whether she believed it would or not.

But Sylvia was different when they got home. She walked into their house ahead of Danielle, her suitcase in her hand, and she went into the living room and stood in the center of it, under the ceiling fan, and looked around without speaking. Danielle guessed that she was processing the reality that she was back home, and she was trying to settle herself back into her usual context, and the revelations she had confronted at the beach made her feel more ill-suited to the house than she had felt when they left.

"It's good to be home again," she said, smiling in a way that Danielle recognized. It was her way of acknowledging that she was thinking about something she shouldn't be—when she thought she could let the thought run its course and be rid of it, she smiled like that, like she was making a joke to herself.

Danielle left her alone and went into the kitchen, where their packing list was still written on the chalkboard. She erased it and replaced it with:

SJM

DLM

And around the two she drew a white chalk heart, and she left it there for Sylvia to notice when she noticed. Sylvia went up the stairs, and Danielle could hear her taking measured footsteps overhead as she unpacked her things. Danielle went to get her own suitcase and realized that Sylvia had taken hers up too, and she was putting away both of their things. She went up to their room and found her with both suitcases open and both of their dressers open.

"I can handle mine," Danielle said.

"Okay," Sylvia said, and Danielle got the sense she would have said "okay" to any statement in that moment.

She loosened up later that evening, though. They went to Guido's Octopus for dinner and got a window table, and Sylvia wasn't talkative, but she wasn't as impassive as she had been in the bedroom, either. They stayed at their table a long time, and the sun was setting when they finished. They walked all the way home, which was more than two miles, listening to the cicadas and talking just frequently enough to constitute conversation. Sylvia seemed okay.

When they woke up the next morning, she seemed better, almost normal. She went downstairs and made coffee for them both, and Danielle found her sprawled on the living room couch as usual, coping with the notion of the upcoming workday.

"I like these two-day workweeks," she said. "I should do them more often."

But while Danielle was getting ready to go to her office, Sylvia came in from the shower and asked, "Do you think Preston's restaurant will be successful?"

"It depends on how well I do," Danielle said. "But if it is, we'll be set for the time I spend away from work."

Sylvia nodded and went into the bathroom to brush her hair.

She came back, still brushing. "Do you know when you'll be done working on it?"

"Soon," Danielle told her. "It's coming together nicely."

Sylvia nodded and went back into the bathroom to finish brushing her hair.

Preston was different too, but in the opposite way, when Danielle drove down to the future restaurant space to meet him around midmorning. He was there already, and he smiled at her and tapped the wooden chair next to him when she arrived. He said, "I've been thinking all morning, and you're going to love this."

Danielle couldn't tell, at first, exactly what it was that tipped her off. It was a normal thing to say, but not a normal thing for Preston to say. He normally treated her like she was so enigmatic, almost mysterious, and yet he had just outwardly presumed to know what she was thinking, and his statement involved the word love, and it sounded weird when he said it.

He put his hands up in front of him, facing a wall. "Plant museum."

Danielle looked at the wall. "I don't think I'm picturing the right thing."

She was picturing the inside of the Virginia Museum of Fine Art, where Sylvia and she had gone to see a number of special exhibits— only instead of art, she imagined the galleries full of plants, and people were wandering around looking at the plants, and they were all trying to have important thoughts about plants.

"A wall that shows you what you're eating," Preston said. "It has a potted coriander plant, and a potted tomato plant, even an onion, all alive and growing, and while people are eating, they can look at it and experience this visceral connection to the Earth."

His tone was somewhere between "entrepreneur bro" and "stoner." The idea could be fine, even good if she did it right. Danielle just couldn't quite free it from the overgrowth of Preston's demeanor. He sounded desperate to have something for her to think about, for them to discuss, and she couldn't tell whether or not he wanted her to save him from himself and shoot down the idea of a live onion on the wall; and she realized mid-thought that she was thinking a lot about how he wanted her to interact with him, and she was thinking about that more than how she wanted the restaurant to look, when up to this point he had been consistent in telling her that he'd hired her for her ideas and not his ideas.

She said, "I'll think about it." And she said "I'll think about it" many more times before the day was through.

Maybe, Danielle mused to herself as she drove home after work, maybe the change was in herself, and not in Preston—or Sylvia—and she was just anxious, and she was just on edge, and she was just trying too hard to hold things together instead of moving on her own path; and that seemed like a mistake, because other people tended to follow her, and everything seemed to work out when she had a handle on herself and was setting her own courses.

Later that afternoon, Danielle went across the street to see if Harriet was also acting like someone had swapped her with an impersonator. Sylvia wouldn't be home for another half hour, and while Danielle was crossing the street, she devised a premise for coming over, and it wasn't the greatest premise, but that was okay. Harriet already found her enigmatic and strange.

She stopped by their mailbox. A lot of people found her enigmatic, now she thought about it. In fact, she couldn't think of a single person who didn't find her enigmatic.

Harriet answered the door cautiously. She said, "Come in," in a hushed tone as she guided Danielle through.

After she had closed the door, she let out a long breath and stood up straighter. "Sorry to shuffle you in like that. When I went out to get the mail earlier today I couldn't get back in because there was a bee guarding the door, and when it flew off, another bee swooped in to take its place, like a bee changing of the guard, and I was just standing there holding the mail, and somebody driving by stopped to ask if I was locked out, and I had to tell him no, just that I was thinking about something, and I could tell he was kind of watching me as he drove away, so I had to charge right past this bee, and it almost got in, and I've been on edge about having the door open ever since. I texted Tyler to tell him to come around back when he gets home and to come in quickly. I'm sure he knows it's bee-related, since it's not the first time I've done this. I'm making lotion in the next room."

Danielle followed her into her kitchen, where a bucket of coconut oil and various cooking appliances were laid out on the counter. Harriet picked her apron up off the back of a chair where it had been slung and said, "Coconut oil stains, and I made this apron. Anyway, how can I help you?"

Danielle almost laughed, and at the same time she seized up with worry, because Harriet was the same as ever, and that meant Sylvia and Preston really were both off-kilter. "I realized earlier today that Sylvia and I never thanked your parents for having us over for the crabs this week," she said. "I just wanted to ask you to pass along our thanks."

"That's so thoughtful!" Harriet said, turning on the blender just then, apparently for emphasis. "They refuse to have crabs just on their own, though," she yelled over the blender, "so to be honest I doubt they noticed, or that they minded. They had my dad's pastor over for dinner one time as an excuse to have crabs. It was a sight, them marching around and acting like they had been to church in the last—how old was I?" Harriet stopped the blender and looked up at the ceiling, counting silently. Danielle thought about Sylvia trying to convert her. "Ten years. I think my mom even practiced some things to say about Jesus. And then one time they tried to have the mailman over because he was retiring, but he acted real weird about it. But I'll let them know you liked it."

"Thank you," Danielle said.

"Close the door really fast when you leave," Harriet said.

Sylvia came home that afternoon looking tired. "We were off just long enough for me to forget what work is like," she said.

"It's no picnic," Danielle said.

Sylvia was about to say something when the chalkboard caught her eye. She looked at it, and took it in, and then reached her arms out to Danielle to hug her. "Let's leave it like this for a while."

Danielle still sensed distance in the way that Sylvia hugged her. She put her arms around her enough to draw her in, and she leaned forward so their cheeks would touch, and the motion felt mechanical.

Mechanical was the right word—better than impassive. Sylvia was going about things like a Sylviabot. They cooked together as always, and they ate dinner and discussed their day, and everything Sylvia said had to do with the office, or with her drive, or with the ten-day fore-cast; and she laughed at reasonable moments, and she displayed empa-thy at reasonable moments; and when they went into the living room after dinner she poured them each a glass of wine, and the two glasses were filled to the exact same height. It was almost eerie how precisely she had filled them. Danielle spent the evening waiting for Sylvia to say something, though she was unsure what Sylvia would have to say, and as they got further from what had happened at the beach it became less a series of events and more of a movie title—*What Had Happened at the Beach*—and she was struggling to remember why it had felt like all the plates she had been juggling so successfully had reversed their spin—because if she replayed the sequence of events in her mind, and then paused the reel at their journey back home—if she tried to ex-trapolate what should happen next from there—then what came next ought to have looked like their life before they had left Richmond, instead of this.

When Danielle replayed the sequence of events in her mind, it boiled down to a series of strong emotions between three people; shock and disappointment for her, then dismay and vulnerability for Preston, then sadness and insecurity for Sylvia, then tepid reassurance for both her and Sylvia and, she imagined, muted impatience for Preston up-stairs. She was again beginning to feel like the change was in her, and not in Sylvia or Preston.

But then she said, "I went over to Harriet's today," intending for it to be a funny story about the bee, and Sylvia looked away from her and stiffened.

"How was she?" she asked.

"She wouldn't talk to me with the door open because she was afraid a bee would fly in."

She expected Sylvia to laugh at that, but she remained still and expressionless. "She wants to get into beekeeping eventually," she said after a moment.

Again, mechanical. Saying something careful and specific but thinking about something else; not vague enough to come across as distant, but somehow not fully there.

Danielle said, "Is something bothering you?"

"No," Sylvia said, and she leaned back with her wine. "I'm sorry. How was your day?"

She seemed to mean it that time, and Danielle realized that whatever Sylvia was dealing with right now was as ephemeral for her as What Had Happened at the Beach was for Danielle. When questioned, it vanished.

Danielle didn't have a meeting with Preston on Friday, so she put her head down and worked. As she worked, a revelation came over her. People did follow her. They cued into her, tried to read her signals, and adjusted accordingly; and she needed a foundation for herself outside of people and their frayed complexity, and she had that foundation in her work. She had been thinking of it as Preston's restaurant, but in reality it was not Preston's restaurant, and it was not Danielle's restaurant either. All things belonged to God, and it was God's restaurant. While feelings around her ricocheted in arhythmic bursts, Danielle could bury her head in her work and make it perfect, and if she made it perfect then God would make everything else perfect. He would make Preston satisfied, and He would make her and Sylvia pregnant, and He would make her uneasiness distant. She and Sylvia would conceive when the time was right, and in the time before the time was right, she would work; and if Danielle worked hard enough, other things would work out, because work was one way of deepening a relationship with God, who made textures, and colors, and space, and food, and hands, and eyes, and feet, and tongues; and if she could deepen her relationship with God, everything else would work out. That was what they had missed about Danielle in *R-Home*, that her line of work had a visceral relationship with creation, and she viewed that aspect of design as its life force; creation itself was God's domain, but her work respected creation, unveiling relationships between forms, colors, and textures, all of which were dependent on light; light revealed ugliness or it revealed harmony, and the soul of her work was that preparation for light, arranging everything in such a way that light would settle upon entering and find a home had been made for it; and she hated the way others walked around dubbing themselves "creative"—or worse, "creators"—when in truth their work was arrangement; artists arranged colors, musicians arranged sounds, sculptors arranged materials, and yet some would denigrate her art because what she arranged were lights and furnishings—which were somehow worse, or inferior—when the only difference between what other artists did and what she did was the category of thing she chose to arrange; and yet those who worked in "important" mediums would blather on about how they were "creating" something, which drove her to the brink when she considered that there was only one place in which God invited people to join Him in the act of creation, and that place was conception, and everything else anyone ever did was arrangement, and at best it was arrangement in preparation for something, something like light coming into a space made for it, or a baby coming home for the first time; Danielle's work didn't impersonate creation but rather venerated it, and her dismay over her and Sylvia's infertility had caused her to drift from that aspect, and from God; and she needed to come back, and she would do that through her work.

But on Saturday, Danielle ran into Preston at Oilwick Café. She had left Sylvia sleeping in a ball on her side of their bed and drove to get them both breakfast, and shortly after she ordered, Preston walked in.

He didn't notice her at first; Danielle was hovering away from the register, at the threshold between the room where people ordered and waited for their coffee and the room where people camped out with laptops at mismatched tables; she watched him for a moment, and she realized that he was studying the space carefully, avoiding looking at any of the people so he could focus on dissection. For a moment she wondered what stood out to him. The corrugated metal fixtures, painted brick walls, and enormous windows all played into an industrial vibe; it could've been mistaken for a holdover from the mid-2010s, when every restaurant was exposing ductwork and opting for concrete over drywall, but here the style came across as more sincere, and more lasting, because it was so lovingly battered, and because all the machinery steaming and hissing behind the counter made the place sound as if it really were a factory. Danielle wondered if he had noticed that, how the space worked with a mythos, which made it feel even more honest when at its busiest; and she labored a little over whether to make herself known or slip soundlessly away, until she realized that in a moment, someone would walk out with her order and call her name. So, she went over to Preston and tapped him on the shoulder. He looked wide-eyed and surprised, and said, "It's been a while. What is it, forty-eight hours since I've seen you?"

She smiled. "I got a lot done on Friday. My to-do list is the shortest it's been in weeks."

"You'll be done with the whole thing by Wednesday, then," Preston said. "I'm going out of town for a week."

Before she could ask what he meant, the college girl in front of Preston finished ordering, and he stepped up to the register. While he was ordering, an employee stepped out of the kitchen with her order and called, "Danielle?"

Danielle took the paper bag, sliding it into the crook of her elbow so she could carry it along with the two coffees she was already holding.

"I'll see you next week," Preston said, stepping away from the register and into the spot she'd occupied a moment ago. That same brimming, energetic smile was back, the one he'd worn when he told her she was going to love the plant museum, and on her drive home Danielle puzzled over where he could be heading for a week; and she didn't understand why he hadn't mentioned that on Thursday or just texted her about it; and it seemed odd that someone as communicative as Preston would tell her that in a chance encounter at a coffee shop; and she considered that maybe he hadn't intended to tell her; and she dismissed that, because he wouldn't have had to tell her right then, in a chance encounter at a coffee shop, if he didn't want to.

Danielle wanted to tell Sylvia she wouldn't be seeing Preston for a week, but she didn't want to tell Sylvia she had run into him on an outing she had taken, without telling Sylvia, while Sylvia was sleeping. She decided she would wait until Monday, and then after she and Sylvia both got home from work, she would mention that she didn't see Preston, and she wouldn't be seeing him for a few days.

But Sylvia was awake when Danielle got home, sitting at their table and working on the jigsaw puzzle they had started before they left for the beach. "I love you," she said when Danielle walked in.

"Now say it to me instead of the bag," Danielle said. "Coffee's on the porch. I had to put it down to get the door unlocked."

Sylvia stood to go get the coffee, and when she stood Danielle noticed that she was wearing one of her old flannel shirts, and it might have been the oldest one she had—Danielle remembered it from when they were in college. Sylvia had worn a lot of flannel in college, and she had mostly stopped, but she still had her shirts for sentimental reasons, and she was wearing one now. She opened the front door and sneezed, and Danielle thought the shirt must have been dusty when she got it out.

Impulsively, Danielle said, "Preston texted me. He's going out of town for a week."

Sylvia was holding both of their coffees now, and Danielle realized that she had stepped outside with her shirt unbuttoned, and she wasn't wearing shorts either. "Why?" she asked.

Danielle got plates for each of them, and they sat down at the table together. "He didn't say."

"Weird," Sylvia said, sipping her coffee.

Danielle unwrapped her sandwich on the plate. "I think it must be restaurant-related, given how focused he's been this whole time. Especially since we lost a couple days this week."

"I wouldn't call them lost," Sylvia said.

"You know what I mean. We had a couple days where we didn't work."

"Ah," Sylvia said.

Danielle said, "You're acting strange."

A wide smile formed on Sylvia's face, and she pointed her eyes down for Danielle to follow. Danielle glanced at the floor, and Sylvia's underwear were next to the table legs. "Not right now," Danielle said.

Sylvia's face flushed.

Danielle said, "We need to save up for when I ovulate."

"Right," Sylvia said. "You're right." She stood. "I need to get dressed."

"Eat breakfast with me."

Sylvia was already on the stairs. "In just a second. I just need to get actual clothes on."

Danielle now sat alone, eating her sandwich while Sylvia's footsteps creaked above her. She took a thoughtful sip of her coffee, then leaned forward and picked up one of the jigsaw pieces, and squinted at the puzzle box, and held the piece above the partially filled frame, trying to determine where it should go.

A week passed, during which Danielle continued work on what she could and heard nothing from Preston. When the next Monday came, she was unsurprised that he didn't contact her. She asked his prospective sommelier and his head chef and even a few of the contractors if they had heard from him, and all gave similar answers. Most hadn't been told Preston was leaving town, and the ones who did know had been told he'd be gone a week, just like her, and no one had gotten any update on why he hadn't returned.

Danielle's work naturally slowed, and by the third week she was only working mornings at the office she shared with the rest of her collective. The silence from Preston unnerved her, but it seemed to bother Sylvia more. Danielle hadn't realized how much Sylvia needed her and Preston's working relationship to stay predictable until it wasn't. When Preston became unpredictable, Sylvia became uneasy. Danielle disliked the developing push-and-pull effect of his actions on Sylvia's actions, and she wanted to sever the connection, and it would have been easier to sever the connection if she wasn't having a hard time figuring out what to do with herself, because that made it harder to figure out what to do about anyone else.

One night during the third week, they were sitting out on the porch together, and Sylvia asked, "Did you see Preston today?"

Surprised, Danielle said, "I haven't heard from him since he left."

"Weird," Sylvia said.

"What?"

"I just thought I saw his car earlier."

July Fourth arrived a few days later. Sylvia and Danielle wore red, white, and blue and grilled burgers in the little Weber grill they kept outside, and they had to call Tyler over to get the coals lit for them; and Tyler and Harriet were having their own cookout, and Sylvia and Danielle didn't go, and the burgers weren't very good. They ate them, though, and they walked down from their neighborhood to the Carillon to watch the fireworks; and they made it as far as Boulevard, and they were still walking across the highway bridge when the fireworks started, and they and all the other people around them just stopped and looked up and watched from the highway bridge; and then they went home, and after they'd gone to bed, Danielle's period came again, and she and Sylvia both cried in bed together while stray fireworks continued in the distance.

Danielle took up yoga during the fourth week of Preston's absence. She pulled up YouTube videos and got good at a few poses and at feeling her breath, and she knew it was working when she could have thoughts like, *This weird dead period at work is a practice run for the time with the baby*, and not follow them up with thoughts like, *If there ever is a baby.*

July took over the neighborhood with its typical sweltering gloom, and every trip outside felt like a dirty bath, and every trip outside required a shower; and all the women younger than Danielle and Sylvia walked around shining with possibility, like the summer didn't affect them. Danielle became increasingly certain that Preston was never coming back. It occurred to her that she was in stasis in the house, just waiting for him.

During the fifth week Sylvia asked again, "Did you see Preston today?"

"No," Danielle said.

"Weird," Sylvia said. She thought some more and added, "It's just really really weird." And then she retreated back into her misty silence.

Silence seemed to be falling along all the channels of Danielle's life. It was as though, by leaving, Preston had pulled the plug on whatever circuitry created noise around them, and everything was becoming quieter as the battery power gave out. In the current landscape, time seemed to gush forward, unimpeded by sound. Her evenings with Sylvia seemed shorter than they ever had as the two of them drank tea, their exchanges becoming too infrequent to be called occasional. Danielle had stopped driving to her office, where there was commuter noise and outside street noise; and she worried about the birds around the house, and the crickets, and the cicadas, thinking one day they'd stop too, and one day she would go to her car to visit the store and it would start up as usual, only she wouldn't hear the engine. It would just start, and rattle, and the lights would come on, but she wouldn't hear a thing; and one night in the fifth week she and Sylvia had raucous, glorious, emboldening sex that made her shout all around. But when they'd finished, the silence seemed to come back swifter, thicker, and bolder, and she worried that her shouts had consumed most of the sound left in her world.

Seven weeks passed before Preston came back. Danielle was alone in the house when his car pulled up, its vivid blue exterior gleaming in the sun. He got out with his sunglasses on and slung that leather backpack over his shoulder, while Danielle watched breathlessly from the window.

He came up the walkway at an uneven pace, first quickly, then, glancing down at his shoes, slower, standing straighter. He didn't notice her at the window, watching from the sink, and he exited her field of vision as he stepped onto their porch. Danielle waited for his knock, which didn't come, and she waited more, still watching the window to see if he went anywhere. Finally, she moved to open the door in front of him, and as soon as she took a step toward the door he knocked.

Seeing him in the flesh, this close to her and not through a window, the relief Danielle had felt a moment ago turned to anger, and she let her anger assume its stance and speak for her, and said, "Where have you been?"

Preston said, "Can I come in?"

Danielle moved away from the door to let him through. It was a Tuesday, and an early afternoon; and as she was closing the door, she glanced at Harriet's house to see if she was home. It was a habit she had developed over the last few weeks as she had spent more and more time alone in the house.

"You can sit in the living room," she said.

"Thank you."

Preston sat down in a series of jerky motions, as though lowering himself down invisible stairs, and placed his leather backpack beside him on the couch. She thought she heard bottles clinking against each other as he lowered it. He didn't make use of the back cushion. His hands were at his sides, and he seemed to be using them to steady his balance. "I have news."

Danielle was still standing. She waited, now fearful that he had come to tell her he was shutting down the restaurant.

"As you know, we've been targeting an October opening for the restaurant."

Danielle nodded. The intensity of her anger had died down, only to reemerge for a second life as anxiousness. She realized what he was here for, and she couldn't risk it. If he wanted to move the opening back, then it could be moved back again; and if it kept moving back, then it could conflict with her due date once she was pregnant, if she got pregnant.

Preston moved his hands to his lap. As he talked, he studied them. "These last few weeks, I've been with my dad."

Hearing him say "dad," Danielle realized he'd always used the word "father" before.

"I left because I'd heard he was in the middle of a cancer scare, and I went out there thinking he might be in the mood for a talk. He wasn't, but my sisters were all around, and I realized I was the only one who hadn't gotten on the first flight out when I heard. I stayed, though, and I guess it did some good, because now he wants to come to town when we open."

Danielle's anxiousness cascaded into relief, then bubbled again into anger. Why hadn't he told her where he went? Why hadn't he told anyone?

"My dad changes his mind on things, though," Preston said. "And I know things haven't been moving while I've been away, so I'm here to ask you personally to help me with this last push."

"I'll work hard on it," Danielle said.

"More than that," Preston said. "I need someone in my corner."

Danielle understood what he was asking, and she felt dusty about it—not dirty, but dusty, and she wished he hadn't come to her house to ask; and she would support him, and help him, and give her best effort; and she wished he had taken that for granted instead of asking. Eight weeks had passed since they spoke at the beach, and even before that, there was the suggestion of going to the beach at all; and she felt that she had returned from that trip hoping things with him would never again strike the tone they'd struck that morning, when Preston had dropped all of his barriers; because after he had dropped his barriers he had reached out and touched her, and now he was in front of her, asking her to keep things in that tone, the exact tone that had preceded his hand on her knee, and he was asking for the good of his family.

She said, "I will be your partner." For the time being, he could read into that whatever he chose. She would make things clear to him over time.

"Thank you," Preston said. He stood. "I feel like I can go straighten things out with everyone now. I don't expect the others to be as understanding as you. Chefs aren't known for their even temperament."

Preston picked up his backpack slowly without letting it swing. Then he raised it to his head and unzipped it partway, only a little wider than his hand. "This is for you, to say thanks," he added. His hand emerged holding a copper mug and a folding knife.

He gave his hand a little tremor, causing the knife to fall back into the backpack, and held out the copper mug. As he held it out, Danielle noticed how gaunt his face looked, in contrast with the copper's polished warmth. "It's engraved on the bottom."

Danielle turned it over and read, "For the one person more obsessed with design than I am."

She looked up, intending to tell him that she couldn't accept it, but he held up his hand.

"Getting it engraved didn't cost much. I mean it didn't cost much, even with the engraving. I promise. I'll see you on Monday."

After Danielle had showed him to the door and watched him leave, she sat on the couch and turned over the mug in her hands, thinking about what she would tell Sylvia.

All at once she realized that an engraved hunk of copper was an unnecessary complication and went outside to dig a hole.

Sylvia got caught in a summer lightning storm on the way home, giving Danielle more time than she'd wanted to think about what she would say about Preston. By the time Sylvia trudged through the door, wet from the short walk to the porch and unzipping the back of her dress as she crossed the threshold, Danielle had played the scenario in her head so many times she couldn't remember which endings went with which beginnings.

"Can we get delivery tonight?" Sylvia asked, plopping herself down on the couch so that her dress spread out horizontally over her like a blanket. "Today was miserable."

"That sounds okay," Danielle said. "What do you want to get?"

Sylvia shrugged. "Let me look." She pulled her phone out of her bag.

The wise thing to do would be to wait until Sylvia had decided on food, and they had ordered food, and the food had come, and they had eaten the food, and they were passing time together in silence. Danielle figured she could get through one or two of those stages before she lost the ability to wait any longer, and she decided that telling Sylvia in the middle of their evening activities would be worse than if she told her right now. If Danielle told her now, then she could cope and then they could have a pleasant night together, and she would work on reducing the silence then, because it had grown from Preston's disappearance, and it would wither with his reappearance, and she could work on replacing it with something better.

"Preston is back," she said. She immediately disliked how vague that phrasing sounded. She added, "He stopped by."

Sylvia continued looking at her phone. "I'm glad you'll be able to finish the restaurant."

Danielle didn't doubt that she meant it, and she knew that Sylvia had chosen her words with the intent to make them sound more important than they felt, in the hope that saying them out loud would make them grow bigger than the thoughts she *wasn't* saying out loud; and Danielle assessed the moment, unsure whether or not she should go along with it. She thought there was a chance that Sylvia had the right idea—that by leaving it at that, she had consigned those other thoughts to shrivel up without attention; and Danielle wanted the chance to be bigger than it was, and she would have left it at that if she'd thought the chance that Sylvia could ignore her doubts was on par with the chance that Sylvia would hold everything in until she exploded.

Outside, the lightning had slowed, but the rain remained hard, battering the windows.

Danielle said, "He still wants to open on time, even though we've lost a month and a half."

Sylvia glanced up at her, then went back to scrolling on her phone. "I assume that means you'll need to work longer hours with him."

"No," Danielle said, saying it before she thought about it. "I mean, yes, probably, but it also means I'll be done sooner."

Sylvia's head rocked up and down slowly, as if she were demonstrating what a nod looked like. She locked her phone and put it down beside her, then turned her whole torso to face Danielle. "Can you explain your role in this to me again?"

Surprised, Danielle said, "You've seen me do restaurants before. It's the same thing, only I get to see more of the process than usual."

"Right," Sylvia said. She seemed to be checking each word she said for quality as it exited her thoughts. "I've been confused about it for a while now. It seems like you're designing the space, but you're also meeting the staff and planning the opening. Just seems like you're doing a lot."

Danielle was puzzled, unsure what Sylvia was moving toward, or if she was moving toward anything. "He's very passionate about design."

She wished she hadn't used the word "passionate."

As she waited for Sylvia to speak, an icy sense of isolation settled in. Danielle could tell Sylvia any number of soothing nothings, and none of them would work. If she told Sylvia she hated Preston, Sylvia would know she was being lied to, and it would be worse to peddle a lie when peddling the truth had proved difficult enough.

Sylvia said, "I'm glad you're going to finish the restaurant, but I don't trust Preston. And lately that's not even notable. Lately, I don't trust anything."

The truth was that Danielle got along well with Preston, and that she always had, and she had enjoyed working with him, and she was proud of her work, and the truth didn't go any further than that; and Sylvia had a hard time seeing how some relationships simply stopped where they were supposed to, instead of piddling out to their extremes, where everything inevitably went wrong.

Danielle said, "That's the hormone changes, right? You always used to talk about how your thoughts went in weird directions."

Again, Sylvia's head moved up and down. It was eerie, how robotic the motion was. "Before I got myself straight, I had a good system where I just didn't trust my thoughts at all, and that kept me in line. Then my life got so much better, and I got in the habit of listening to myself, and I'm finding that habit hard to give up."

She was still staring straight at Danielle, looking guilty and lost. "Every time you leave the house, I tell myself not to picture you heading toward a bed. And yet I do, and it only gets more vivid."

Danielle was dumbstruck. How had it happened this fast?

"You don't have to say anything," Sylvia said. She tapped her temple. "There's more than one me up here right now, and the one I like the most is sure you'd never do that. She's just outnumbered."

Danielle said, "You weren't like this before."

Sylvia breathed out, her eyes turning downward. "I'm half of what I am and half of what I was, and I've got the wrong halves."

"I don't understand," Danielle said. "Are you accusing me or not?"

"I'm not," Sylvia said. "I'm just saying I've convinced myself that all my worst fears have come to pass. Even that they've been actively happening over the last two months. I've been seeing Preston's car all over the city while he's supposed to have been away."

"He's been in Maryland," Danielle said.

"But I've been seeing his car," Sylvia said. "I didn't say his car was around, just that I've been seeing it."

There were two kinds of arguments between them. The first kind was a safe argument, in which the bottom was defined and sealed before they started, and that bottom stayed within redeemable bounds, so that even if they sunk to the argument's lowest possible point, whatever they said could still be taken back, and reversed, and erased when the sun came up the next morning. The second kind of argument was the dangerous kind—the kind that had recurred in the early months of Sylvia's transition, where unspoken agreements could be breached and customs could be sunk and everything was exposed; and Danielle's instincts told her that this was a dangerous argument, and she felt alone, unable to trust Sylvia to pull herself away from the edge; and she felt pressured to go out to the edge and meet her there and pull both of them away, and she resented it.

Danielle said, "I don't understand. You're telling me you think I'm cheating on you, but you also don't think I'm cheating on you."

"Pretty much sums it up," Sylvia said.

Danielle walked out of the room. She was dealing with a crazy person. She was dealing with a person who'd lost her marbles. The person with whom she was dealing had gotten on the boat to nowhere. At the same time, she was dealing with Sylvia, whom she loved, and who loved her; and she had no way of talking to Sylvia alone, without this aberration listening to their conversation.

"I'm sorry," Sylvia said. She had followed Danielle into the kitchen, and she had re-zipped her dress, and she was standing straight up, looking formal in a way that only made her seem more robotic.

"I just don't get it," Danielle said. "I'm not sleeping with Preston."

"I know that," Sylvia said.

"I'm not partial to him at all."

"I know that too."

"And our marriage is important to me."

"Me too."

Danielle said, "Can we leave it at that?"

Sylvia was trembling. "Help me do that," she said.

Danielle had helped her so much already, and once again she needed more. An urge to slap the countertop and yell rose up inside Danielle, but she didn't know what she would even yell, because the words that could pinpoint all the unrequited ways in which she had opened the walls around Sylvia never materialized in moments where she would actually say them; when she was minorly angry—or even when she was hugely angry but about something that didn't matter— she always knew exactly what she would say to gain the upper hand, to zap Sylvia with a one-liner that left her dazed, and she always knew she wouldn't say any of it; and right now, if the words came to her, she knew she would say them, and they would never be recovered; and somehow the words themselves knew that, and they were hiding from her like children from an enraged parent. The only word she had left was, "How?"

Sylvia shook her head. "I know you've put your heart into the space and not into Preston. I don't want you to quit on it. I just don't know how to keep myself under control when I can't know anything for sure."

A question came to Danielle's mind, and she asked it, and asking it felt like holding a rain-slicked iron rod up to the storm clouds outside. "Do you want to quit trying to have a baby?"

Sylvia didn't move. "No. There's nothing I want to do less."

As the meaning of the words unspooled in Danielle's mind, the silence around her completed its descent. She could no longer hear the rain, or the thunder, or the hum of the refrigerator, or the breath in her nostrils. The silence she had feared encircled her, but instead of destroying things, it clarified them. In place of hearing, she was feeling. She was feeling the water in the raindrops, and the ions in the lightning, and the chilled air in the refrigerator, and the flow of breath in her lungs, and the blood in her pulse. Her emotions became crystalline, and her thoughts came into focus.

But Sylvia hadn't joined her yet. She was still the algorithmic Sylvia, the inconsistent Sylvia, the entangled Sylvia—acting out the motions of a living body, mired in a lurid haze. The robotic Sylvia said, "The other night I woke up at four in the morning and I felt optimistic, like I'd just forgotten a good dream. I left you sleeping there, thinking I could go watch the sunrise from Libby Hill and maybe feel like myself for a while. I didn't, though, because when I got downstairs, I heard a car idling. I looked outside and there it was, without its headlights on. I sat in the dark, relieved I hadn't turned on a light, until dawn cracked and the car drove away."

Danielle ignored her. Sylvia was lost in her illusions, but the illusions had reached their melting point. Danielle wasn't interested in them. Instead, she said, "A baby won't fix things, if we let them break."

"I know that," Sylvia said.

The sound of the rain came back, louder now. The refrigerator hummed with renewed vigor. Danielle said, "We're placing our faith in God to give us what we can handle."

"I know that too," Sylvia said.

Danielle was swaying a bit, imperceptibly to anyone but her, each sway perfectly symmetrical, creating equilibrium and living in it, still feeling everything around her, still alive in that intense, clairvoyant focus. "Trust God first, and then trust me."

"I will try," Sylvia said.

Danielle studied Sylvia's face. She studied her eyes and her nose and her skin. Then a big blue flash filled the room, and the lights cut off. A few seconds drifted by in the rainy twilight, and then the lights returned, and all the appliances started whirring and thumping and humming and beeping at once.

"I will," Sylvia said. "I will trust God."

"We should pray," Danielle said. "Let's say a rosary."

She walked out of the kitchen and up the stairs, and Sylvia followed her into their bedroom, where both of their rosaries lay. They came back down and sat around their kitchen table and held hands and said the Apostles' Creed; and they said the Our Father; and they said three Hail Marys for Faith, Hope, and Charity; and they said the Glory Be; and they announced the First Mystery; and they said the Our Father; and they said ten Hail Marys; and they meditated on the First Mystery; and they said the Glory Be; and they announced the Next Mystery; and they said the Our Father; and they said ten more Hail Marys; and they meditated on the Next Mystery; and they said the Glory Be; and they said the Hail Holy Queen; and they said the Final Prayer; and they made the sign of the cross; and when they finished they went back upstairs together, and Danielle smiled, and she felt both full and empty, and she felt light and free, because she knew what she would dream about that night.

4

Harriet said, "I knew they were having problems because Sylvia had taken an atypical interest in their yard. I get gardening, and I can understand somebody wanting to get out there and drizzle the soil through her fingers, but I've grown enough plants to know how instantly disillusioning it is. I've been growing tomatoes, peppers, coriander, basil, grapes, lemons, peaches, cucumbers, potatoes, pears, rosemary, plums, figs, and even olives since I was seventeen years old, and every single year there's a point where I just stare at a big patch of soil and think, *Is this worth it?* So when somebody's just starting out, you expect to see them get disillusioned like that, especially after their first couple of plants die. But Sylvia was out there every day with some new garden implement, churning or planting or watering something.

"That was the other thing that tipped me off that Sylvia was a beginner: the boxes. I don't like being called a housewife, but I do spend a lot of time at home, and of course I look out the window a lot, so I saw Sylvia out there unloading big hardware store boxes at least twice. It wasn't hard to discern that she was a novice, knowing she was buying all of her equipment alongside her plants; and again, novices in gardening are a wonderful thing, but they're sprouts in a frost. Most of them just don't make it.

"It's possible that she was out there trying to bludgeon it into a habit. You could maybe convince me that she thought, *If I do this every day and do it a lot, then eventually I'll do it without thinking about it.* But there were other signs too, in addition to her newfound gardening lark. She had also taken an interest in bird watching, for example. In the mornings I'd see her out there on her porch with binoculars and a book, staring into the trees, even after the mornings started getting chillier.

"I guess the other thing that's relevant is that I know her pretty well. At that time, we weren't really talking, and we hadn't really talked much over the summer, for reasons that didn't exactly make sense to me. I'm guessing they had to do with the problems she and Danielle were having—the ones that had driven her to birdwatching, which I knew she didn't have a prior interest in because I had spent a whole evening trying to get her interested once. She'd just said no, she didn't have the patience, and I told her she's a very patient person in a lot of ways, so she switched to saying no, she didn't have the time. But people with problems in their marriage always have time on their hands, and they hate it. They wish they had less of it. They want to go out on the street and just start handing out time, but they can't because that's entirely too metaphysical, so instead they start gardening and birdwatching.

"The other thing I noticed about them was that Sylvia just always seemed sad. I know that one is a little more dubious than gardening or birdwatching, but she had this way of carrying herself where it looked like her body was leading her around while her head and eyes lay dormant. She'd never had a hunch in her walk before, in fact I'd always admired her a tiny bit for standing straight up the way she did, not shying away from the fact that she was taller than most women. I'm sure her gender caused her some kinds of insecurity in some places, but you wouldn't know about it from the way she walked. Out there in their yard, though, she had a distinctive hunch. Her shoulders were always slumping a bit forward; her legs kind of dragged her around. I'm making it sound more perceptible than it realistically was, but the picture was bleak once you saw it. Once you saw it, it was the first thing you saw when you saw her.

"But I should mention one more thing before I go to the more definitive proof. Sylvia looked sad, and in her own, less outward way, Danielle seemed sad too; but I wouldn't venture to say that Sylvia seemed angry or fringy. Her demeanor was heavy-hearted, not flaming-hearted. I've always thought she was a gentle person—I mentioned patient earlier too—and I have a hard time picturing her otherwise.

"But to get back to what I saw, I was working on the theory that they were having problems and that was causing Sylvia problems, but it's not an assumption a person should be walking around with in their head. I did my best to hang back and not let it drive me to any kind of long-term formulations about them. It's not like Tyler and I have never had problems. We've had plenty, especially early on. And I was still holding out hope that my friendship with Sylvia would snap back to the way it was going in the spring.

"It really was like a fall breeze between us for a while. I'm very good at sensing people, and at the time, I sensed that Sylvia was aching for female friendship quite a bit, which makes sense given her history. I reached out in a few ways, and she was surprisingly receptive, and after a while, things just sort of took off. Everybody wants to be on good terms with their neighbors, but this was a dream of a neighborly relationship. We got along famously. We were so interested in one another, and we did lots of different things in that epoch. She brought this soothing, watery calmness with her, and I needed that. Tyler's a lot of good things, but one of the bad things is, he's a bit high-strung, which is why all of his jokes are so exuberant; he's perpetually decompressing himself. And then I'm pretty much a worker bee myself, although I'm afraid of bees. But when Sylvia was around, I just felt like time moved at the best possible pace. There was always the right amount of it, like nailing the pH of soil around a hydrangea to turn the bloom the exact right color.

"The intensity with which she and I liked each other did make me a little uncomfortable at some junctures, particularly when Danielle was around. I'm not saying I saw Sylvia differently from any other women; in a lot of ways, I saw her—actually, no, scratch that, I already don't like the thought I was getting toward. I'm not saying I saw her differently from any other woman, full stop, because I didn't. I just also happened to be aware that Danielle might have developed certain reflexes earlier on in their relationship, and that those reflexes—one could assume—might lead her to make assumptions about a burgeoning acquaintanceship between her spouse and another lady. I never saw it that way in the slightest. As dismissive as I tend to be toward men, I'm attracted to them, full stop, and I doubtless didn't see Sylvia that way. I was constitutionally incapable of it. But a lot of the times when Sylvia and I were doing something and Danielle was around, I sensed a bit of covetousness toward the relationship Sylvia and I shared. I'm not a psychologist, but I like thinking about people and drawing conclusions about them, and the conclusion I drew about Danielle was that she wasn't jealous, per se, but she had come to realize that having a female friend, unencumbered by any past perceptions of Sylvia, meant something to Sylvia; and Danielle herself couldn't mean that same thing, and that bothered her. Our culture tends to talk about jealousy a lot, and normalize jealousy a lot, and dramatize jealousy a lot; and I think the result is that a lot of people experience these multilayered feelings toward the way their spouse interacts with other people, and they don't have a word for it, so they depend on what the culture is telling them and just label it jealousy. In that sense, then what I was sensing in Danielle was jealousy, even though I don't think she ever seriously worried that Sylvia and I would, well—I don't think she really believed that would happen, even if she maybe backed into the notion after she decided that jealousy was the right label for her feelings; even though in this case, I think that was only partially accurate, and wrong in some damaging ways.

"I don't think, though, that I had anything to do with the marital troubles they were having, because Sylvia only seemed to get sadder and sadder in my absence. I don't mean my absence was the thing making her sadder and sadder, just that I was absent from her life while she was getting sadder; and even if you discount the birdwatching and the gardening as circumstantial evidence, it's hard to argue with what I saw the night Preston's restaurant opened."

Harriet said, "The restaurant? It was phenomenal on the inside. I had no doubt that Danielle was talented, and from what I'd heard and seen, I gathered that Preston was fairly invested in her, so it wasn't really a surprise that the place was nice, but it did surprise me how intensely nice it was. I'm of the opinion that anything a person makes reflects, in some sense, the frame of mind they were in when they made it, and I guess she and Preston really liked working together, because everything just seemed to come together so noticeably well. I'm not saying it was glitzy on the inside, or in any way overdone. If I had to pick between understated and overstated, I would say it was understated, but every infinitesimal detail just lined up. When you were in there, you just felt like you were in a restaurant. Other restaurants seemed awkward by comparison. I remember being at a table with Tyler, ticking down the list of my other favorite restaurants, and realizing each of them seemed to have a flaw I hadn't noticed before that this one somehow made obvious.

"The other thing about it, and I don't exactly know how this worked out, was that it made you feel like you and your companions had this crowded place to yourself. I'm not saying it felt like everybody was in private rooms, more like it felt like you and your companions— in my case my companion was Tyler—were on a stage in a play and under the spotlight, while everyone else in the restaurant was an extra. When you got up to walk somewhere, the right path seemed to magically materialize before you. It was almost spooky the way the place enveloped you and kept you feeling private and yet surrounded by energy, but I've been back one time since then and had the same experience. I'd heard Danielle talk about design and emotions before, on one of the days she wasn't being covetous, but I didn't entirely understand until

I spent a night in that place. Tyler and I talked about it, even, how the surroundings made us feel special and alone.

"That sense of privacy was so thick that I admittedly didn't notice Sylvia and Danielle all that much, and when I did notice them, I had to make an effort to hold my focus on them and see them and observe—but I observed enough to observe what I observed. I observed Danielle getting up to go outside, and I observed the fact that she still had half a salad on her plate, and I observed Sylvia looking at her own salad, like she was deciding whether or not to continue eating. It was Danielle getting up and walking past that initially caught my eye, but from there I watched Sylvia, who sat there looking at her plate for a little longer, then took a bite, and then changed her mind and got up to walk out to where Danielle was. After I saw that, I turned to look out the window for Danielle, to see if she was on the phone, or even smoking or something, but she wasn't doing anything. She was just looking down the street.

"Sylvia finally joined her out there, and they stood a few feet apart from one another. They were talking, but they didn't move much, and I felt like I was being invasive by observing, so I went back to chatting with Tyler. We really were having a great time. I remember Tyler being able to drink a lot more than usual without his speech or demeanor changing, just a greater sense of energy that he could even share with me. I didn't even feel uncomfortable, despite being eight months pregnant, and we were touching each other across the table, leaning toward each other when we talked—the sort of thing that makes a good date a good date.

"Eventually I noticed Sylvia and Danielle walk by again, and this time they were holding hands, though it didn't strike me as romantic. I got this sense as I looked at them that they were holding hands because all the other things that held them together were stretched out and wearing thin. They sat back down and talked some, but they didn't talk a lot, and Danielle seemed really dismayed by her food, which seemed very odd to me, considering if anyone knew the menu, it would be her. In fact, Danielle looked sick most of the times I remembered to look at them, and maybe that was what it was. Knowing what Sylvia told me afterward, though, it might've been both.

"It did cause me some pain to look at them, both because I knew they were having trouble and were sad about it, and because of how pretty they looked at the table together. They really are beautiful with each other in a lot of ways. I've always been struck by how each of them seems to reflect the other, like well-choreographed pieces of jewelry catching each other's light. Like everything else that evening, their collective loveliness came across with peculiar intensity, even from twenty feet away. I suppose that was another aspect of the restaurant—maybe even how Danielle got it working the way she did. When you did look at someone else, they seemed framed just for you to see. I had noticed that effect earlier in the night as I watched Preston personally seating his sister and her family, smiling with an almost whimsical formality as he held the chair for their daughter, then grimacing as he walked away. It must have been laborious smile night, because Sylvia and Danielle were eating together with their own uneasy smiles, grins of chagrin, if you will, framed for me to see, and it was hard on me. I did forget to look at them most of the time, but I should admit that I didn't like looking at them. It bothered me, almost made me feel crawly. One time, just as I looked at them, the baby kicked.

"I know: I'd been watching Sylvia gardening and birdwatching, and now I was at a restaurant on a date with my husband, maybe even our last date before the baby arrived, and there I was looking at them again. It makes me sound a bit voyeuristic, especially considering I met them as neighbors. Maybe I even introduced myself so I could know just enough about their lives to spend my time speculating on their problems. I know that's the impression, but that wasn't the reason. I did have a special fixation on them. I'll admit that. It didn't come from a voyeuristic place, though.

"The fact is, I don't like men at all. Aside from Tyler, about whom I'm often mystified, and my dad, about whom I'm mystified even more, I would spend all my time with other women if I had the ability. I don't think there's anything grandiose about it, like men are diseased or malfunctioning or morally derelict by disposition or anything like that; it's just an intense personal preference. I just connect with women in a freer way than I do with men. I'm not sure that I feel something around women that I don't around men, and I'm not sure that I *don't* feel something around women that I *do* feel around men. I just seem to have an easier time with things in female company. Even Preston, whom I would rate as my first genuine male friend, gives me this little hum in my head that drains me over time. I'd call myself an extrovert by nature. People give me lots of energy, and I do seek them out, but maybe that's too generous of a term. If I got to spend my time around other women all the time, I'd call myself an extrovert, because women don't leave me feeling drained, even the exhausting ones. But men pretty much all do, with the exception of Tyler and my dad.

"So when I think about Sylvia, I get a lot of thoughts about that, and the fact is I root for her. I know there are some women who don't like women like Sylvia for what they see as an intrusion, but I also know that being around Sylvia has consistently replenished my well of personal energy, and I know that men don't have that effect on me—except for Tyler and occasionally my dad, whom I've already mentioned—so I just don't buy the stance that women like Sylvia are pseudo-women. Not that I ever bought it anyway, given that I'm more than a little progressive, but it's especially hard for me to buy that idea now, having had the personal experience with women that I've had. I mean, since I became old enough to notice trends in my personal energy levels, I've witnessed a constant phenomenon of increases around women and decreases around men. It strikes me as patently ridiculous to assume my energy levels increase and decrease due to the clothing choices and names of my companions, so there has to be some deeper divide at work—some kind of gender-sense that's deep enough to make it hard to circumscribe, but tangible enough for me to physically sense and consistently react to, again and again.

"I root for Danielle too, even though I don't like her on a personal level. In fact, Danielle is a really good example of what I mean. Danielle dislikes me too. She's not very subtle about it. Most people would be frustrated by someone who doesn't like them, right? Not me. When I spend time with Danielle, I'm on pins and needles until the moment I'm back home alone, and each time I still end up feeling like a coiled spring, all scrunched together and desperate to just, *boing*. It's negative energy with Danielle, but it's still energy, and it converts from negative to positive fairly easily. I never get that well-run-dry feeling from her like I do around Preston, and Preston likes me. He's been my friend since I was a kid, and he treats me nicely, and still, after a couple hours with him, I feel like I need to go lie down. There's something I'm able to sense, a meaningful divide made out of an invisible force. I just don't know what that force is."

Harriet said, "Gloves? No, I don't have any strong memories of Preston wearing gloves. Sylvia wears gloves a lot, though. She has at least two pairs. I know that because she had a pair of knit gloves when we met last winter, and I'd always see her wearing them while she cleaned off her car in the morning. I was always thinking she was going to ruin them, but I suppose she only had the one pair, and last winter was snowy and sleety for Richmond, so she did what she had to do. I know about the second pair because she made them under my tutelage just a few weeks ago.

"It was sudden, actually. We hadn't spoken in months, even though observing her that night at the restaurant made me feel like we *had* spoken. But I wasn't expecting her to reach out, given that it didn't seem like anything had changed—in fact, it seemed like she was only getting worse. But then on a Saturday afternoon in the middle of October, she knocked on our door.

"I was the only one home at the time. It was a Sunday afternoon and Tyler was traveling again. His job makes him travel a lot, which sometimes makes me anxious and lonely but other times makes me happy to have so much space for my imagination—and now it just makes me scared since we have the baby. He's on paternity leave right now, and I'm doing my best to not think about what happens when that ends and to just take things one at a time. We had an interesting and difficult experience in the delivery room, and I'm still sorting through that. As of right now I'm a little afraid to go outside, and I know that isn't healthy.

"But Sylvia knocked that afternoon, which was typical, because Sylvia and Danielle's doorbell is broken. So most people ring our doorbell, but Sylvia doesn't. That's how I knew it was her, or at least knew to assume it was her. I was excited, and as I was coming around the stairs, I hoped I hadn't been wrong and it was really someone from the Census Bureau or a package delivery. But when I opened the door, Sylvia was there.

"It was getting cold outside, that dry cold that comes after the first slate of fall rains, and she wasn't wearing a coat, but she had on a scarf that I made for her back when I was trying to get her to take up knitting with me. I say that because I had never seen her wearing it before, probably because I made it for her in April, but I think she had partially put it on to complement her message. I don't remember if we had any small chat or if she went right to her question—and I don't think it's important, aside from the fact that it tipped me off that she had apparently completed her descent into misery.

"She said, 'Can you show me how to be like you?'

"At first, I didn't understand, and I said, 'You just have to drink lots of different teas and have opinions on plants,' thinking it would make her laugh.

"She didn't, though. She just kept that frozen demeanor around her, and said, 'No, I mean, how to make things. I want to learn how to be self-reliant.'

"Admittedly, I was flattered by the phrase 'self-reliant.' I mostly ignore people's negativity, but I've been privy to some unflattering things I know some people have said about me, particularly people with corporate-cog-type jobs who really don't like them, and I appreciated Sylvia recognizing how I felt about myself. Maybe she had always done that, and that was why she always made me feel so at rest.

"She was really a sight, standing at my door in the dress I'd made for her—I just noticed that after she asked—and in the scarf I'd made for her, asking me how she could be even more like me. I suppose I'd made the things I made because of how I saw her, though, so maybe it's not fair to characterize it that way. In either case, I invited her in.

"I was going through a basket-weaving phase at the time, I think because the baby was coming soon and we had acquired a lot of baby items as gifts. You have your first pregnancy—and in my case probably only pregnancy—and all of a sudden this whole industry of baby items stretches out its pastel-colored tentacles for a hug. Sure, there's strollers, car seats, bassinets, and crib mattresses; and those you don't want to try and make yourself for safety reasons, so you buy those. But then there's also baby soap, baby clothes, and baby blankets; and those you just have no business buying, in my opinion. I feel the same way about toys. But along with clothes, soap, and blankets, people kept giving us toys, and books, and by the time my labor was imminent we had this utter mountain of purchased objects before us, and it made me queasy. We're fairly popular people, Tyler and I, I think because we both have sunny dispositions and I make things for people; so we were really inundated with gifts—a lot of them the same gift just doubled up. I didn't want to be ungrateful, but the whole ordeal ran so contrary to how I think about things that I was having trouble coping. I was having thoughts like, *Everyone wants me to abandon my self-reliant ways of stocking the house now that I'm a mother and submit myself to the economy of specialization*, which had no basis in reality and is really just kind of paranoid.

"I suppose I was particularly sensitive about it given that I have this terrible open secret all ensconced in my surroundings: I don't work. I used to tell people that I make things and change the subject, but they'd keep asking questions until they understood that, no, I didn't want to talk about it, and they'd get that look of pity and loathing—the ratio is different for different people—and then finally the subject would change. Now I tell them I'm a freelance artist because three years ago, Tyler had a friend who wrote an archaeological article for which I drew a speculative rendering of an early human sea vessel, and it's much easier to change the subject off that. I'm aware that I should work. Everybody works nowadays, and it's a universal good thing, but I just can't do it. I know I'm living mostly off Tyler's salary, and I've apprised myself of the implications for my gender, so to speak; and there are days where I feel dizzy with the conviction that I'm living contrary to all of my values, and I have to remind myself that it's hard enough to live consistently with my values, certainly it would be even harder to live completely opposite them, right? But I just hate the way the economy makes us all so dependent on everything. Nobody can move an inch without forty-seven different systems making space for them, and that drives me crazy. I think about it all the time, and the baby gifts just brought all of it out. I spend hours in this kind of manic place where I'm trying to produce my way out of that horrible dependence—a dependence that, in working, I'd have to accept as the only mode of living in the world. And I think to some degree, I was immediately partial to Sylvia because I sensed in her that same insecurity, that same feeling that she'd have so much trouble explaining herself to someone else that it wouldn't be worth trying and would probably even backfire. But I'm getting beyond myself. Self-aware paranoia aside, I was uncomfortable with all of the baby gifts that people had plucked out of the big, enormous economy. So I'd decided to make homemade baskets to sort all of our baby items into, and then at least when I looked around, I'd see my house, by my hand.

"It wasn't the best environment to bring a depressed person like Sylvia into: basketry items all strewn around, since I had the house to myself; and bright-colored baby objects tossed and sorted on the floor; a couple failed basket attempts discarded underneath the window; but in my defense, I hadn't expected to see or hear from another human for days, much less a human like Sylvia. She didn't react well. Remember I mentioned how everything a person makes reflects their temperament in some way, so I hate to think about what my mess told her about my temperament. But in addition to that particular postulate of mine, I have a corollary: that how a person reacts to something made by someone else is every bit as reflective of what's going on in that person's mind as the item is of the maker. Actually, let me try that again. That how a person reacts to being shown a handcrafted item reflects that person's state of mind as much as the item itself reflects its maker, which is why it's possible to love something at one point in your life and despise it at another. My mess must have been a bad fit for Sylvia's worldview in the moment, because when she looked around at all my baby items and basketry, I thought she was going to cry. She fixated on different items for longer than a person typically fixates, and Sylvia is and always has been a fixator, but she fixated for a long time. And then in the end the only thing she said was, 'Are you making baskets?'

"I told her I was, and that I would be happy to show her if she was willing to learn with me. I had my laptop open on the coffee table and was watching a YouTube video about the four core basketry methods. I had been annoyed about that particular video when Sylvia showed up, because it seemed helpful, but it also had a long windup about the history of basketry with dramatic music and National Geographic-type shots of women making baskets in some remote, vaguely non-Western European location. It's just insulting to everyone to get too mystical with the ancient culture aspect, especially the video's target audience, which I assumed was people like me who were already there to try and learn to weave baskets. I really didn't need the exotic footage with the flute music and the voiceover and the rushing water sounds to talk me into it, but each time I skipped ahead I landed *too far* ahead—I had been trying to pinpoint exactly where the instruction started, because it went back and forth between all the solemn village shots and a smiling, definitely Western European woman explaining how to weave.

"Even in her aggrieved state, though, Sylvia had her typical effect on me, and I was able to sit through those scenes and watch until the instructor came on without getting antsy or frustrated; Sylvia watched with me, then she and I tried following the instructions together. I had bought enough materials to make a second home out of baskets, so I didn't mind her helping herself to some of them, and I think it did her good to get something between her fingers. She started to open up and talk to me some, even smiled a few times over how her basket was going. She was weaving it really tight, and I remember looking at it and thinking it could probably hold water, which amazed me since mine was turning out pretty loose and flimsy. I really think the secret to my success learning how to do things is that nothing I've ever made has turned out well the first time, so I've just gotten used to making terrible versions of things until one day they magically turn out well. But Sylvia's basket was going well, and it possibly would have made me jealous if I hadn't been so grateful that she was talking to me again, even if the subject we were discussing was a YouTube video about weaving baskets.

"I felt happy, the way usually I feel when I'm making something. That's one thing I think people fail to understand about eras earlier than ours—and I'm not speaking from experience, because I'm not a time traveler. But in this urban homesteader act of mine, I've discovered there's a meditative, contemplative mental tone that you can reliably induce through repetitive handiwork. These days, everyone wants to be at rest. They want to be still, supine on couches, sedentary and uncomplicated, and they think their problem comes from moving too much. They think they would be relaxed if they could just get more of this rest, so they try to use their rest time for the best rest possible. They learn to meditate and they make tea and they go to Montana and they watch these agonizing TV shows, all in some vague gray attempt at relaxing, and they don't realize that all this rest is what's making them so tired. They don't realize that rest is addictive, and rest is tiresome, so your brains will demand more and more rest, until everything around you is some form of rest, and even that's too taxing. People look at past eras and wish things could be slow like they used to be, without realizing that the world was pointier and deadlier then, and it demanded so much more of people that rest was never in excess. Rest is killing us, and that's why I keep myself busy with things. People think I sit in this house and rest all day, and I don't, but I end up more relaxed because I sit here and make things.

"While we were weaving, and I was feeling happy, Sylvia asked me, 'Is this how it works for everything?'

"In context, it was clear that she was asking: do I always just watch a YouTube video and attempt to make something, and learn skill after skill that way? I told her this was actually the worst of the various ways to learn this stuff, and the best way is to ask someone. I've found farmers' markets really useful, because they're so full of people who make useful products, although I can't remember if I told Sylvia that.

"Then Sylvia said, 'Does asking you count?'

"The phrase bounced along like a joke, although it was clear from her tone that she didn't mean it to be funny, and I said, 'Of course.'

"And she asked, 'What else can you show me?'

"So I took her around the house and just pointed out all of what I'd made or was making. She was already acquainted with the lotions, clothes, soap, subsistence plants, and knitting; but I showed her various examples of all of them, along with the olive oil, leatherwork, pickling, candles, and sunscreen. She was particularly interested in soap, I remember, and I remember thinking I suddenly couldn't remember what had driven me to learn about making soap, but that after Sylvia asked, it seemed so right and so natural that a person would make her own."

Harriet said, "A folding knife? No, I don't remember Sylvia having any kind of folding knife. Cooking knives, yes, which I realize is obvious, but I can't recall ever encountering her with any kind of utility knife, folding or otherwise. Actually, let me take that back at once. There was one time that I saw Sylvia with a folding knife, but it wasn't hers. It was Preston's.

"This was early in the summer, on this ill-fated trip we all took together to relax at Preston's beach house and pop in to visit my family. I say it was ill-fated because it was that trip that seemed to turn the tide for Sylvia and me. I mentally sort the trip into two halves: the half where Sylvia and I got along famously, and the half where she and Danielle had a big Do Not Disturb sign hung around them. I mean that figuratively, of course, but things did turn on a dime like that. Although I didn't really notice until the knife incident, which is probably why I'm able to call it up with such lucidity.

"Near the halfway point of the trip, while Sylvia and I were still having fun together, we discovered these two vintage beach cruiser bikes in the carport of Preston's house. They were beautiful, well-maintained, pastel-colored wonders—one the color of a robin's egg and the other the color of a clownfish—both with white wheels reminiscent of Caribbean sand. We tried to take them out on our own one morning, both of us perfectly aware it was an activity so cutesy you could practically hear 'Just the Two of Us' playing in the background. The snag was that the tires were low. Not totally flat, but flat enough that they would've been miserable to pedal any significant distance, so we went upstairs to get Preston, hoping he had a pump. He told us that he did, but then he went to find it and it was nowhere. So Sylvia and I took Tyler's car to the store right across from the neighborhood. The point of that store—as with most stores in the Outer Banks—is to sell as many things with the OBX logo on them as possible, and we figured, reasonably I think, that they might be selling OBX-branded bike pumps in addition to the OBX frisbees, T-shirts, mugs, tumblers, journals, shot glasses, baby towels, and everything else you can imagine. We didn't have any luck, though, so instead we bought an OBX kite and went back to the house.

"After that, Sylvia went upstairs to say something to Preston and Danielle, and she was gone for a while. She was gone long enough that I got pretty antsy out there on the beach, just sitting in the sand waiting for my friend to come back. When she finally showed up, she brought Danielle and Preston with her—or more accurately, she brought Danielle and Preston had come too—and we went to fly the kite, which worked out pretty well, since the wind was blowing hard, making whitecaps in the distance.

"I'm not sure what happened then, because the kite seemed to be doing fine up there with Sylvia letting more and more of the string out. A lot of people don't know that kites aren't always tied at the bottom, so I reminded her to keep an eye on that, and she acknowledged me, but then something caused the kite to take a nosedive. For a minute it looked like it was going to recover, bobbing violently in the wind, but then it just flung itself down and out of sight and we all ended up running after it, just leaving the line on the ground behind us. When we found it, it was tangled up in some weeds on the other side of the dune, really gnarled in there like the weeds had grown around it. We tried to just yank it out by the string, but there was no give at all. The weeds had claimed it with newlywed zeal. Preston observed that we'd need to go in, and he did so gleefully, although his glee didn't become evident until he pulled his hand out of his pocket. Sylvia and I stood there on the nearest beach access, mostly in silence, while he lowered himself into the weeds, and that was when I noticed the folding knife in his hand.

"He was wearing linen shorts that looked relatively new, though they could have been ten years old if they were among his beloved possessions. Preston is an odd duck with the objects he owns; he either takes such fastidious care of them that they never show any wear, or he annihilates them with reckless use. I'm guessing he liked his linen shorts, since he lifted them up a little as he moved further into the green. He looked almost like a lady lifting a skirt, holding his shorts up like that as he took his slow steps. Finally he got close enough to the kite to cut it free. He pulled it carefully and—I remember thinking—tenderly from the weeds, and when he'd finished, he smiled at us on the beach access and held it up in triumph. Sylvia, Danielle and I applauded, both polite and mocking, probably with different ratios—or maybe Danielle was being polite and Sylvia was mocking and I was just clapping—and he climbed back over the dune, holding the string so the kite wouldn't get snagged again. Tyler had arrived at some point, and all of us converged on him, myself and the other two ladies coming down the stairs, Preston sliding down the dune, and that was when we noticed the cuts on Preston's legs. There must've been thorns in the weeds, because his legs were covered in bright red, enough that we could see the blood pooling and streaking. It looked worse than it was, I'm sure, but it looked bad. I think I even gasped, or whatever the normal person equivalent of gasping is, because he looked down and said, 'I guess I didn't notice.'

"We were all silent for a moment, and then Sylvia repeated Preston's answer as a question, saying, 'You didn't notice?' She's often cagey like that. From what I can tell, her belief is that a sparsity of words is superior to an abundance of them; but Preston seemed more than happy to ping it back at her, because he repeated her question as an answer, saying, 'I didn't notice.' And lest we continue the cycle of interrogatives and declaratives, perhaps culminating in exclamations, Tyler intervened to change the subject, and said to Preston, 'Cool knife.'

"I do wonder what would have happened had Tyler not jumped in, because it did seem like Sylvia was intentionally needling Preston. Not that it was the only time she spoke to him in that anodyne sort of tone—so intentionally anodyne as to become a bit pernicious. She's not always great about eye contact, but she did make the effort with Preston, always finding his eyes whenever she spoke to him. She even had a posture she tended to assume when she had something to say to him, again something quite devoid of any apparent significance. She'd stand very straight, very narrow, with her shoulders turned slightly away from him but her head directly facing him, and her neck extended, almost like a dancer waiting for the first beat. I don't think she did it out of any particular antipathy toward Preston, but rather a desire to obscure her discomfort around him. She doesn't like to indicate discomfort, which I know she equates with indicating insecurity, so I would conjecture that she stood so straight so as to conceal herself, though I don't think she concealed very much. I first saw her do it in Ellwood Thompson, when we ran into Preston before a party I was hosting, and she did it again after the kite incident, even though she was standing on sand. She had done it earlier in the trip, too, after we came home from my parents' house and everyone but me started drinking—as though they had all completed some difficult collective obligation by seeing my parents. Sylvia walked over to Preston and assumed her Talking-to-Preston Stance, again making eye contact with him, and asked, 'What are you making?'

"Preston told her he was making a Moscow Mule, and Sylvia, having moved a millimeter at most, said, 'Sounds lovely,' and that was it. And a day after the kite incident, when she and Danielle were in their insular Sylvia-and-Danielle bubble, she was holding hands with Danielle and she stood that way again to say to Preston, 'Thank you for inviting us here.'

"I said I don't think her behavior came from a desire to needle Preston, but if you know Preston, you know that nothing would make him crazier than those expressionless pleasantries. He doesn't like it when things are opaque, or even translucent. When we were teenagers, he made me read a book by Ernest Hemingway because he needed me to understand how much he disliked it. He kept saying, 'Why do these people act like this?' He couldn't stand how certain details about the characters had been withheld. I'm not saying I loved the book, because in truth I found it uninspiring, but the worst I took from it was boredom. We were sitting on the beach one evening and he said—and keep in mind he was a teenager—'I just feel like I'm getting owned by this guy.' Imagine, a man who doesn't like Hemingway because he feels dominated by him. I was under the impression that all men get a pass on not being as manly as the mythical man-of-all-men that Hemingway supposedly was, but Preston seemed to think he was in some sort of male rivalry with the man, whose only provocation was leaving some explanatory clauses out.

"It's a silly way to think, but I'm intrigued by the idea that—much like jealousy acts as a *deus ex machina* explanation for any complexity of feeling involved in the stubborn coexistence of friends and romantic partners—men find a certain eagerness in vague concepts like rivalry, competition, and domination. They're vague enough ideas that one can find traces of them in lots of more nuanced frustrations, but in the male mind writ large, those ideas will insist on being the whole thing—the rock on which any nuance is built. In Preston's case, I think his aversion to brevity developed outside of his taste in literature. His parents are quite private and his sisters rather cliquey. He has a cultivated instinct to find enormous significance in what he has and hasn't been told. His thinking can veer conspiratorial at times, or at least it did when he was a teenager at the beach.

"In fact, that was far from the only time his thinking veered toward the conspiratorial, even as a teenager. The one that instantly comes to mind happened the year after the Hemingway thing, or maybe the year before. It was late in the summer, as the summer was turning to fall, and we had said our goodbyes the previous evening. But I woke up to a pair of texts from him, sent at something like seven thirty-six and seven forty-one a.m. I'm not sure if those were the exact times. I just remember them being five minutes apart and sent in the sevens, which might as well have been the fours to a teenager. The first read, '*were* staying another week.' No apostrophe. And the second read—lowercase I—'i didnt know.'

"And I remember the questions that came to mind when I read those texts: Did he wake up at their usual departure time of his own accord? Did he frantically pack his things, or had he packed them already? Did he eat breakfast by himself, or did he wait in his room? Did he go and wake someone, or did someone realize he was up? Were his sisters as unprepared as he was, or had they all been told? Why did he wait five full minutes before sending the second text? Did he type several different variations before sending it? Did he type a big, long confessional and then remove everything other than those three words? I was a teenager at the time too, so I had some fun with it, thinking about all my questions, and I was looking forward to laughing at him over the seriousness of his tone. But then we met on the beach that afternoon and I could see he was really bothered. He didn't want to talk about it, which I found curious, given that he had been so severely deflated by his family withholding something from him. But thinking about it now, with all the psychoanalytical benefit of hindsight, it seems clear that he wanted to withhold something from someone else, even if the someone was me and the something was his troubled feelings about withholding. It was a sort of reclamation for him; a situation in which he was withholder and not withholdee.

"But I don't think Sylvia was attempting to dominate Preston any more than his sisters were, or his parents, or Ernest Hemingway. Honestly, I suspect her truncated sentences and Talking-to-Preston Stance were a way of interacting with him without interacting with him— mustering as much peace as she could with someone she clearly didn't like. But I doubt Preston interpreted it that way, and it may have come to a head right there on the beach if Tyler hadn't so deftly intercepted the tension by saying, 'Cool knife.'

"Preston looked proud and launched into an elevator spiel about how it was a French knife with a history of affordability, how Picasso used the same brand, etc. etc.—still bleeding quite profusely mind you. I zoned out some, to be honest, but Tyler seemed enraptured. Men seem to get that way around certain objects, and actually, Tyler ended up making us buy the same type of knife, so we have an identical one in the house right now."

The attorney said, "Can I see it?"

Harriet said, "Of course. It's right here. He keeps it down here because most everything we do that would require a knife—which, I never realized before, is kind of a lot of things we do—we do in this room. It's up here on the mantel, in the back corner. It's the exact same one as Preston's—Tyler sent him the link before purchasing to confirm it was the same, although Preston's was bought in France at a store that's been selling them for a hundred years, so maybe ours isn't quite as authentic—but if you put the context aside, it's the exact same knife.

"Preston showed his to all of us that day; we all passed it around and looked at it and acted suitably impressed. Well, maybe Danielle or Sylvia actually was impressed. I didn't particularly care, so in my case I was just acting impressed, but Sylvia did look at it for a little longer than I expected, and she folded it and unfolded it and twisted the guard around before giving it back to Preston, who put it in the pocket of his linen shorts and then waded into the ocean to soak his cuts in the saltwater.

"But as I'm talking about that trip to the beach, I'm realizing I never totally finished where I was headed when I mentioned that Sylvia and I made her a pair of gloves together, and I do think it's relevant. Not really the gloves themselves, as they were kind of an incidental output of our arrangement, but the things I became privy to while tutoring Sylvia in the ways of self-reliance.

"The first thing I should say is that Sylvia quickly proved she would be a dedicated pupil. She spent several more hours at my house after our foray into basket weaving, during which I taught her all about making soap, and before she left that first evening, she made it clear that she would be willing to come and learn more every night if I would have her. While under normal circumstances that would have qualified as a bit much, there was a smattering of other factors at play.

"One was the fact that I was, as I've mentioned, quite pregnant, and the dark homemaker energy that medical professionals call 'nesting' was in full swing. Considering my propensity for finding things to make even under normal circumstances, I was perpetually on the precipice of consuming our entire house with projects in progress, and Tyler was pretty vocal about how uneasy it made him; I suppose he worried that I would go into labor with a hundred half-done projects lying around, and we'd bring the baby into an unlivable mess. When I was telling him about Sylvia over video chat that evening, I think he sensed an opportunity to point me in a direction that would keep the house reasonably under control, and so he told me, enthusiastically, that I should teach Sylvia everything I knew.

"The second factor was that I really, really, really, really, really, really, really, really wanted to know what went wrong between Sylvia and me at the beach last summer. The truth is that I would've rooted for Sylvia from afar if she were anyone else, but I genuinely liked her a bunch and felt like our friendship could become something profoundly positive in my life. When I say that I think Sylvia was hurting for female friendship I do mean it, but I'm also self-aware enough to admit I sensed that need in her because it was a need I felt in myself. I have lots of female friends, but making friends is easy for me, and I'm naturally prone to finding things to like about people. It's a way of living that I enjoy, and I wouldn't trade it, but sometimes it leaves me feeling—I'm not sure . . . superficial? I have all these friendships that I've formed out of the fact that I can make myself enjoy other people's company, and as you get older and get married, you see people less often, and for shorter periods of time when you do see them; and you see them in public instead of in private; and you spend more time catching up than you do learning new things about each other, until you're confined in all these old friendships where neither of the original two friends exist anymore; and then you're out there making new friends, but you never have the opportunities to get to know and understand your new friends the way you used to understand your old friends; and it can become very isolating, especially when you're pregnant; and I wanted my friendship with Sylvia back because there was something so magical, so blissful, so mystical about the way she broke through all of those barriers so quickly.

"But maybe I'm building it up too much, because for all my talk about breaking barriers, I failed to out-and-out ask her what had gone so wrong. I wanted to, and on several of those fall nights when she was over, I very nearly did, but she always seemed so fragile. I hadn't sensed that in her previously, or at least not to this extent. We were having an okay time, and from the outside I think it was probably indistinguishable from how we had been before the trip, but there was an edge to it; and I couldn't escape the notion that asking her would be unfair, because with how fragile she'd become, it would be harder on her to tell me than it would be on me to hear it.

"She came over a couple nights a week and spent long stretches of several weekends at my house. I expected Danielle to eventually accompany her on one of these outings, but she never did, which only made me more suspicious that they were having problems, and I was unsure whether I was allaying those problems or exacerbating them. I couldn't ask Sylvia, though, and she continued coming over.

"Had we continued along with that pervasive off-ness and little else, our awkwardness would likely have dissipated over time; but there were also two incidents where things clearly took a turn. The first occurred on a Saturday. I was supposed to start teaching her how to sew. I had been cranking out baby clothes for the past few weeks, and baby clothes struck me as a good thing with which to show a beginner the ropes. They're small, but they hit all the difficult parts very quickly because of how little work it takes to get to each phase, and Sylvia and I had agreed two nights prior that we would have a sewing lesson with a little onesie, for which I had found an adorable fabric.

"Sylvia was at the door on time, as usual. She's very punctual as a rule, which I find unsurprising because, for all her virtues, she is decidedly not an optimist. I've read articles about how optimism correlates with lateness, because I'm a very late person, and people know that about me. Eventually someone sent me an article about how optimists tend to think things like, *The GPS says it'll take twenty minutes to get there, so I'm sure I can drive fast and get there in fifteen,* and, *Of course I can start this task right now, it only took me five minutes that one time I did it incredibly fast and that'll probably happen again.* Sylvia's not walking around shooting everybody's hope in the foot or anything, but you'd never catch her assuming things will go well.

"She seemed normal when she walked in. She was quiet, but she's often quiet, and she was hugging herself some, with her arms folded in around her cardigan, but it was cold enough that walking around in a cardigan and a scarf would make a person hunch up like that. If I had been looking harder, then it's plausible I would have noticed some tics in her mannerisms, but nothing jumped out at me until she sat on the couch instead of following me to the sewing table, and when I looked back at her she was shaking.

"In the moment, though, even that didn't tip me off—I think because the optimist in me wanted to think it was a simple, easy-to-fix discomfort. I said, 'Are you cold?' Again, thinking that the cardigan was undershooting it.

"But she shook her head, and then she says, 'A moment.'

"I didn't understand. So I said, 'Pardon?'

"And she says, 'I just need a moment.'

"At this point I'm on my feet again, unsure if she wants to be left in private, despite it being my house. I remember that Sylvia leaned downward, with her hands still folded inward so that it looked like she was inspecting a spot on the floor, and then she sniffed.

"Well, with the sniff et al., I'm aware now that she has a need, but I'm still unsure if she's here because I can address that need, or if she's here because someone else tried and missed their shot; and all I can think to do is get her a handkerchief—realizing right at that moment that a handkerchief would have been a better thing to make with her on her first try sewing. She takes it, and after a second, I realize she's not going to blow her nose on it; instead, she just sat there squeezing it like a stress ball. I didn't know watching someone squeeze a handkerchief could be so flustering, but it very much was. Her hands were just terrible to this little light blue cloth square; just truly abysmal to witness as she kept squeezing it, occasionally shifting it in her hands so that the pattern of folds changed.

"At that point, I decide that no person in distress ever felt worse after being offered water, so I start to walk away; but as I'm turning, I hear her say something so faint as to be inaudible, and I so badly wanted to think she was talking to herself, but no, I know she's talking to me. So I took a step toward her and asked her to repeat what she said.

"And she says, 'We had it.'

"I'm even more confused now, but again, it's entirely obvious that she wants me to understand; that it's important to her that I understand. So I said, 'What did you have?'

"She tried to speak, but then she shut her mouth tightly and rocked back instead, holding the handkerchief with so much tension I thought it would rip. And she tried again, failed again, and then tried again. But when she finally got the words out, they were cryptic at best: 'We had it. We did it, and then two weeks later it's just . . .'

"I understood that she had tried to say 'gone,' but I still lacked any sense of what she was talking about, and I'm far too deep in the moment to figure it out. I realized then that I would have to figure it out later, in a quiet moment, when the answer would simply come to me.

"Although, it never did.

"And Sylvia just said, 'It was all over.'

"I didn't understand, which I've said, but I was trying my best to help. As I mentioned, I was too frazzled to discern what was happening, but I had intuited that it was something to do with Danielle, and the word 'over' never sounds good in the context of a marriage, so I tried to reassure her by saying, 'It'll never be over.'

"She gave me a long look, from which I could tell I said the wrong thing, so I quickly pivot to, 'It will be over soon,' which didn't sound great coming out, either.

"She teared up again and shook her head, then she stood up and said, 'I'm sorry. I shouldn't have come over here like this.'

"But I didn't want her to leave—in fact, I sensed an opportunity to cut through the walls with her at last and have a moment where it felt like we knew each other again, so I rushed to the door saying, 'It's all right.' I even reached out and touched her forearm, which I noticed made her shiver. 'It's all right. It is,' I said. 'I'm glad you came.'

"She stopped her rush to the door and looked at me, I think to decide whether she had it in her to politely excuse herself again. Thankfully, she decided she did not, and she came back into the house and back to my couch, and then she made a curious request.

"She wanted to make a candle. It struck me as not only curious but also inconvenient. I had been going lighter on the candles since flammable objects are more or less at the top of the babyproofing 'Don't' list. But if friendship and siblingship and relationships all share one common ground, it's that occasionally you do something inconvenient for the sole reason that another person's feelings depend on it; and if you have to understand exactly why their feelings depend so much on it, then it doesn't count.

"So, we made a candle. She wanted it to be an unscented, rolled candle, and she left quickly after we finished, holding it up and admiring the natural honeycomb pattern from the beeswax as she crossed the street.

"The encounter left me feeling at loose ends, so I went back to sewing baby clothes. I finished the onesie I had meant to make, and I moved on to making a baby sweater, because our baby would be a newborn entering the coldest part of the year. While I was working, I thought about that cold, and thoughts about my newborn shivering made me shiver along with him, and just like that I couldn't get thoughts about my baby in danger to vacate my head. That was new to me. Every mother has thoughts about her baby in danger, and the internet is laced with techniques to banish those images, but while I waited for Tyler to get home, those thoughts stuck in my mind.

"I don't remember much of what I spent that afternoon doing, even after Tyler got home. When I try to, my mind skips to dusk, when we went on our daily walk. I've mentioned that this was a cold fall all around, and the nights seemed particularly chilly—I think because the afternoon sun was still strong enough to push through gaps in the tree canopy and blanket your shoulders—but at dusk the contrast really started to sink in, with that sun giving way to bristling wind. We cut our walk short because of how cold it was, even though I was eight months pregnant and pregnancy makes it so you can hardly stand the summer, smothered as you are by your own body, like you're under a blanket with a toaster. We cut our walk so short that we were home before nightfall, which was unusual for us, as we're typically crossing through that ghostly haze of commercial lights on Lafayette Street around the time the trees turn to shadows. But I recollect being back to our door before dark, because I only barely caught the flicker in their window.

"I thought I had seen a firefly at first, and I looked around hoping to see it again, thinking about how lonely a firefly must be in November. I was a little off kilter still. My experience with Sylvia that afternoon had primed me to see loneliness, and now the world seemed soaked in it. I guess I do remember what I had been doing all afternoon after all: I had been seeing loneliness on the tree branches, hearing loneliness in the birds, walking through the loneliness in my house, with my various sprawling projects, which suddenly all felt solitary. So I turned to see this lonely firefly I thought I'd spotted, and as my eyes hunted for another flash, I realized what I had seen was a flicker from Sylvia and Danielle's window. I left Tyler on our side of the street, not wanting to be loud, and walked toward it. I suspected it was the candle Sylvia and I had made, and in the moment, it felt important for me to know what had happened to it. I crouched down, as much as a person can crouch down when she's threatening to go into labor at any second, and I walked in awkward steps across their grass, just kind of drawn to the flicker, until I was close enough to realize I could see their faces too, illuminated only by the candle—all their other lights out—and they were sitting on either side of it, holding hands and speaking in unison, with a necklace of some kind in Danielle's hand. I watched them for a few seconds, speaking and holding hands around the candle in the dark together, Danielle running the beads of her necklace through her hands, until I felt certain they would notice me if I didn't turn around. So I went back to Tyler, who asked me what I was looking at. I told him I thought I'd seen a firefly, and we went inside."

Harriet said, "Panicky? No, I never witnessed any instances where Sylvia was panicky. She's the antithesis of panic in my mind, actually. There was a moment in the spring when she was over, and I opened my door to show her something. I forget what I was showing her, because as I opened my door, two bees flew into the house, and I'm deathly afraid of bees. So I was ready to run flailing to Carytown, but Sylvia was there, and she just calmly smiled and said, 'You know what I've never tried?' She didn't say anything else, just dipped her finger in some apple juice to lure the bees over, and as soon as they both landed on her finger, she took them to the door and set them free.

"She's just not a person who's quick to react to things, panicky or otherwise. The day after I witnessed her and Danielle with their hands interlocked around my candle, she showed up again, again wearing the scarf I had made for her; and again, things were about to take a turn. But she had brought me a present. She was holding it between her arms so that I could see a synecdoche of it, from one corner of which I could tell it was wrapped and rectangular. She asked if she could come in, and I said of course, so she came in.

"She said, 'Thank you for helping with the candle yesterday.' She was looking directly into my eyes when she said it. Sylvia doesn't always make eye contact, and sometimes it can make her appear shifty or suspicious, but in truth she's as shy as she is stoic, and she uses eye contact strategically—mostly when she's saying something of importance. It's not great as a general practice, but when you know her, you recognize it. It's a shame that she does it, really, because her eyes are beautiful. They're blue-tinted, but mostly gray, and quite pale. When you look at her eyes you see a mournfulness befitting someone older and more preoccupied, yet at the same time, if you know her, you know she has a storm inside, with the way she thinks. Her eyes are pretty when you don't know her, but when you do know her, they're different. I suppose Danielle knows all this too.

"I was so distracted by her eyes that I almost didn't hear the next thing she said, which was, 'It sounds strange to say, I know, but having something like that helped us . . . cope.' She looked up and out after she said 'cope,' like she was looking at the word.

"'I'm glad it helped,' I said.

"Then she smiled and said, 'I don't think I should keep coming over here, asking for lessons on how to do things. It's gotten a little too transactional for me, and I think I owe you for all the thread and beeswax.'

"I told her, 'You can still come over,'

"'I know that,' she said. 'But I'll come over to help with your baby while you make things. It would be a tragedy for you to be too busy to roll candles of your own.'

"She shifted a little, and at first I thought she was going to hand me the present, but she just sort of held it by her hip and I wondered if maybe she was on her way home, and maybe the present was for Danielle.

"And she asked, 'When are you due?'

"She had moved her eyes away from me, breaking the line she had created with them earlier. They were now studying my bump. 'Yesterday,' I said.

"It's typical for first babies to come late. I knew that intellectually, but as an optimist, I had assumed mine would come early, and I had been wrong. Sylvia was the first of a parade of people who would ask me that question in the coming days, vexing me more each time. It seemed like everyone in the neighborhood, and everyone working at all the stores, and even the mail carrier all suddenly needed to know when I was due, and each time I had to tell them I had already passed my due date, feeling more frustrated and nervous each time. Frustrated because I was starting to detest being pregnant, and nervous because the idea of an induction repulsed me. You can't go more than two weeks past your due date, or the baby is at risk. But in the five days between then and my eventual labor, it seemed like everyone was asking, as if they were all mimicking Sylvia.

"But Sylvia nodded and told me, 'He'll come, and it'll be fine. I was a C-section baby.'

"The air quaked a bit—that's the only way I can describe it. It wasn't a comforting thing to hear, but in the moment, it seemed like an intimate thing for her to tell me. She raised her eyes up from my bump, again making eye contact with that cloudy blue peacefulness, and asked, 'Are you going to get him baptized?'

"The question threw me. I wasn't sure what to say.

"Sylvia nodded sadly, and then she brought the present up from her side, into both her hands, and held it forward, and said, 'I don't think you're going to like this, but I feel like I have to give it to you.'

"I took the present. It was carefully wrapped, but not perfectly wrapped. It hadn't been wrapped at a store, I mean.

"'Thanks again for the candle, and everything else,' she said, and she left.

"I should say I wasn't offended by the suggestion of baptism, just discombobulated by it. I don't like the way I handled it. She left the house with the wrong idea, I think. I'm not a militant atheist. I've even been church-curious in my life. When Tyler and I were engaged, we considered having a church wedding, since both of us are technically Christian. By technically, I mean both our parents had us baptized. Everyone had their kids baptized in the eighties and nineties, though. It's not like that today. Today there's no real pressure on you to do anything religious. Most people are unreligious and mistrustful of the whole ordeal. Tyler and I never considered ourselves atheists until we went to church to test out the church wedding idea. The couple of times we went, it was pretty. The music was nice, the pews were austere, and the people were an interesting mix of solemn and upbeat, but there was just this feeling. I felt this instinctual revulsion whenever they talked about God with certainty. Tyler felt it too. It's not a thought, and maybe not even a feeling—just a powerful, pervasive uneasiness that drops into you. I didn't think I was smarter or better or more morally sound than anyone there. I just couldn't stand it. I couldn't stand that uneasiness.

"I unwrapped the present after she had gone, although I had guessed what it was from our conversation. Under the wrapping paper was an illustrated book titled *Baby's First Bible Stories*. I held it for a while, looking at the cover. It was all pastel colors and smiling faces, and when I looked inside, it had cute drawings of various saints and the like. I had a thought like, *Maybe this book is what pulls me into religion*, and I felt that uneasiness. But I respected Sylvia too much to throw it away or bury it, so I put it in the book basket to lay with the others.

"You asked me if I ever saw her panicky, and like I said, I never have. I don't think she could ever panic in the traditional sense of the word. But she moves on a wavelength other people don't have access to, and I'm convinced it must be lonely."

Harriet said, "Me, a witness? Of course, I'm willing to do whatever would help get all of this sorted out, but I truly didn't witness anything. I was in labor in my living room when it happened. I had gone into labor late, right around midnight, which I expected to happen, because my doula had informed me that melatonin is one of the key hormones involved in labor, so most first-time moms go into labor when it's dark out and all the blue light from the sun and the bulbs and the screens has been whisked away. I didn't even witness anything through the window, because melatonin is also important to continuing labor once it's started. So when the birds went into their dawn chorus, Tyler and my doula went around and blacked out all the windows with heavy cloth squares I had made for that exact purpose. After that we lit a few beeswax candles I rolled months ago, because firelight doesn't cinch the flow of melatonin, and for a while my contractions were going well. We had the birthing ball out and I had spent some time laboring in the tub. It was all progressing fairly slowly, but again, that's normal for a first-time mom. My doula was glad that labor was progressing steadily and slowly, in fact, because we had hoped I would be in position for a home birth with a midwife, so we had one on standby. I was happy with the way it was going too. Waiting for labor had challenged my optimism, but going into labor spontaneously restored it, and then some. I wasn't just letting myself believe I would give birth at home—I started to think I was on the way to fetal ejection reflex. Have you heard of that? Fetal ejection reflex is this mysterious phenomenon wherein the mother is so relaxed during labor that the baby appears to come out all by himself. It's also called orgasmic birth, and it's tremendously rare, and rarer still in hospital births. That was why we were hoping to give birth at home, as a means to an end, so to speak; but my doula had been transparent with me that if there was any sign of trouble at all, we'd scrap the plan. I did appreciate her being upfront, but at the same time I worried that she had stressed me out by saying it and thus diminished my chance of it happening. Still, things kept going well all morning. I say it was morning, but in truth I had no idea what time it was. No clocks were visible, and the cloth squares were doing their job with the windows, plus the firelight . . . the whole experience was a bit dreamlike, with the pain being the only thing reminding me I was technically awake, and the space between contractions the only reminder time was still passing. I was about five centimeters and going strong when we heard the scream.

"I don't want to say that that scream—and only that scream—was the reason I didn't experience fetal ejection reflex, but it did shake me. One of the other things my doula had told me about hospitals was that they can be stressful because of all the gore that you're privy to. You can hear other people screaming when things are going bad—feel the occasional running footsteps of nurses in a hurry—and over the PA system there's all those inscrutable codes, each of which reeks of concealed desperation. In staying home, I had supposedly avoided all that, but then that scream burst into our home, shattering the illusion of a candlelit inner space populated only by myself, my doula, and Tyler. It wouldn't have shocked me if it had shattered the windows too, and blown candles out, it was such a shrieking call. And I'm not sure how, but I knew it was Sylvia's voice.

"I had just made my way through one of my bigger contractions and was trying to catch my breath before the next one. My doula and Tyler had both frozen and seemed to be having a silent debate over whether or not one of them should go outside. I wasn't thinking all that straight, but I wasn't having an out-of-body experience, either. I knew they were trying to spare me somehow, but I was in labor, and any thoughts beyond that straightforward conclusion felt miles out of reach. Finally, Tyler said, 'I'll be right back,' and went to the door, leaving me with my doula in our candlelit den as another contraction revved up.

"My doula massaged my leg through the contraction, which was more effective at reducing the intensity than it sounds like it would be, and I was on the downswing where things loosen up a bit when I realized Tyler hadn't left yet. He was still standing at the door, and my doula was holding out a pair of sunglasses. They didn't want the sunlight from the doorway to jeopardize my labor, I realize now—and I also realize now that they were extra concerned because they knew the scream had thrown me—but I didn't realize either of those things right then. I didn't really think at all, just trusted my doula and followed the prompts. I took the sunglasses and put them on, and then Tyler was gone, and I sat there in darkness with the candle flames around me all muzzled and muted and the glasses fogging up, and the fog mixing with the wisps of smoke as I waited for the next contraction.

"The second scream came a moment later. I was still wearing those sunglasses—I assume because my doula wasn't certain when Tyler would come back, thus exposing my delicate labor to the horrors of sunlight—and the scream affected me differently this time. My eyes were dimmed, which likely intensified my ears' sensitivity to the scream itself, and with the candles and fogginess around me, I felt as though my world was doused in illusion, like what I imagine sensory deprivation to feel like, such that the limited sights around me seemed to also jump at the sound of Sylvia's fear, and I remember becoming afraid myself. I'm not sure I could've taken another scream in that state. I may have tunneled through reality and found myself in her kitchen, facing whatever terrible specter had come to visit. The scream bled into another contraction, the biggest one yet, one that peaked and ebbed, then peaked again, and it was only when that contraction ended that I realized my hands were over my ears.

"My doula was saying something to me. I wasn't sure what it was, because another contraction came then, the same kind of giant contraction as the previous two, with that big, eviscerating peak and that second peak on the end. My senses felt disconnected from my head, and things were swirling. I tried to listen to my doula and focus on where I was.

"It's funny: having a baby goes in the domain of things like checklists and schedules, so I had devised my birth plan and written it all down in detail. I realize in retrospect I was operating under the falsehood that labor responds to a person's mental approach. Were I planning to do it again, I'd know next time that labor is like breathing, only violent. It happens at a pace determined by the body, and the most peaceful approach is to relinquish control and let the body be apart from you, because it *wants* to be apart from you. It doesn't like hurting you.

"But now I realize I've been rhapsodizing, when the only pertinent detail for you is the scream. I can't confirm it was Sylvia, and I don't have any corroborating details, like her car in the driveway or anything like that. But I'm sure it was her, and I'm sure it was fearful; and because of how she is and how she thinks, I'm sure that to me, the scream was a bee in my house—a terrifying, flying menace—but to her it was merely a point of interest. I can imagine her listening, even while she's screaming, interested in the sound."

5

Sylvia could call up exacting details of what had happened; every word and image, thought and echo. She could remember details as infinitesimal as individual drops of rain, set against enormous landscapes of sound. It was all there, emerging unprompted any time some wisp of familiarity opened the vessel of her memory, and she would never be able to transmit it to anyone, to articulate it, to unburden herself.

"Are you ready?" Danielle asked.

Sylvia shook herself. "Yes. Sorry. I was thinking again."

Danielle said, "Let it come, but let it leave."

"Right," Sylvia said. "I'm trying."

They went out into the December night air. In the cold, Sylvia felt attracted to streetlights. Snow was falling in big, distant flakes, still melting on contact with the ground. *Let it come, but let it leave.*

Harriet answered the door with the baby in her arms. He was too small to move his head, and his eyes looked up toward Harriet, a product of how his head rested. Danielle smiled wide and leaned in to say hi to the baby. Sylvia was glad to see her react that way.

Tyler was standing with his back to their fireplace, wearing a Christmas sweater and holding a mug. "We made mulled wine if you want some," he said. "I have a feeling you won't regret yours around midnight."

Both Danielle and Sylvia laughed politely. The house was warm, lit with a mix of soft incandescent bulbs and the glow from the fireplace. Sylvia slid her coat off her shoulders.

"I can take that for you," Tyler said.

"The mulled wine is this way," Harriet said. She led them into the kitchen. Sylvia realized that both she and Tyler wanted them to have some. She felt as though, if she could intuit the exact reason, she would learn something about parenthood.

Danielle's doctor had told them to take a month off after her miscarriage, and then they could resume trying. They were doing as they had been told. Coming into this night, Sylvia had worried. She had worried that Danielle would take the sight of Harriet and Tyler's baby hard, and she had worried she wouldn't have the energy to mediate.

"How are you sleeping?" Danielle asked.

Harriet shrugged. "We were warned not to expect any sleep in the first three months, and things are playing out that way."

"Coffee still works, though," Tyler said, sipping from his mug of mulled wine.

Sylvia held her mug in both hands, feeling no desire to sip but enjoying the warmth. There was a pile of baby books by the fireplace, and she noticed, without intending to, that hers was not among them.

She had expected that. Harriet and Tyler weren't religious, and they were unlikely to cultivate religion in their child. She had felt called to try, though, and recent events had only intensified the call. It wasn't a divine call, a summon from above to go forth and evangelize. Nothing like that. She felt called by her personal experience with religion. So much of her life had quivered with anxiety, fear, dread—and now the breach. She had experienced a breach in safety, and it was here in this room with her. But religion was in this room with her too, as it had always been, alongside the breach—as it had been alongside her dread for so long now. The breach was with her at this moment, threatening to drain away her warmth. But there was also God here.

"What are you guys doing for Christmas?" she asked.

Tyler and Harriet shared a glance. "We're not really in a position to travel, so we'll be here."

Sylvia caught herself in a thought about Harriet and Tyler and religion and Christmas. She was letting her intellection take people away again, and she needed to stop and be present instead. She would have fun tonight. Harriet was a friend, and an important one that she liked. She wouldn't allow her mind to dissect their friendship. There was no reason to do that. She wouldn't allow it.

Danielle spoke to Tyler: "You know, I just realized I don't know where your family is from."

Tyler said, "I grew up here, but after I went to college they moved back to Pittsburgh, where the rest of my extended family lives."

"I can't believe we've never talked about this," Danielle said. She put her hand on Sylvia's back. "Sylvia's from the area too."

"What part?" Tyler asked.

"Henrico," Sylvia said. "I went to Tucker."

"No kidding. I went to Deep Run. We were probably at the same basketball games, if you ever went."

Sylvia said, "I would've been on the court."

"Me too," Tyler said.

Harriet and Danielle were both smiling at her. Sylvia realized what she had said, and she realized she had said it easily, without freezing up.

She took a sip of the mulled wine. It tasted as warm as it felt.

"Let's go sit down," Harriet said after a moment. "We don't all have to gather 'round the mulled wine pot."

They took their seats around the fireplace. Harriet lowered herself down to the rocker on the floor and laid the baby in it gently, rolling his body out and cradling his head. She pulled her face away from him slowly. The baby watched but did not cry. Finally, Harriet was standing all the way up, and she took a step away. "Their eyesight is still rather poor at this age, but they love the faces and voices of their caretakers."

Sylvia saw the baby turn his head when Harriet spoke.

"Most of the time he protests when I put him down, but I've learned that if I do it just right, he's happy."

Sylvia looked at Danielle again to see if she was still taking it okay. *You treat her like she's going to combust.*

"How are you guys adjusting?" Danielle said.

Harriet shrugged. "It's definitely hard. He's often fussy, and I can't keep him awake during the day, and I can't keep him asleep during the night. But we're learning how to do things, and we're getting better at them."

Tyler said, "To put it in my language, quantity of effort is equal to quantity of diaper changes multiplied by difficulty of diaper changes. So if you get better at diaper changes, it matters less that there are a lot of them."

"That seems like a healthy approach," Sylvia said.

She liked this version of Tyler. He was more muted, less theatric. Less engaging, more honest. She assumed fatherhood had left him with enough energy to think about what to say, but not enough to think about the cloud of irrelevant factors that seemed to guide how he acted. Maybe this was how he looked to Harriet.

And for that matter, perhaps the way Tyler usually looked to Sylvia was the way Danielle looked to Harriet. And perhaps the way Harriet looked to Danielle was the way Sylvia looked to Tyler. Perhaps this was what made it so easy for a person like Preston to hide out, as long as every series of relationships became a web of angles.

"It's healthy for the moment," Harriet said, "but the moment may change."

Sylvia thought she sounded wishful. There was a segue there, if she or Danielle took it, but Sylvia didn't want to tell them about their plans yet. She worried that she and Danielle were bringing their news into the wrong moment. Harriet and Tyler were tired. Sylvia didn't want them to take it poorly.

If they took it poorly, though, they would be fine once they got some rest. Tyler and Harriet were people with friends. It wouldn't bother them to hear that their neighbors were moving away. It wasn't fair to assume they were fragile.

She talks about you like a sick pet.

Danielle said, "Is it okay that we're talking about babies? It's dawning on me that we're likely the twelfth couple you've had this conversation with."

Harriet smiled. "I like to listen to how my answers change."

Sylvia liked that way of thinking about interactions. She noted it. It was something she would come back to when she was alone. She could plot herself out on a map of questions, then scrutinize the different answers she would give to different people. Alone. She would think about it more when she was alone.

"Why are you shaking your head?" Tyler said.

"Just clearing some cobwebs," Sylvia said.

"I was worried you disagreed with me."

Sylvia said, "What are we talking about?"

Danielle put her hand on Sylvia's knee. "Breastfeeding in public."

"Oh," Sylvia said. "How does everyone feel about it?"

They all laughed. Danielle spread her fingers out to encompass more of Sylvia's knee and gripped it tighter, but not so tight that the change in tension would be visible. "We're all for it," Danielle said.

Sylvia nodded.

Tyler said, "I was saying that babies are everyone's favorite. People always want to see the baby, talk to the baby, hold the baby, but they always want it to be on their terms."

"Cute baby," Harriet said. "But don't bring him to my wedding."

"Exactly," Tyler said. "So it becomes about where babies are and aren't welcome, because they fuss or they throw food, but then it becomes about where mothers are and aren't welcome, because the baby doesn't care that she's exposing her boob in public."

"You could use some finesse on the words," Harriet said.

Tyler sipped his mulled wine. "This is why I work with numbers."

"I had a client tell me once that kids wouldn't be coming to his restaurant," Danielle said. "If I remember right, he brought it up too."

Sylvia kept a lid on her thoughts. They were coming with too much attached. The baby began to cry.

"Looks like I'll get to demonstrate," Harriet said, rotating her torso to reach for him.

Sylvia noticed as she turned that there was a milk stain on the shirt she was wearing. It was a black T-shirt, and Sylvia wondered if she had chosen it to obscure stains in the presence of others.

"You're both sure you don't mind?" Harriet said.

"Breasts aren't new to us," Sylvia said. Tyler laughed uneasily, and Sylvia regretted saying it out loud. She had intended it to be jovial, with a bit of matter-of-factness. Instead, she had sounded defensive.

Harriet pulled up her shirt and cradled the baby, guiding him toward her. Two mismatched pillows sat beside her elbow, and Harriet's elbow came to rest on them as the baby's mouth rose higher. "There you go," Harriet said to him. And to the rest of the room, she said, "I've been getting the hang of latching him."

"You handled it like a veteran," Sylvia said, trying to clear out the tone she had spoken with a moment ago. She didn't like that she had sounded defensive; she didn't want to be defending anything. She had spent years assembling an image of herself from what she knew about women and what she knew about Sylvia. Her body would fall short of many of her ideals, and she believed she had accepted that. She tried not to think about anything for a few seconds.

"Changing the subject, we have some news," Danielle said.

Sylvia turned to study Danielle. Had she noticed the tone?

She talks about you like a sick pet.

"We're moving up north," Danielle said.

Harriet raised her eyebrows and shifted her neck, smiling. "How far north?"

Sylvia put her mug of wine on the coffee table. She was drinking it too fast. "Way up north."

"Acton, Massachusetts, just outside Boston. It's where my family lives," Danielle said.

"Oh wow," Harriet said. "That's north, all right."

"Very north," Tyler said.

Danielle was still gripping Sylvia's knee. "We wanted you guys to know before you see the For Sale sign go up outside our house."

Harriet shifted the baby. "We want to interview your poten-tial buyers."

The mulled wine was back in Sylvia's hands. "We can arrange that."

She was relieved. They were taking it fine, in keeping with what she had expected. Harriet and Tyler had the gift of making each person feel like they were part of a circle of select friends that didn't include the rest of the hangers-on. But the truth was that they felt the same toward each of their friends, and people like Danielle and Sylvia came and went from their lives as easily as the tide.

Sylvia wished she could turn down the dial on everything for a while. At the moment, she was floating. The last year had gradually taken her out of herself, and now her thoughts and feelings drifted about without her input. It was how it had been before—the way she'd feared. Titrating off hormones had separated her strands—the knot of beliefs, values, ideas, thoughts, feelings, impressions, and self-deceptions that her transition once delicately secured had loos-ened and loosened, and then Preston had cut it apart. Now Sylvia was an observer again—afloat—again waiting to discover the last plot twist: how she would meet her end. The only difference was that this time, "her end" didn't mean death. Sylvia's worldview had become more nuanced than that rigid binary of dead or not dead. She no lon-ger feared herself, but she knew she didn't have any input over where she or anything else went. It would all play out as the paths had been written, under God's detailed eye. She felt distant from God, and at the same time alone with God. Only God could decide whether or not the baby came, or the house sold, or if she could regain the closeness to the world that had marked her transition, or whether or not that was possible in Massachusetts, or whether or not she and Danielle would hold together.

"I hope you're not moving because of that business with Preston," Harriet said.

Danielle and Sylvia shared a glance. "He hasn't been back," Sylvia said.

Harriet said, "Still, I hope that's not the reason you're moving."

"The design opportunities are bigger in Boston," Danielle said.

"And I've never lived outside Virginia," Sylvia said.

It's a codependent hoax and I'm tired of it.

"I'm just saying I hope that's not the reason," Harriet said.

"It's not," Sylvia said. Again, her tone betrayed her. She couldn't have said any more clearly that it was.

Harriet nodded. All four of them were silent. The baby popped off Harriet, throwing his head back. "He always does that." She was smiling down at him. His neck was completely stretched. He was looking at the world upside down. "Little milk drunk guy," Harriet said.

"We'll be back in town a lot," Sylvia said. "My parents still live here, and they'll . . ." she trailed off.

Harriet and Tyler were looking at her.

Danielle said, "What she means is, her parents will insist that we come down to introduce them to the baby. We're trying to have one of our own."

You treat her like she's going to combust.

"Congratulations!" Harriet said. "On making the decision, I mean. I hope you guys have a boy. The world is in need of more boys who can handle themselves."

"We're a rare breed," Tyler said.

Harriet leaned forward so that her face was blocking Tyler's from view. "You'll have to excuse him."

So that was it. They had officially told someone they were trying. Maybe now, it would become clear that concealing their intentions had been the issue. They had kept their attempts secret for fear of creating pressure for themselves. In doing so, perhaps they had silently conceded to each other that it was a long shot. If they had confidence, they would tell people. They would tell people, if they had faith.

Harriet was looking at Sylvia thoughtfully. That day on her couch, Sylvia had told her without telling her. Maybe she was realizing now.

"Now we really hope you don't move," Harriet said. "How will our kids end up with crushes on each other long-distance?"

"We'll have to arrange phone meetings," Danielle said.

Tyler turned to the baby and assumed a stern tone. "Young man, you are not going outside to play until you've sparked a romantic interest in a kid we know from Boston."

The milk drunk face faded, and the baby whimpered.

"He doesn't mean it," Harriet said. "Shhhhhhh."

The baby went back to being strung out.

"I need to work on my parent voice," Tyler said.

"They say that babies teach you how to raise them," Harriet said. "I'm going to walk in on him giving Tyler voice lessons."

Sylvia liked the idea of a baby teaching his parents how to raise him. At the same time, it made her think back to being little and wonder how she'd taught her own so little, missing the specifics, the important points, the parts they should have been warned about. She understood Harriet. Harriet believed there was harmony out there, as long as you were looking for it. She was like Sylvia. The difference was in where they chose to look.

She was getting distracted again. The buzziness was so thick in her mind, she could hardly observe a thing. Sylvia tried to observe as many things as possible about the room to bring herself more sincerely into it. The baby's onesie was green. Harriet's shirt had milk stains. Tyler's mug had a football on it. The room smelled a tiny bit like vanilla.

They stayed for a little more than an hour, then wished Tyler and Harriet good luck with the night and went back outside. The snow had picked up some, enough that the grass in the porch light's radius showed a light dusting. Danielle walked quickly and then, once they had gotten onto the street, she said, "Harriet's got it bad for you."

"What makes you say that?" Sylvia said.

Danielle shrugged. "The way that she talks to you, and looks at you when you're not talking, and the way she always seems a little disappointed that Tyler isn't you. She was devastated that we're moving, if you didn't notice."

"You sound drunk."

Danielle skipped ahead some. "I think it's cute, really. Dealing with all the change in her life, and she ends up with a very confusing crush. It's not very courteous of you to expose her to these feelings that puzzle her. I bet you make her feel so mysterious."

She stepped up to the door of their house but turned around before she unlocked it. "You know, I'm not feeling tired. Let's go out tonight."

"Where?" Sylvia said.

"Carytown." Danielle stepped onto the sidewalk and began to walk away, spreading her arms wide. "I'm sorry, I'm just excited that I'm not the only one with a crazy admirer."

Sylvia said, "I don't know where this is coming from."

"Come on."

"I mean it. I don't think it's true."

Danielle looked at her, open-mouthed. "You really haven't noticed."

"I don't think there's anything to notice."

Danielle laughed. "Sylvia, she's crazy about you. If you walked into her house right now and said, 'Pack your things,' she would get into the car and hold the baby tight while you drove."

"How much of that mulled wine did you drink?"

"I'm not mad," Danielle said. "I can hear it in your tone. You think

I'm seething mad and acting happy about it, but I'm not. I'm deliriously amused that you're still maintaining this illusion."

You treat her like she's going to combust.

"You asked me point blank if she was in love with me."

"That's what makes it so amusing."

"She's married," Sylvia said.

"So are you."

"And I'm a woman."

"So is she."

"Let's talk about something else," Sylvia said.

"After I've made my point."

Sylvia was watching her closely now, waiting to see if she would reach for a flask. They had been advised to take the month off from trying, and she had taken it well, but she hadn't taken it perfectly. Not this imperfectly, though.

"My point," Danielle said, "as I was building up to it, is that Preston's approach was all wrong. I don't doubt that he was in love with me for a while, but over time he fell in love with hating you. I think it made him feel special to have an enemy, but he got stuck: He needed to consummate his hatred and free me up at the same time, and so he couldn't follow the easy path to the latter, which would've been to speed you and Harriet along until you left me."

"I would never leave you."

"No?"

"Never."

Danielle stopped to let a car pass. "But don't you feel like it's something along these lines: We met each other and we loved each other, then things got really really complicated. You came out and I tried my best, and I wanted to have a baby and you tried your best, and then things kept happening before we could sort anything out, and it turned out we couldn't ever get back to normal."

Sylvia understood now. Danielle felt the same way she felt, only she had said it better. They had gone so far from normal. "Normal" was the shape they had traced around themselves when they first came together. As things changed, they held on to each other as their forms became stretched and bent. They could still hold on to each other now, but they wouldn't fit that shape anymore.

"I don't feel that way," she said.

Danielle ventured into the intersection. "You can say you do. You don't have to deny it."

175

"Do you?"

Danielle said, "No."

Each of them laughed. They were so frustrated and discombobulated, so distant and imperiled. It was funny to realize it.

In the silence that followed, Sylvia became aware that there had been a witness with her, one who could listen to her, who could help her carry the memory. *Angel of God, my guardian dear . . .*

Danielle said, "You know, Father Stephen asked me about you once."

Sylvia crossed her arms and looked down, finishing her prayer before she spoke again. "What did he say?"

Danielle said, "Nothing. I didn't tell you about it because it was nothing. I left feeling this warm feeling, and then I thought about what had actually transpired, about the actual words, and I realized I had nothing to go on. No indication of anything, other than that I had come to church with you. And I realized how careful he had been to express only that, nothing else. You have been coming to church, and so has that person."

Danielle kept talking. "I was thinking about that when I talked to Preston, after I went to tell him I was packing up my Sylvia and going home, and he was not to follow me, nor even look for me. I left and I knew I'd expressed the only thing that could make him realize the pointlessness of all his subterfuge. I'm in an endless marriage, and so is that person."

Something occurred to Sylvia. "Let me ask you this," she said.

"Ask me anything."

"Do you actually think Harriet is in love with me?"

"I wouldn't deny it."

Sylvia said, "That's not what I mean. I mean, do you think that Harriet is—" she paused "—*smitten* with me?"

Danielle nodded. "I think she's quite taken with you."

"So let me ask you this too," Sylvia said. "What does that say about Danielle, that she sees it?"

Danielle said, "That's clever."

"You didn't answer."

"I'm thinking about it."

She looked up at the constellations, thinking about it.

Danielle said, "So odd. All of a sudden, I'm feeling quite puzzled; maybe even a little mysterious."

They were quiet.

"I've missed you this year," Sylvia said.

Danielle said, "I've missed you too."

It's a codependent hoax and I'm tired of it.

Sylvia put her hands to her nose. The leather of her new gloves felt cold, but it was soft and wet. Her breaths pushed against the stiff new leather and then circled warmly back in. She didn't want to think about something else. She wanted to think about what was here right now. She wanted to think about this, and not something else.

"You know what?" Danielle said. "I don't think I want to go out after all."

She turned around and walked back in the direction of their house. Sylvia drew in her breath and followed.

What had happened to Sylvia? She was sure she could make peace with it all if she opened herself from end to end and let the story pass all the way through. In her early twenties, Sylvia met a woman she loved. That woman convinced her to start going to church regularly, and she found she liked it. She married that woman, whose name was Danielle. Later, Sylvia came out as transgender. She and Danielle stayed married and tried to have a baby, but they miscarried. Later still, Danielle's jealous stalker emptied out their cabinets in front of Sylvia and the crashing of ceramic made her shake.

But she hadn't opened herself far enough.

In her early twenties, Sylvia met a woman named Danielle and loved her. She loved Danielle because Danielle made the world seem like its own real thing. Danielle convinced her to start going to church regularly, and Sylvia found that she liked it. The values seemed different from how she remembered them. Later, she came to realize that her feelings of alienation from the world flowed from the alienation she had endured from her gender. She developed into a more stable person, capable of straddling different realities. She and Danielle decided they should have a baby, but it proved difficult. They got close, then they weren't anymore, and it hurt them so much that Sylvia had to make a candle. Later still, Danielle's jealous stalker came to the house one morning while Danielle was out and started talking to Sylvia. He kept on talking to her, first uneven and twitchy, then frantic and angry, until he opened a knife and said, "There's something that's mine here," and went into the kitchen, where he didn't find what he wanted, and instead he found her gloves and he called them her hands and started breaking things, just breaking everything he could find, warding her off with a knife as he did.

That was better, but she needed to open further.

In her early twenties, Sylvia met a woman named Danielle and loved her. She loved Danielle because Danielle evaluated the world in such a different way from anyone Sylvia knew. She interacted with the world as a tenant, making things as right as she could without believing in any true level of ownership, neither for herself nor for any other person. One clear night, she made a comment about the stars, and it started to rain. Others found her confusing because they didn't understand how she saw things. Sylvia didn't understand how Danielle saw things either, but she found endless fulfillment in trying to see the world the way Danielle did, and it made her love Danielle more. Danielle convinced her to start going to church regularly, and Sylvia found that she liked it. The values seemed more grounded in human freedom than she remembered from her childhood. The further she progressed in her faith, the more she began to understand that the teachings of the church could bend in the way a physical church built from wood does. It swells in the rain, contracts in the cold, and bends in the wind, with just the right amount of give to withstand external force while still holding itself up. Later, Sylvia came into intimate contact with the idea of values swelling in the rain and bending in the wind by realizing that she was transgender. She fought with herself over whether her faith and her identity could be reconciled, with little resolution. She came out to Danielle and took steps to discover how real her revelation was. Over time, it became clear that the fog in which Sylvia had lived all her life would fall away if she completed her transition. It became clear to Danielle too, and they took the step together. They took that step believing that things between them could still be the same. They believed they could be in the same marriage in the same house with the same jobs, and have the same genes, and have sex; and through sex, put those same genes together and bring a baby into their house, and support that same baby with their same jobs. Later still, a man who desired Danielle was deeply offended by the step they had taken together. He couldn't stand it. He thought their marriage needed to fall apart for the good of all things because he had confused the good of all things with the good of himself. He came to the house while Sylvia was alone and asked to come in, and once he was in, he started talking. He kept on talking to her, first uneven and twitchy, then frantic and angry, until he brandished a knife and said there was something in their house that belonged to him, and he went into their kitchen to find it, and he said to her, "Where's the mug?" And she didn't answer, so he came closer with his knife and said, "Where is it?" And she didn't know what he meant, and then he saw her gloves and put them on, and he said, "See these? These are your hands, and this is what you're doing." And he pulled a stack of ceramic plates that had been a wedding gift out of the cabinet and threw them on the floor, and she was so startled she screamed; and he continued, and she tried not to look at the kitchen table, but she made the mistake of looking.

But still, that didn't answer the question. What had happened to Sylvia that made her this way?

In her early twenties, she was fortunate enough to come across a woman named Danielle, and soon she found she loved her. She loved Danielle because Danielle situated herself in continuums. At the time, Sylvia suffered from a confined and solipsistic worldview; her isolated perspective made her process every second through layers and layers of her own interpretations, until nothing remained but the layers. She was captivated by death, even believing she would eventually bring it upon herself. She drank to unravel her hypotheses, fearing their conclusions. Danielle challenged her notions with grace. Danielle had opinions about the world, but her opinions all assumed a dignity in the messiness around them. The work of God lay around Danielle in the way that time had jumbled it, and she was alive to arrange it a little better. She was lonely in her own way, so confident that she had found the exact level of humility a person should have—frustrated with others who were too humble to try to make the world more harmonious, and equally frustrated with those who were too audacious to confront their limits. Others found Danielle confusing. Sylvia found her wonderful. At Danielle's behest, she began to take church seriously. Rather than a Catholic by blood and baptism, Sylvia became a Catholic by practice. They went to Mass together every Sunday in Sylvia's early twenties, Danielle explaining things that Sylvia hadn't been taught. Over time, Sylvia became enraptured by the church. The church assured her that the world around her was not a projection or a falsehood. She came to realize that being close to God required participating in the context set out by God. Sylvia began to feel that all of the supposed demands of the church—among them Mass attendance, prayer, and confession—looked small in comparison to the ceaseless toil of maintaining her elaborate worldview. She and Danielle were married in Charlottesville, in a Catholic ceremony in a Catholic Church. Near the end of Mass, they presented a gift of flowers to the Blessed Mother, and together they said Hail Marys while those they had invited watched from afar, excluded from a moment that belonged only to them and to Mary. Sylvia became so fully integrated within the church and within her marriage that she felt empowered to be humble, free to live vulnerably. She got to living so vulnerably that she discovered she was transgender. She didn't believe it at first, not exactly, but she told Danielle, and once she told Danielle, all the doors opened at once. Everything made sense, and she was dizzy. She talked about it to Danielle, and she talked about it to friends. But after some time, she realized that she could only talk about it if she was drinking. When she realized that, she noticed other things, like the way she assessed a situation for alcohol access before broaching the subject, and the way her internal monologue had always become incoherent by the time she finished. She sought help from a carefully chosen psychologist and was told to take hormones. She sought help from a carefully chosen priest and was told not to irrevocably damage her fertility. Danielle struggled, but she was strong. Together they reworked their world. They talked long into the nights, learning about each other's points of sensitivity. Danielle confessed that she would have a hard time with the word "wife." Sylvia confessed that she felt jealous that Danielle had memories she never would, rites of passage that had passed her by. They spoke openly to each other, proceeding together in faith. They proceeded together in faith until the time came for them to have a child. It was unclear when the time became clear or what changed to make it so, but both of them felt it. Sylvia realized that she had been living on a delayed-release capsule. She and Danielle wanted kids and the Catholic Church had strict guidelines about the acceptable methods of conception. Sylvia had bent her faith but, in her opinion, had not breached her faith, and now their attempts to have a baby would test her faith. She and Danielle proceeded together, once again, in faith. But unbeknownst to Sylvia, earlier news of them proceeding together in faith had made its way across the ocean to England, where a man who desired Danielle was coming off a depressive episode that ended with him in a jail cell. He came back across the ocean and offered a job to Danielle, who agreed to work with him because her and Sylvia's relationship had reached a blissful peak and they felt insulated from the potential dangers, and the money he had offered would secure their ability to support a child on one income. Danielle became pregnant soon after, but she miscarried. They prayed a fervent, desperate prayer under the light of a candle Sylvia had made. The man who desired Danielle was unaware of all of this, and he proceeded with his incoherent plan to enrapture her. When things stubbornly turned away from his desired end, he became angry and came to their house. He asked if Danielle was home, and he didn't leave when Sylvia said no. His foot moved as though trying to walk him away on its own, but his face stared straight through her. He asked if he could come in. And Sylvia didn't like him, but she didn't want to create a petty conflict. He told Sylvia he had a knife she'd think was neat, and he showed it to her, opening the blade and showing her how the guard worked. She said she'd already seen it once before, but he left it open. Opening his knife seemed to open the entire stream of himself, and he began to say things. They started out pleasant and unsuspicious, even vulnerable, but they grew into a frenzy. Sylvia realized he had crossed into a different mental state when he told her that her marriage was a codependent hoax and that he was tired of it. He told her that she treated Danielle like she was going to combust. He told her that Danielle talked about her like a sick pet, and he asked her, "Why do you matter so much here? Why do you matter at all?" He became increasingly agitated in a way that Sylvia couldn't follow. She thought he may be drunk. He kept calling her a sick pet, still holding the knife. He spoke faster until he was babbling. Sylvia didn't follow the chain of his logic, but his logic escalated until it was no longer logic, and then he stopped for a moment, and his silence thickened around him, and his eyes became twitchy, and he told her, "You have something of mine," and directed her into her kitchen with his knife, and prodded her over to the window; and he began to search, and she didn't know what he was searching for, and she said nothing; but he went on, saying, "The mug." And each time he said, "The mug" he pointed his knife at her, until he noticed her gloves. Then he put his knife down within his reach and out of hers. He put on her gloves and said, "These are your hands, you see? And this is what you're doing with them." And he threw a stack of their plates on the floor; and Sylvia was so startled she screamed, and again he lifted his knife and pointed at her, and said, "Quiet." He kept smashing things, everything he could find: their wine glasses, their pint glasses, their ceramic mugs, their vases, their coffee pot, their jars of spices, all in a ruinous pile; and all the while, she made herself watch him, because she knew if she looked at the table he would see the candle, the one she'd made with Harriet, around which she had prayed with Danielle after their miscarriage. But she wasn't disciplined enough, and he saw her eyes move, and he asked her, "What are you checking on?" He moved slowly around the table, the knife keeping her away, and he asked, "This?" And reached for the candle, and she said, "Please." She couldn't manage a second word, just "Please," and he laughed at her, then put his knife down on the table, as if daring her to reach for it; and he took the candle in both hands and snapped it, and she cried out in anguish, as if he had snapped her instead; and he laughed at her again—until he saw Tyler out front, taking furtive, anxious steps toward the house, squinting at the window. Then Preston picked up his knife and his horrible backpack and left suddenly, out their back door, still wearing her hands. Sylvia rushed to the front porch and held out her hand, deferring Tyler, who raised his eyebrows and gave her a thumbs-up, asking without words if she was thumbs-up or if she was thumbs-down; and she summoned all of her self-control to give him a thumbs-up so that he wouldn't come to her, and possibly come inside, and she went back inside where she could be alone with herself; and she let her thoughts fall out of her and onto the surfaces of objects, outnumbering her, looking at her, until she saw the ruined pile of their possessions and she couldn't be there with it, so she went back outside and collapsed into the damp grass. She was a crying, disjointed mess when Danielle found her. Danielle pulled Sylvia to her feet, and though Sylvia was far from coherent as she explained what happened, Danielle told her she believed that Sylvia was faultless and she would help her clean, fix, and replace everything that had been shattered. Sylvia quickly realized she would never feel safe in their house again, and Danielle understood. Danielle suggested they leave Sylvia's hometown and try Danielle's, where they could try a second time on the winding spiral staircase their marriage had become. Sylvia agreed, and now she was here.

"Are you coming back to bed?" Danielle asked.

"In a bit," Sylvia said. "My head is swirling when I close my eyes."

She had come downstairs without really thinking about it, so caught up in trying to open herself. She still hadn't succeeded. Every time she went into the clear blue water of her memories, the sand fell away and the bottom receded. It would do so until she became water too, along with everything else in her, and then she would be free.

Danielle moved farther into the kitchen and pulled herself onto the counter. She looked at the chalkboard, which now displayed an image of two long-haired stick figures under a smiling sun, with one of the stick figures holding the hand of a shorter stick figure, and behind them a stick house. Beneath the drawing were the words "Us in Acton."

"I should've given us a cat," Danielle said. "Promises drawn in blessed chalk have a better chance of happening."

"I'm allergic to cats," Sylvia said.

Danielle lowered her voice and raised her eyebrows. "I meant a blessed cat."

Sylvia laughed. She was waking up now. Earlier she had burrowed herself so deep that thinking harder made her less wakeful. She was grateful to Danielle, coming down here and waking her up.

Sylvia was looking at the chalkboard now. "I'm scared, and I don't really know why. I've been there with you, and I know you'll take me all around Acton and help me see it how you see it, but the thought of going there makes me seize up."

"I felt that way when I moved to Richmond," Danielle said. "Charlottesville is one thing. All college towns are pretty much the same town, but Richmond was this whole different mess of weird."

"I know," Sylvia said. "I guess I'm glad I know a local."

Danielle said, "It means a lot to me that you're coming."

Sylvia was surprised. "Of course I'm coming."

"I know. And it's not really the right phrase, saying I'm glad you're coming. But I mean that it means a lot that you would've come if I'd asked you before; that it doesn't feel like we're only going out of fear." She looked into Sylvia's eyes for a moment, then changed her inflection. "I've been thinking about our marriage, and I've been realizing that a lot of what we've been through makes sense if you don't think of us as one unit." Then she sighed and said, "That came out wrong."

Sylvia glanced at the clock. It was past one a.m.

Danielle gathered herself up. "Trying again: I don't think either of us takes our marriage for granted, but I also don't think either of us lets our marriage dictate things. The average of two people is less interesting—because it's an average—than two distinct people with distinct struggles who pursue the things that matter to them and try their best to stay in love, even when they're all over the place."

Danielle dropped her head and shook it. "I'm not saying it right. I'm trying to say that you're you and I'm me, and you're free to take Sylvia to her conclusion and I'm free to take Danielle to her conclusion; and I don't think I can take Danielle to her logical conclusion without Sylvia, and I don't think you can take Sylvia to her logical conclusion without Danielle; and it's powerful that we spend time flying down each other's curvy mountain roads instead of averaging ourselves into this confining little straight road."

She looked out the window. "I don't like that one, either, but I think it's as close as I'm going to get."

Sylvia smiled. She was feeling happy now. It was nice to be awake. "I'll sleep on it, and when I wake up, I'll understand," she said.

Danielle hopped off the counter. "For that to work, you need to sleep."

The For Sale sign went up three days later. Sylvia stared at it from the kitchen. She was thinking it was odd that For Sale signs had such a consistent silhouette. It was always the same one-sided cross, with the rectangular post hanging from its arm. It was a symbol of change, and Richmond was changing. They had been warned not to expect a quick sale in the wintertime, but Richmond was changing fast. Lower-income areas were being gentrified in all directions. Neighborhoods like Sylvia's were moving from middle class to upper class. The wave was cresting, and they were in the tube.

Danielle was still asleep, and Sylvia had left their bedroom quietly to avoid waking her. She finished her coffee and sighed.

In January, they would once again be trying to conceive. It felt to Sylvia like some of the coming changes would go right, but not all of them. But they all pulled on each other so specifically that she couldn't see one aspect going wrong without the rest going wrong too.

She needed to leave now, or she would be late.

Sylvia put on her coat and gloves, swung her bag over her shoulder, and went outside. It was the kind of December day that feels icy, even when everything is dry. The grass was lying still on the hard ground, and the sky was milky white behind the bare, spindly trees. Sylvia stood at her car for a moment, digging in her pocket for her keys.

"You can't leave."

She turned and looked up. Harriet was standing there with the baby in her arms. The baby was wrapped in a towel and wearing a hat.

"You scared me," Sylvia said.

"I'm sorry," Harriet said. "I've been learning how to walk quietly. And you can't leave."

Sylvia said, "Why not?"

Harriet shook her head. She looked at the ground. She seemed to be making an effort to look down in such a way that her gaze went past the baby. "You just can't."

"I'm sorry. We decided it's for the best."

Sylvia noticed now that Harriet was significantly less bundled up than her baby. She was wearing a pair of flannel pants and a T-shirt. Harriet said, "I'm in over my head."

"I'm sure you're just adjusting."

Harriet bit her lip and tightened her arms around the baby. "Tyler has to travel so much. My parents live in North Carolina."

Sylvia shifted her bag. She'd been in the Richmond area with her own family nearby all this time, and what had she done? She had tried to think about her family as little as possible.

She said, "You can ask them to come up."

"I can't."

"You'll be okay."

"For now," Harriet said. "For now, I'll be okay."

"For later too."

"Tyler's going to go off leave soon and he'll start traveling. You're going to sell your house and leave."

"You have tons of friends."

"They don't understand," Harriet said.

"Don't understand what? Having a baby?"

"Me," Harriet said.

Sylvia stifled a sigh. She let her shoulders drop slowly and breathed out in a way that was inaudible. The wind rustled the dry leaves. "Danielle and I will be by tonight. No need to make mulled wine or put up lights. We'll just be by to help."

Harriet paused for a while, then said, "Thank you."

She went back inside. Sylvia watched her go.

If they had a baby, at least Danielle would have her own family there, up where her roots ran deep.

Sylvia got into her car and started driving. As she drove, she thought about Harriet saying her friends didn't understand her. What was there to understand about Harriet? She made perfect sense. She had made perfect sense to Sylvia by the third time they spoke. Was everyone else really that obtuse? And why didn't anyone understand Danielle either? Did Sylvia just have a habit of latching on to people whom other people found opaque? Why didn't people make sense to other people?

Even Preston made sense to her. He was one of those people to whom other people didn't make sense. Nobody made sense to Preston. Not even Preston made sense to Preston. That was his problem.

When she got to work, Sylvia parked on the far reaches of the lot, as she always did, and walked into the office under that milky white sky, stepping carefully because she couldn't convince her feet that there wasn't any ice.

They put up Christmas decorations that year. Sylvia had always found it strange that Danielle wasn't much of a Christmas decorator, given her line of work, but Danielle insisted it was consistent. She believed in an unadorned, disciplined, personal faith, and she believed in subtle, layered, ambiguous design. This year, though, there was nothing subtle or ambiguous about their home, only layers. Layers of lights outside, layers of lights and ornaments on their tree, and layers of tinsel on the thresholds. They made gingerbread men and decorated those too, under layers of icing, sprinkles, and cinnamon. They lived out the phrase "deck the halls," and when they were done, the house looked like a Christmas movie set. Sylvia loved it. As they were working, she concluded that this was the proper way to say goodbye to a house deprived of the chance to hold a family.

"We should put candles in the windows tomorrow," Danielle said. "Real ones."

She was hunched over the coffee table by the tree, stringing a garland out of popcorn and cranberries. There was a clear plastic cup of wine beside her busy hands.

Sylvia was hanging stockings from the mantle. "It's already a miracle we didn't blow a fuse. We shouldn't test our luck with fire."

"Not your best argument, but I'll consider it," Danielle said. "Make some more popcorn if you're done with that. I'm running low on garland supplies."

Sylvia went into the kitchen and put a bag of popcorn in the microwave, then went back to Danielle. Out of habit, she glanced at the open wine bottle sitting on the coffee table beside a plastic cup of cranberries. "Do we have any more needles?"

Danielle didn't look up. "We don't even have one needle, technically. I borrowed this from Harriet."

The popcorn was jumping in the kitchen. "I'll go see if she has another," Sylvia said.

She put on her coat. It was cold out in the way that seems to howl and then fall silent. The cold burst in through the doorway as she opened it, then fell silent as she walked across the yard. The grass crunched under her feet.

As she stepped onto the empty street, itself a dark stream between her home and Harriet's, Sylvia's thoughts converged on Preston. He hadn't called Sylvia a sick pet. No, he had said Danielle thought of her as a sick pet.

Her feet found the sidewalk on the other side, and the image of Preston fell away.

Tyler answered the door. "We probably have some," he told her when she explained what she needed. "Not sure where, though."

"Harriet's not here?"

Tyler said, "The baby's passed out right now. He sleeps like a rock right after the sun goes down for some reason, and we're not fighting it. Harriet's asleep." He was looking around the room. "That looks like a sewing box."

Sylvia followed Tyler to the bookcase, where he took Harriet's sewing box off the top shelf and opened it. "Ow." He pulled his finger out. "Right, it's full of needles." He reached in again, gingerly this time, and removed one.

"Thank you," Sylvia said. "I'll bring it back tomorrow."

She walked back toward the door, passing the stairs in the process. As she left, she thought she heard footsteps above her.

Sylvia walked carefully across Harriet's yard, clutching the needle, afraid she would stumble and lose it in the grass. She didn't want to be on her knees, groping around for the needle with only the streetlights to help her. The moon wasn't out tonight. She held the needle in front of her as if were a compass. Again, Sylvia entered the space between the sidewalks, pointing the needle at her own door in a joke with herself. Her thoughts began to magnetize, rotating toward their own north. She remembered what Danielle had said about Preston, that he'd been consummating his hatred.

She was already on the grass, but her thoughts continued, emanating from her compass needle. Perhaps that was it. Preston had come and broken their things as a final ritual—as much a ritual as any other ritual—chasing his twisted peace through a ritual, a ritual all over their kitchen floor.

She returned home, hearing the cold howl as she sealed the door behind her. Danielle was still working on the garland. "I think the popcorn's done."

Sylvia went into the kitchen to get the popcorn. She placed the bag onto a paper plate and held it level. She noticed there was one gingerbread man left and she placed that on the plate too. When she got back to Danielle, she broke the gingerbread man and held out the chest and head. "It's the last one."

Danielle smiled at her as she took it. "Here," she said, and she poured the cranberries out of their cup and onto the plate, then filled the empty cup with wine. "We can see if they work as a pairing."

"How do I do this?" Sylvia asked, taking the other end of Danielle's thread.

She noticed now how short the garland was, even after Danielle had worked on it as long as she had. Danielle said, "Like this," and ran her needle through a cranberry, and then another, and then a piece of white popcorn. "And then repeat. And don't prick yourself. I don't want blood on my garland."

Sylvia threaded her needle and began. She felt happy now, with the fire crackling and Danielle beside her. She'd believed their marriage was teetering for so long, but what was their marriage, other than this? To be in a relationship with someone was to exchange elements of each other through rituals. She would continue to go to Mass with Danielle and slice onions with Danielle, to say rosaries with Danielle and draw stick figures with Danielle, each time filling the air between them with peace. Sylvia was anxious, wounded, dizzy, exhausted, and insecure. But she believed that she and Danielle would continue to have their rituals, and perhaps over time their rituals would turn every feeling into its opposite. They would string this garland, and when it was done it would be shorter than they expected after so much work, but they would find a place for it, and they would hang it, and they would look at it together peacefully. And the snow would melt, and they would go to Massachusetts where the snow still stood, and even there the snow would melt as the ineffable momentum of spring spread its vast chain of rituals across the Earth. And in that abundance of spring they would conceive, and they would carry their child forward, into the summer and into the fall, and back into the snow, and the child would be born. And wouldn't she be grateful, so very grateful, if all that came to pass? She would be grateful, ever so grateful, if God saw fit to will it.

ABOUT THE AUTHOR

M.J. Sions grew up near Richmond, Virginia, and later moved an hour down 64-West to study architecture at UVA, where she developed a fondness for horizontal buildings and hoppy beers. She currently lives southeast of Charlottesville, Virginia, with her wife and four children.